MARIA MERCURIO

EVERNIGHT PUBLISHING ®

www.evernightpublishing.com

THE SURVIVAL SERIES

Copyright© 2023

Maria Mercurio

Editor: Lisa Petrocelli

Cover Artist: Jay Aheer

ISBN: 978-0-3695-0905-5

ALL RIGHTS RESERVED

MARIA MERCURIO

DEDICATION

This book is dedicated to Celest Amos. You were my first reader, editor, and cheerleader of this series. The world is a dimmer place without your wit, brilliant smile, and massive heart. Cancer stole you from us, but your kindness was forged into our memories.

MARIA MERCURIO

Survival, 1

Maria Mercurio

Copyright © 2023

Prologue

"Please." The word escaped me in a shudder. "You don't have to do this." I watched in horror as he finished duct-taping my legs together. My wrists and hands were already bound all the way to the knuckles of my fingers, as if permanently fixed in prayer. *I will pray forever and a day if I get out of this.*

He chewed at his lip while staring at me. Those eyes, I had once seen as seductive, were half-crazed as they darted about the room. He had taken to frantically pacing the floor and running a hand through his disheveled hair.

"I'm sorry," he whispered for like the hundredth time.

I wanted to scream, but was trying my best to

survive. "You don't have to be sorry. Whatever this is, we can forget about it. Just let me go."

My begging caused him to wince. It made me hopeful that I might be breaking through.

"I can't do that," he replied deflating me. "You have to understand, I don't want to hurt you."

"Then don't."

He looked outside the dirt-encrusted window. The sun was starting a slow descent on the horizon. He squeezed his eyes tightly and scrubbed his face. I could hear him blowing out a few deep breaths before he spoke. "I have to." It was as if he was trying to convince himself. I held my breath. His choice would seal my fate.

I trembled as he reached for the syringe on the nightstand. Panic set in. My stomach clenched and my skin grew hot and clammy. "No!" The tears fell heavily, temporarily obscuring my vision. "I don't want to die!"

He crouched back down beside me as I struggled to move away. I was no match for his large frame and strength. He kept me neatly in place as he injected a burning hot liquid directly into my neck. His eyes bored into mine, remorseful yet determined. "You're not going to die, Chloe. You'll just wish you had."

Chapter One

Three Weeks Earlier

"And what can I get you?" I leaned in, exposing a little cleavage, not enough to come across as slutty, but enough to get my tips up.

"I'll take a light beer on tap." His eyes lingered longer than was polite. He was old enough to be my father, and I found him utterly gross. But on a slow night at a dive bar, I had to make the best of things. Rent was due.

"Coming right up, sugar." I filled a glass and slid it down the worn wooden bar.

"What's a pretty thing like you doing in an ugly dump like this?"

"Ah, my daddy asks me the same question all the time." That was a lie. I didn't have a father. By referencing said father, though, I accomplished two things. First, my customer would now see I think of him as fatherly. Second, it established me as a good girl who loved her daddy. Southern gentlemen are programmed to respect girls who love their daddies.

"Well." He took a sip of his beer, and the creepy leer lessoned by a few degrees. "You should listen to him. A girl like you could do way better."

Bingo! Now he was in the business of watching out for me. I'm free and clear of him trying to get in my pants the rest of the night. "How awful sweet of you to say. Have some pretzels. I just opened a fresh bag."

"It's the truth." He held up his glass in a salute while I smiled and checked on my one other customer.

Damn straight it was the truth. This was the last place anyone I knew would expect to find me working. It was why I drove twenty-four miles from my house in Asheville to work in a dive bar in small town Hendersonville. I've made an absolute mess of my life, and I'm not too eager to share that fact with the world. In short, I was fired from my dream job six months ago and have been having the worst time getting properly employed.

I bartended my way through college, and occasionally after, I would do an event or two for extra cash. I never thought at twenty-seven I'd be doing it full time to keep the lights on. My fellow bartenders marveled at how much I could rake in compared to them. I'd like to say it was because of my skills at mixing drinks, but this place had more of a Jack and Coke vibe. There wasn't much of a call for a mixologist at a dive bar. I poured whiskey straight, shots, and draft beer about seventy percent of the time. My ability to outearn the other bartenders here was more of a natural talent. I have legs that go on for days and huge breasts. Those assets afforded me a confidence level at an early age. I wouldn't sleep with the patrons. I just used every advantage at my disposal. Life was shitty enough.

"Hey, Chloe!" Ray, our bouncer, strode in. "Sorry I'm late. Had to fix a flat."

I gestured to the two old guys at the bar. "No worries. This crew ain't too rowdy."

"The night is young." He winked and set up his stool at the front door.

"Can I get ya something?"

"Club soda."

I had to reach farther back on the shelf to get to the plastic cups. Glass around Ray was a bad idea. He often had to sprint and stop a fight. Glasses always were the first casualty. I tossed three limes in a Solo and jokingly topped it off with a paper umbrella. I smirked when I crossed the room and handed him the drink.

He snorted at the dainty paper decoration before using it to pick at his teeth.

I grimaced. "Classy."

Before I made it back to the bar, the front door opened, letting sunlight into the dingy room. I saw dust particles floating in the air before the entrance closed. This place was better in the dark.

Five guys stood at the door. They looked young enough for Ray to card them. I'd say late twenties, maybe early thirties, except one looked like a teenager. Ray waved them through, so they must have checked out. The group headed to the pool tables in back. I wiped down the bar waiting for them to saunter over for a drink. I covertly watched and played my little game of "guess their order."

One was a hulking brute of a guy. Easily six-five and looked like crushing things was his favorite pastime. *Jack and Coke for the big guy.* After looking at the colossus, any girl's eyes would next be drawn to Hot-and-Dreamy. Full-fledge movie star looks at work. He had soft wavy blond hair, large blue eyes, and pouty lips. Too pretty for my taste. I wanted to be the hotter one in a relationship. *A pale ale for Hot-and-Dreamy.* The youngest of the bunch was a nervous-looking kid. He hadn't stopped chewing on his nails since he entered the place. He hung a little back from his group while they all laughed and talked. *Corona for the nail-biter.*

The final two broke off and headed my way. A wiry, tatted-up guy with a piercing through his eyebrow offered me a sly smile. *Gin and tonic.* My eyes didn't linger long, however, because his buddy was something to look at. He wasn't gorgeous like Hot-and-Dreamy. His features were rugged, as if he spent a great deal of time outdoors. His jet-black hair was slightly mussed in that just-right, sexy way. The confidence he carried oozed off of him. Once I singled him out, it was hard to look away. *Whiskey straight.*

"We'll take five tequila shots and five beers."

Okay, so I suck at the guess-the-drink game.

"Any preferences?" I ask, letting my words sound breathless and flirty.

Tall-and-Rugged stared at me then, interest lit up his hazel eyes. I might have needed to scale it back some before I gave him the wrong idea. The thing was, I'm not sure I wanted to. For me, this was an anomaly.

"Dealer's choice." He provided a cocky grin as if sensing the attraction was mutual. Normally a total turnoff. On him it worked. He deserved to be cocky.

At any other place I bartended this would be an opportunity to pull out the top-shelf liquor and run up the bill. No such choices here, our most expensive hard alcohol would not be considered "well-worthy" at a decent place. With Tall-and-Rugged, I probably wouldn't jerk him around and overcharge him. He looked blue-collar, and if he was from around here, most likely he was not loaded. I poured five generous shots and slung some draft beers on the counter.

"Do you want to start a tab or pay now?"

"What's the damage?"

"Sixty-two, fifty."

He pulled out eighty dollars and laid it on the bar. "Keep the change."

I was disappointed. If he opened a tab, they planned on staying longer. He was the most interesting thing to walk into this bar in months. He signaled the nail-biter over.

"Lowe," he shouted, getting the nervous kid to glance up. Lowe hurried over and between him and the tattooed dude they carried drinks back to Hot-and-

Dreamy and Giant Man. To my delight, Tall-and-Rugged grabbed a seat at the bar.

"I'm Raff."

"Chloe."

He took his shot. I stared, fascinated, watching his strong throat muscles work. I had to remind myself to blink, as if I was in some sort of trance. He slowly placed his forearms on the bar and leaned in, displaying well-defined biceps in the process. His forefinger absently tapped at the condensation on the bottom of his glass, making me gaze at his hands. They were rough hands, no stranger to hard labor. His hands were almost as appealing as his throat.

I expected him to start up a conversation. Why else would he ditch his friends and linger at the bar? Yet, he seemed content to just regard me. Wanting to hear the deep baritone of his voice again, I uncharacteristically broke the silence.

"Did you want another shot?"

His eyes held mine for an immeasurable length before he shook his head.

"I'll take another." My elderly protector held up an empty glass.

I offered him a sweet smile, grateful for the distraction. It wasn't like me to be flustered over a guy. He's not even my type. I like a guy in a suit, not a hard hat. My man needs to be well read and able to manage a 401K.

"Here you are, sugar. Sorry you even had to ask."

My patron nodded in response, clearly not as delighted in my company after watching me flirt with Raff. Feeling a little trapped behind the bar, I took the opportunity to wipe down a few tables. Hollie, one of the other bartenders, had done a real crap job closing last night. Everything was stickier than it should be. In a dump like this, a certain amount of sticky was expected, but this was beyond the tolerable level.

Raff might be a man of few words, but I certainly held his attention. He swiveled his stool and blatantly stared while I worked. I played nonchalant, like I didn't notice, but my pulse sped up as the weight of his inspection settled on me. The other old guy signaled he was ready to cash out, and I nervously returned to the bar to ring him up. Once currency was exchanged and glasses bussed, I attempted to resume my table-washing.

"You live around here?"

Oh, that voice! Hearing it sent shivers across my neck. "I'm a resident of the beautiful State of North Carolina, yet I don't call Hendersonville my home."

He didn't ask a follow up, even though I left a great opening. I gritted my teeth to hide my frustration at his unwillingness to play fair. "I haven't seen you around here before. Are you new to town?" *Ugh!* Now I look like I'm interested in him. I wanted to kick myself as the words left my mouth. First rule of bartending: only comment on what they offer, don't come off as too curious. Be a good listener, not a detective.

"My crew and I came into town last week for a job."

What kind of job? How long are you in town? Where about are you staying? I shook myself mentally. *You will not ask him a single question!* "Well, it's a quaint town. I'm sure you'll enjoy your stay."

"I wasn't sure I would at first, but it's grown on me rather suddenly." He stood up then, dragging his glass across the bar. His eyes lingered on my body before he offered me a killer sexy smile and turned to walk away.

That man was trouble.

Chapter Two

Over the next two weeks Raff and his buddies were present for all my shifts. It would have been flattering if the man had shown more interest, but our conversations were all short with just a hint of flirtation. Only Raff ever spoke to me, and I still knew next to nothing about him. I was starting to think I was off my game.

He's not my type. We do not date patrons from the bar. And we most certainly do not get overly friendly with the regulars of a dump like this!

Yet, when he strolled in the door, a shiver of excitement flared. Raff was alone tonight, and he made a beeline straight for the bar. Naturally I pretended not to notice him right away, making busy adjusting bottles.

"Chloe." His voice was like warm chocolate sauce on ice cream.

I turned slowly for the full effect. My long sun-kissed brown tresses were strategically arranged to look messy, like I didn't bother to look like a siren, it just came naturally. Now, my top was a bit more scandalous than usual, but he forced me into desperate measures. I may not have decided yet if I wanted to date him, but I surely wanted him to want me.

Raff noticed the top, or lack thereof. He took in a quick audible breath and leaned in close over the bar. I could see his arm muscles rippling under his tight button-up shirt.

Well, well, guess he's not made of stone after all...

His eyes drank me in, and I was giddy under his gaze.

"Hope you didn't go to all that trouble for me?" There was a noticeable amount of disapproval in his words.

Giddiness gone. Embarrassment moved in.

"Excuse me?" What a jerk!

"I hadn't noticed you coming to work half-naked before."

"Can I get you something?" Cold professional demeanor snapped in place.

"Because if you wanted me to notice you, you needn't have bothered."

"Okaaay, I'm gonna go check on paying customers."

He grabbed my wrist. It was the first time he touched me, and I was startled by the strength of his hands.

"I notice you."

I stared at him stunned. The entire exchange was weird and deeply personal. It wasn't a packed night, but the bar seats were almost filled, so we had an audience.

"When does your shift end?"

His hand still clutched me. His grip wasn't painful, but it kept me in place when I wanted badly to walk away. If I called out, Roy would be over in a heartbeat. It's what I should have done.

"One."

"Then I'll be back at one."

It took me a moment to compose myself once he left the bar. I was a tornado of emotions. Anger crashed through me, and bewilderment circled my thoughts.

What the hell just happened? Impulse control was always a shortcoming of mine. I generally never waited for things I wanted. As much as I tried to talk myself out of it, I wanted Raff. I thought about him when I wasn't working and wondered what he thought about me. I never gave a shit what a guy thought about me. Why was it so different with him?

I left shortly before one and briskly walked to my car, hoping to escape before Raff returned. I had little to no control of my emotions around that man. It scared the crap out of me.

Employees parked at the end of the lot. My blue Honda Civic sat under a lamppost so I could see it in the dark. Raff was clearly illuminated, lounging on the hood of my car. How the hell did he know this was my car?

I tugged my jacket tighter at the sight of him. "What do you want?"

"Same things you want, I guess."

Images of us naked and sweaty flashed through my brain. "What's that supposed to mean? I don't want anything from you."

His eyebrow lifted in silent challenge. I glared at him in response.

"I need a ride."

"You want me to take you back to your place?" I asked incredulously.

"Well, when you put it that way. I guess you should at least buy me dinner first."

"Are you for real?"

He laughed, breaking some of the tension. "I have a surprise for you, but you need to drive to it."

"I don't like surprises, especially ones from strangers."

"You'll like this one." He dared me with his eyes.

"I don't think so."

"Come on, Chloe. You can always leave me there stranded if you don't think it's cool. Tate has my truck for the night."

"Which one is Tate?"

"The big one."

Don't do it. This is crazy! And stupid! Don't do it. Don't do it. "Fine, get in."

The smirk he delivered made me regret my words before I even closed the car door. Bad decisions are something of a specialty of mine. I've even been crazy enough to pick up a hitchhiker on a long car ride because the element of danger enticed me. Of course, I know better than to go off with a man I barely know. Raff sounded off all my alarms, but I was drawn to him. There was a strange pull to be near him I had never felt before with anyone. Starting up my car, I pulled out of the lot and let the doubts drain away.

"You'll need to get on seventy-four heading south."

"South? From here? Not much there."

"Sometimes a whole lot of nothing can be an amazing thing." His smooth voice made me almost believe it.

"Seriously. Where are we headed?"

He sighed and took my measure. "The construction site my guys and I are working at."

Oh, information about himself! "Your crew is a construction crew then?"

"No, Chloe. We're a dance crew, and I picked you up to act as referee at our dance-off."

The idea was absurd. I actually snorted while laughing. I covered my mouth with my hand to stop myself from further embarrassment, but could not hold back the giggles. My reaction earned me a heart-melting smile and a sexy chuckle from Raff.

"We're an excavation team. We specialize in cut and fill and setting up proper foundations for the future construction. I'm an engineer."

A college boy. Just what I needed, another reason to like him more. "What's at this site, may I ask, that's worth seeing in the middle of the night?"

"Are you tired?"

"No," I admitted. "I'm pretty much a night owl."

"Yeah," he said knowingly. "I figured as much."

"Why is that?"

"You are a bartender," he said and shrugged.

"I guess late nights do go hand in hand with the lifestyle." I glanced over at him when I changed lanes wondering again why I was breaking all my rules. He wasn't the kind of man I went for, yet I desired him. "Bartending isn't my real job, though."

"Paying the bills between gigs?"

"Something like that." I chewed at my lip, nervous about how much I wanted to open up and share. "My regular job was late-night hours too."

"Ah," he grimaced and smirked. "Call girl?"

"Ha ha, funny." I swatted at him with my free hand. "I was in hotel management."

"And you got stuck with night shifts?"

"Stuck. No. Night management is never the most coveted spot. If you want to move up and are willing, it's a faster promotion. I didn't mind, though. I loved working nights. I guess I feel more alert when everyone else wants to be sleeping."

"I hear that. Night is the best part of the day," he said with a wink. "I enjoy when a project allows us evening work. Most guys would feel like they drew the short straw, but for me the night holds its own magic." Raff gazed out the window at the crescent moon, a small smile tugging his lips.

"Definitely the most I've heard you speak about anything since we met." I grinned at the warm and fuzzy I was feeling hearing him talk. I'd been working hard all week for just a few scraps of information about this man.

"If you're looking for a man to talk your ear off,

you'll need to talk with Weylin."

"Which one is he? Biker Gang or Hot-and-Dreamy?"

It was Raff's turn to laugh hard and choke. "I guess Biker Gang. Hot-and-Dreamy would be Rollin. But, God, I hope he never hears either of us calling him that. Do you have a nickname for me too?"

No way would I admit it! "No," I lied smoothly. "You introduced yourself the first night. I had to make up names for the others. Your friends have never spoken to me."

"Glad to hear it." Raff looked pleased.

"Oh?"

"I like having you all to myself." His eyes, filled with a warm fire, gazed steadily at mine.

Oh, yeah, this man was trouble. In one night he has offended me, embarrassed me, flattered me, and caused my pulse to race. "Is that where you're taking me, then? Someplace to be alone? Tell me right now if it's to drop my body in a deep hole you dug."

He chuckled again. "You weren't kidding about not liking surprises."

"And you're an expert at evading direct questions."

"Ten more minutes max. Anticipation is the best part of the surprise." I felt the sexually charged double meaning from the tone of his voice alone.

"Well, in that case, it better be good. You have me driving in the opposite direction of my home." I held my scolding tone but it didn't faze him in the slightest. Many men have crumbled worrying about disappointing me. I'm not exactly high maintenance, but I'm not low maintenance either.

"Why did you get fired?"

The man could have caused me whiplash forcing

me to turn and stare at him sharply from that doozy of a question. "Who says I was fired?"

"Why did you quit your job to drive to another town and work at a crappy bar?" He raised his eyebrows at me. "If you like that question more."

Well, here goes nothing. Might be nice to get it out of the way first. "I have a bit of a temper, coupled with a birth defect of being born without a filter." *Guys love to hear this, Chloe. Maybe you should mention PMS too.*

"You pissed off the wrong person?" he guessed.

"I had a crazy busy night at the front desk. Random power outages and tons of complaints. Everyone needing to talk with the manager. I'd been yelled at, cussed out, talked down to, and even had a receipt thrown in my face."

"Sounds like a full moon kind of night."

"I'll say. So, when this snooty old bitch got in my face and talked down to me like I was a moron, I lost it. Never good to scream at the hotel guests, but this was worse. Turned out to be the hotel owner's mother. He fired me the next day, and I've been having a horrible time even getting interviews. The jerk must have put the word out." I grunted softly. The whole situation made me disgusted at my own lack of control. It was strange. I usually felt like a normal person, but every once a in a while, I wanted to punch my fellow man.

"Don't beat yourself up. Your reaction was normal."

It was sweet of him to try and console me. "Thanks for saying that, even though it's a lie. I messed up, plain and simple. It actually feels good talking about it. I haven't told my family I was fired yet. I'm too embarrassed."

"Family?" He sat up and turned toward me.

"They haven't figured it out yet? Are you close with them?"

"Well, my mom is on husband number five. It's only been a few months, so she's blissfully in the honeymoon stage and not as involved in my day-to-day as she usually likes to be when her life is crap. My sister is Susie Homemaker with three highly intelligent and active children. It's not hard to keep things from them." *Enough with giving him the life story!* "What about you? What's your situation?"

"I travel a lot. Moving around wherever the work takes me. My folks are still together after thirty-two years. My parents own a ranch. Mom oversees a wildlife preserve. Dad is a scientist. They are great, but I had a strong need to move away and do my own thing."

"Siblings?"

"Yep. Seven."

"Seven! Yikes. Your mom have a litter?"

"Only a litter if it's all at once. I'm the oldest and Hot-and-Dreamy, aka Rollin, is one of my six brothers. The rest are still at home."

"Wow, all boys. Your poor mom."

He shrugged before pointing out the window. "Take the next exit."

I'd gotten comfortable talking and having him open up. Nerves reemerged as my car traveled down a dimly lit street. We were in the middle of nowhere, and I was back to questioning my sanity.

"Pull in here," he directed.

"I'm beginning to think my surprise sucks." I parked the car and drew a deep steadying breath.

He reached over and grazed his thumb across my jawline ending with a light tap on my chin. "Ye of little faith." He sprung out of the car.

Should I follow him?

Chapter Three

With my hand frozen on the door handle, I watched him turn and look back at me expectantly. *This is crazy! He could be an axe murderer!* My hormones overrode common sense when he smiled and dared me with his eyebrows. I was a sucker for dimples. I popped the center console and reached inside, palming a can of mace, just in case things went south fast. I exited the car.

He hadn't lied about it being a construction site. Points for honesty there. As I gingerly exited the car he trekked back and held out his hand to me. The desire to place my hand in his was supercharged, and when his hot digits curled around mine, I wanted to cuddle up by his side and nuzzle his neck.

Wow, I've been away from men too long. Cool the jets.

He tugged me past a newly poured foundation, helped me over a few obstacles, and headed to a makeshift office structure. Pulling the keys from his pocket, he rifled through them quickly in the dim light selecting the correct one on the first try.

"You wanted to show me your office? I'll have to warn you, I'm not really into filing."

"You're a crack-up." He chuckled and flipped on the light.

My eyes adjusted as I glanced around, marveling at what I saw. Raff read the look of wonder on my face.

"I said it would be worth it."

The office was like a museum. A room filled with Native American artifacts. Pottery was displayed on tables, weapons hung on the walls and shelves, and stone jewelry rested in plexiglass boxes. It was a massive collection, and many would have been impressed. I was thrilled. I adored Native American culture, was one of the few girls obsessed with Westerns, and regularly visited tribal lands. My mom said I was part Cherokee, but too small a part to be recognized. Ever since she told me as a little girl, I was hooked on learning everything I could about it.

"How did you know?" I asked breathy.

"That this would be worth it?"

I turned to appraise him. "How much I would like it?"

"What's not to like? It's some freaking cool stuff," he said and smirked.

"Why is this here?" I walked forward and lightly brushed at a clay pot. "An odd place to store a collection."

"Better than a hotel room. I move around a lot. This trailer comes with us from site to site."

"This is yours?"

"Benefits of the job."

"You dug this stuff up?" I looked at him in wonder. "Why did you keep it? This should be in a museum or returned to a local tribe."

"My brother is an archeologist. His part in all this is to assess if a site needs to halt construction or if we need to halt for artifacts." Raff placed a wicked-looking spearhead in my palm and I ran its smooth surface over with my finger. "We often work with local tribes. A lot of what you see here are the thank-you gifts at the end of a job. Not everything has value, but I like it."

That made me feel less guilty exploring the objects. I relished being able to touch and feel everything. Way cooler than just looking behind glass.

"Would you like something?"

The question caught me off guard. At first, I

thought he meant a drink, but he had his hand out signaling the room.

"A generous offer. You hardly know me." It would be amazing to have any piece here. My eyes could not help but rove around the room. "I can't accept."

"Nonsense." He stepped close behind me. I felt the contours of his chest brush against my back causing a liquid flame to heat me through to the core. His arms swept forward and he fastened a pendant around my neck. It was beaten silver adorned with turquoise, not a sophisticated piece, but I loved the roughness. It felt ancient.

My hand clutched the cool metal. "It doesn't feel right."

"No?" he challenged.

I shook my head, yet my hand still clutched the pendant. Strangely, I believed it should be mine, but my mind warred with such a notion.

"I want you to have it." His hungry stare scorched me as he looked at the necklace settled between my breast.

"Huh," a puff of air escaped my dry lips. "Do you always get what you want?"

I expected a cocky "most definitely" in reply. Instead, he kissed me. It was unexpected and certainly not gentle. His hand clasped the back of my neck taking full possession of my head. His lips crashed into mine, startling me into opening my mouth, giving his tongue entrance. I was a passive observer for a brief second before my body automatically responded.

I swear if it was any other man I would have reared back and belted him for his aggressive liberties. With Raff, I softened, melting against him. I welcomed the intrusion of his tongue in my mouth. My senses lit up tasting him. His scent was intoxicating, making me almost dizzy. I was instantly aroused and completely ignored the little voice in my head screaming for me to get a grip on the situation.

He pulled away still holding my neck, and stared deeply into my eyes. I was panting, trying to remember to breathe. I needed him to kiss me again. Not wanted. *Needed*. I leaned in trying to encourage him to resume, but he dropped his hand and stepped away.

"I'll walk you to your car," he said abruptly.

"Wait. What?" Is he kicking me to the curb?

"It's late and you have an even longer drive home now."

He acted like the kiss didn't meet his standards, yet the clear bulge in his pants said otherwise. "You're asking me to leave?" I asked bewildered by the turn in his demeanor.

His hand snaked out and clasped mine before I could think to deny him. "Are you working tomorrow?" he asked.

"No."

"Good." He tugged me out the door. "I'll pick you up at noon."

"Are we having the same conversation here?" As we headed out, I tried to free my hand from his, but he held on tightly until we reached my car door and he opened the driver side for me.

"You know how to get home from here?"

No way am I letting him see his craziness affected me! "Of course." I wanted to hop in, slam the door shut, and gun it, when Raff's warm hand splayed open over my collarbones. His fingers tickled and caressed me, driving me to distraction. I started to lean into him again thinking things were getting back on track, when he pushed me gently into my seat. He fasted my seat belt as if I was a small child requiring assistance.

"Drive safe. Go straight home."

He shut the door and strode away before I could tell him to fuck off.

Chapter Four

I almost had myself convinced last night was a dream. What guy gets all hot and heavy and sends a girl home? It had to be some bizarre nightmare brought on by the frustration I felt around him. I wanted him and it made no sense. I don't fall hard for complete strangers. In fact, I never fall hard at all. Guys are a fun distraction, never an obsession.

"What is it about you, Raff, that has me hot and bothered?"

I stretched, reaching for my phone on the nightstand to check the time. It was a quarter to eleven, but when you get home after three, it was reasonably early. I turned off airplane mode and the junk emails poured in. No responses to the slew of resumes I'd sent out. No texts from my friends either. I wasn't surprised. Since I lost my job, I'd been a bit antisocial, shooting out a negative to every invite, and rarely answering calls.

I had a pile of bills to attend to, groceries to buy, and a long overdue trip to the gym to round out my day. Groggily, I made it to the bathroom where the mirror reflected Raff's pendant still dangling around my neck. I reached to unclasp it but changed my mind. As much as the guy drove me to distraction, I adored the necklace.

Normally I would skip the shower before heading out to the gym, but enough beer had spilled on me last night to require a rinse-off. No one wants a girl to smell like a brewery on the treadmill. Besides, it was one of those Indian summer, early fall days. I'd be dripping in sweat as soon as I stepped outside. After the shower I was mentally ready to tackle my mediocre day.

While hunting through the sad remains of my

fridge for nourishment, the doorbell rang. Expecting some kid trying to sell me junk food for fundraising, I swung the door open with a politely bland expression. Raff stood there instead. He was dressed in swim shorts and a loose tank top, exposing toned arms and beautiful tanned skin.

"Oh, good. You're ready." Raff offered me a sexy smirk while his eyes wandered all over me. I was showing less skin than I usually do to tend bar, but his gaze made me feel like I was naked. Just the idea of being bare in front of him caused the sweetest throbbing.

"What are you doing here?" My response was way more breathless than I wanted it to be.

I should have shut the door on him, but he managed to squeeze past me and enter my home uninvited.

"Live here long?" He perused my condo at his leisure.

"Oh, not again. When I ask a question you should just answer it. Like, how the hell do you know where I live?" This called for a hands-on-hips, no-nonsense stance.

He swung around to face me, clearly not intimidated, based on the amused glint in his eyes. "I said I would pick you up at noon. Don't you remember?"

"I don't remember agreeing, *or* telling you where I live." Hands on hips moved to arms folded across chest.

"Why don't you go put on a swimsuit? I have everything else packed."

"You're doing it again! You're avoiding answers by changing the topic. It's making my head spin."

He moved in close, invading the boundaries of personal space. I could smell the sun on his skin mixed with a sent uniquely his: woodsy and wild. I had the strongest urge to nuzzle against his neck. "I'm just trying to speed this up. Get us on the road faster and start our day. We could have this long dragged-out talk about what a jerk I am or why things ended abruptly last night, but the day is beautiful and I have another surprise for you."

"You are nothing but surprises. And, like I said before, I don't like surprises." Was this guy for real?

"Hmm." His index finger slid down my throat and made little circles around the pendant he gave me. "Chloe, I'm not going to ask you to come with me. I can tell, even if you can't, that it's what you want."

"Why, you arrogant—"

"I want," he interrupted my rant. "To spend the day with you. I want to hear that sexy laugh of yours. I want to watch you lick those full lips while you debate how much about yourself you are willing to share. I want to see that beautiful body dripping wet and lounging beside me at the lake."

His rumbly deep voice and seductive words made my nipples harden and my body heat up. It was as if he had woven a spell over me. My irritation vanished. I wanted … whatever he wanted.

"Does that seem like such a bad surprise?" he asked softly.

I could only swallow and shake my head.

"Then go get dressed. I promise to provide you a memorable day off."

It was only when I was in my room, bathing suit laced up and pulling on my cut-off shorts that I wondered about my reaction to him. This attraction was like nothing I'd experienced before. I was always in control. I called the shots. Being the one with the power in the relationship was as necessary to me as breathing. Yet, I grew bored after a short while, hardly ever satisfied. Raff was hot enough to melt the polar ice caps, but I'd dated hot. There was something desperate in my desire that both frightened and intrigued me.

He presented a challenge. I loved a challenge.

"Ready," I called out as I sauntered back in the room. My candy-apple-red bikini showed through the sheer white tank I tied up high, leaving my midriff bare. The cut-off shorts I threw on were barely more coverage than my bikini bottom. Those shorts coupled with high wedge sandals made my legs look fantastic. If I was going to pant like a wild animal over this guy, I, at the very least, had to take a shot at him doing the same over me.

"Did you eat?" The look he cast my way said he would like to eat me.

I smiled, pleased at his reaction. "Nope. Not much here."

"I know a place on the way to stop. They make a mean picnic lunch." His big warm hand enveloped mine as he led me to his giant Ford pickup truck.

No surprise this time. It's the perfect vehicle for a construction guy. I had to hop up to make it onto the seat. Note to self: *Never* wear a short skirt when he drives. The thought made me giggle. I was already planning on seeing him again.

"What?" His cocky, seemingly all-knowing smile made an appearance.

"Your truck suits you."

"Yep." His smile turned into a cheeky grin. "It's big and built for performance."

I rolled my eyes but laughed, some of the tension leaving me.

"That laugh of yours does things to me."

This I like. A bit of the power shifting to me. "Oh? What kinds of things?" I poured on the sultry.

"The kind of things that make we want to do all

sorts of things to you. Breathless, sweaty, lip-biting, deep moaning kind of things."

This guy had a direct hotline to my groin. As a bartender, I excelled at casual flirting. It was different with Raff. I felt everything more intensely. I swallowed noticeably and remained uncharacteristically quiet.

His throaty chuckle sent a dark blush across my cheeks. "No smartass response, darlin'?" He paused as his eyes caressed me and I remained mute. "I'll have to remember how much you react to dirty talk. With a woman like you around, that's gotta come in handy."

"Around?" I tried to put as much scorn in my voice as possible. I didn't like him thinking he bested me. "What makes you think this is more than a one-time date?"

The engine roared to life. He left the gear in "park" as his hand grasped my thigh. Fingers rubbed the skin under the edge of my shorts. He angled his body in front of me, skimming his lips up my throat and across my jaw. His stubble left a delicious burn in the wake of his movements. "With you, Chloe, once would never be enough." The words spoken in my ear were warm and silky, and I shivered despite the heat.

He leaned back and shifted into "drive." The truck lurched forward, breaking the spell. "You are one cocky bastard," I breathed out.

A sly smile spread across his face and he gave me a knowing look. He could have been a real dick and called out my reaction to him as proof, but he didn't need to. He had me beside him panting and ready with a quick thigh grab. I needed to turn the tables around and not play the bitch in heat.

Old-time country music blasted out of the speakers making conversation, not only unnecessary, but impossible. I used the time during the drive to devise a game plan. For this man, I would be pulling out all the stops. *No more simpering nice girl!*

Chapter Five

"Um … how much food do you eat?"

Raff rattled off an order for lunch that would feed a small army.

"I'm good with a sandwich and bag of chips," I added.

"I might not have even ordered enough. My crew is at the lake. They left earlier to launch the boat and are probably close to gnawing on each other right now."

"Oh," I tried not to sound disappointed. I thought it would be just the two of us. "Are you throwing me a surprise party?" I teased.

"Something like that." His hand settled on my hip yanking me forward. I collided with his hard chest as a gasp escaped my lips. He took advantage of my open mouth to kiss me, right in the middle of the crowded restaurant. It was unexpected. He had numerous chances at my place that he passed on. Instead, he waited for an audience. PDA is not my thing, yet I didn't pull away. His kisses were addictive. I involuntarily arched my back and pressed in closer as if my body needed to rub up against him. They called our order, to my disappointment. I didn't get enough of him. The secretive knowing smile of his made another appearance, mirth danced in his eyes. He was excruciatingly aware of the effects he had on me.

Raff one, Chloe zero.

Raff stacked all the boxed lunches and carried them out the door. I balanced the drinks and followed behind. The lake could be seen from the front of the sandwich shack, making the remainder of our drive only a matter of minutes. Despite the warm day, it wasn't too crowded. The campground he parked at housed one trailer and a four-wheel drive Suburban. A lone ski-boat floated in waist-high water just off the launchpad.

Three picnic benches, painted a dark forest green, sat in alignment at the water's edge. All were empty save one. Tate the Colossus, Rollin Hot-and-Dreamy, Weylin the Biker Dude, and Lowe the Nail- Biter were all laughing and cutting up. No girls at all.

"Do the guys know you're bringing a date? Looks like man time to me." My stomach felt a bit unsettled as I fidgeted with my outfit.

Raff shook his head and snickered before swinging his door open. "Get out of the car, Chloe. They're going to love the fact that you're here."

"Why is that?"

He took the drinks from my hands and replaced them with a few boxes. "Because you're bringing food."

"Ha-ha," I griped but some of the flutters faded. I talked to strangers for a living. Most men loved me instantly. *How hard could this be?*

The guys all stood as we approached and helped us set down our burdens. The Hot-and-Dreamy Rollin was the first to shake my hand. I knew most of them from the bar but strangely we never spoke, everything had been filtered through Raff before.

"Chloe, I'm Rollin." He sauntered up, and I smiled my big dazzler before I shook hands. His were smooth for a man in construction, but as the archeologist of the group, perhaps he didn't do any physical labor.

"Nice to finally talk with you. I was thinking perhaps Raff's crew was mute," I laughed.

Hot-and-Dreamy even had a perfect dimple when he smiled. "My brother is a bit territorial."

"Raff did tell me you were brothers, but not much else." I examined Rollin and Raff side by side, only seeing the resemblance once it was pointed out. On close inspection I could see similar lip shapes and almost identical bone structure. Rollin was blond with blue eyes, like a Nordic god, where Raff's black hair and olive skin depicted him as more of a Roman god. Both very deserving of their divine origins.

"What, he doesn't talk about me endlessly to you?" Rollin teased. "He sure talks about you enough to me."

A pleasant warm and fuzzy feeling settled over me. *So, he talks about me to his brother. Score a point for Chloe.*

Raff shoved his brother to the side and pointed at Colossus. "Chloe, this is Tate."

The bolder of a man didn't offer me his hand, instead he tipped his hat. "Ma'am."

"Hi." I nodded in return.

"And I'm Weylin." The full-sleeve tatted-up biker dude introduced himself before Raff could. He took my hand in both of his and shook it warmly. "I'm so glad we get to spend the day with you. I hope you like boats. Do you ski?"

"Never tried before," I confessed.

He gave me a toothy smile and wiggled his pierced eyebrow. "I'm an excellent teacher. I guarantee I will get you up and riding in less than three tries."

I'm not one to back away from a challenge. "Sounds like a generous offer."

Weylin would have continued to talk with me, but Raff nudged him aside and signaled to the Nail-Biter. Being the youngest, he was always the one they called to carry drinks or get the balls for the pool table.

"Say hello, Lowe," Raff instructed.

"Hey," the kid croaked. I knew he was over twenty-one since my bouncer let him in the bar, but it was hard to believe. Lowe looked like a pimple-faced teenager, unsure of himself and completely worried about what others were thinking of him. I generally ignored men like him, but when he awkwardly thrust his hand out and lowered his eyes, I felt strangely protective and wanted nothing more than to make sure he felt comfortable around me.

"Hey back at you, Lowe." I squashed the natural sultry in my voice completely and spoke in a higher, more soothing pitch. It worked enough for Lowe to make a second of eye contact before he smiled shyly. Raff watched the exchange silently, but I noticed approval in his eyes.

"Let's dig in," Raff announced. A flurry of opening boxes and setting out plates followed. Raff snaked a sandwich first and piled his plate with every side dish. It always surprised me how much guys could pack away.

The others were more gentlemanlike, and treated me like a guest. Rollin offered me the perfect dimple with his smile. "Ladies choice."

"Oh, I'm not picky. You boys take what you like."

Not one of them made a move to do so, however. Realizing we were at a standoff, I opted to be gracious so they would eat. "All right, then." I laughed. I didn't fill my plate to the brim, but I did attempt to try a little of everything, it smelled and looked amazing. While Raff was munching away, his crew waited for me to take my first bite before they helped themselves.

The day went on much like that—Raff doing what he pleased and his crew trying their hardest to please me. While there were times I didn't know what to make of it all, the attention was nice. I was desperate to have Raff eating out of the palm of my hand, but it didn't look possible. What I lacked from him, the others made up for tenfold.

Tate was a man of few words, but he was a gentle giant. After lunch the guys stripped down to just their swimsuits to swim out to the boat. I stressed over it slightly. I didn't relish just being in a skimpy bikini with five guys, but knew my white tank top would be soaked and little better than see-through once wet. Tate offered to carry me all the way out. He was so tall the water didn't even touch me. After depositing me softly in the boat as if I was made of glass, Tate smiled, clearly pleased he could be of service. The big guy just made me feel safe.

Rollin was a complete flirt. I wondered if he did it to get a rise out of Raff, but his brother clearly wasn't the jealous type. I hated jealous boyfriends, yet Raff getting a little green would have thrilled me. Rollin showered me with compliments about my laugh, my hair, more than a few about my red bikini, and even waxed poetic about my badass drink-making skills. In any other situation I would assume the guy wanted to get into my pants in the worst way, but instead I felt appreciated.

Weylin was as good as his word. He did make an excellent instructor. I was up and skiing on my second try. He was also the most inquisitive man I'd ever met. He bombarded me with questions about myself, and genuinely seemed interested in every answer, even the mundane ones. My dead-end job, lack of amazing friends, and little apartment took on allure and fascination in his eyes.

Lowe warmed up to me. He was a bit of a joker and prankster. I imagined he'd make an excellent little brother and dastardly deeds co-accomplisher. Together we managed to hijack Rollin's phone and installed a series of apps that sent him constant notifications during the day. Lowe told me that Rollin was a bit of a phone junkie, and the dings would drive him crazy. We snickered to each other as he pulled his phone out and stared in confusion when it prompted him to make sure to drink more water, or notified him about current events unfolding like weather patterns or beauty pageant results for Miss North Carolina.

Raff remained an enigma. His guys were awesome. I felt instantly connected and comfortable around them. Raff left me on edge. The worse thing was, I wanted to please him. Why I cared, I couldn't begin to fathom. I was being lavished attention by the others, but it was Raff I wanted. My eyes were drawn to him. Every simple touch brought a rush of warmth and pleasure. Every sexy stare had my core burning. I ate, I swam, I skied, my hair whipped wildly in the wind while the sun kissed my skin, yet all I wanted was for Raff to take me home and get in my bed.

Shit, I had it bad.

Chapter Six

"I had fun today," I simpered while I played with my hair. This man made me use all the tricks. Raff had parked his truck in front of my place, but made no move to get out. "Would you like to come up? I can make coffee, or something stronger."

"Say what you're really asking for, Chloe." Those hazel eyes of his were half-lidded yet intense.

"Sometimes you can be such an ass." I wanted to crawl under the seat and hide in embarrassment, or scratch out those penetrating eyes. *Why am I sticking around for this shit?* I grabbed my purse in a huff and shoved open the truck door. Stupid thing was too heavy to slam as loudly as I would have liked, but that didn't stop me from trying.

Raff hopped out after me and started leisurely following. I whirled around to face him. "What the hell are you doing? In case you didn't get the hint, I'm kinda pissed off right now."

He chuckled deep and throaty before scratching at the stubble on his chin. "It did not escape my notice."

"Well, then?" My glare brought plenty of men to their knees.

"I'm ignoring it, obviously." He strolled past me as I stood stunned and flustered.

I wanted to rage. I wanted to tell him to go to hell and to ask who he thought he was. Something stopped me. Some crazy force had me walking up the steps after him and handing him my keys when he gestured for me to do so. I was mute as he flipped on the lights. I tossed my purse on the table by the door and waited. Whatever his next move was I wanted to see it.

He made a beeline to my bedroom door then leaned against the frame while crossing his arms. "Come here," he said gruffly.

Damn me, but I did.

"You had the boys eating out of the palm of your hand today," he spoke with his lips twisted in a side smirk. He took his index finger and pressed it lightly against my lips before I made a snarky comment. "You did good with them, as I knew you would. Had them falling over themselves, eager to please you." He dropped his hand from my mouth and circled it around my waist bringing me in close. "But that isn't ever going to be me. I don't mind you trying, in fact, I often enjoy the show. I certainly don't mind when you throw a fit and the claws come out. I like that side of you too. Be yourself, darlin'. From a woman like you, I expect nothing less. Just know that I will be myself too."

"And who is that? A cocky bastard?" I asked with all sweetness.

His grin was wide but his eyes held a lot of heat. "I'm the one in charge."

"In charge?" I titled my head up to meet his stare. "Are you for real, Caveman?"

His answer wasn't a verbal one. His lips explored my neck, marking their journey with warm kisses and soft nibbles. The sensation shot straight down my spine and had me curling my toes. He tugged aside my bikini top exposing a nipple. My protest died suddenly when he closed that magical mouth over it licking and sucking until I cradled his head against me. He walked backward as he feasted on me, and I stumbled along in a fog of lust.

Raff tossed me on the bed. I bounced a few times while I watched, slack-jawed, as he removed his shirt. All day I had enjoyed the sight, but seeing his sculpted abs and toned shoulders in the privacy of my bedroom was a real treat. He covered me with his warm body and captured my lips in a searing kiss. I was encouraged that my plans for sex were finally mutually shared by the ridged length of him pressed against me.

I made a move to touch him, but he stayed my hand. Instead, he undressed me. First unlacing my bikini top and tossing it to the floor, then with one forceful tug my shorts and bikini bottom followed. I was completely bared to him, and I could tell he liked what he saw. His hands explored my breasts and traveled down my stomach almost reverently. I sucked in a sharp breath when he cupped my sex and rubbed me gently. I was ridiculously wet for this man, and he slipped a finger into me with ease.

"This is what you were really asking me for in the truck. Isn't it, Chloe?" His tongue flicked over his bottom lip while he watched his finger glide in and out of me.

I sure as shit didn't want him to stop. Who needs pride anyway? "Yes," I admitted.

"You want to be with me. You want me inside of you?"

"Yes," I nodded barely able to think as his clever fingers moved.

My answer satisfied him and he dedicated all his attention to my pleasure. Between the steady rubbing and force of his invading finger, he wrung an orgasm out of me faster than I had ever managed by myself.

Magic mouth and magic hands.

As soon as the flutters and pulsing ended, I wanted more. I couldn't explain my body's strange awareness and needs around Raff, but that man played me expertly. I came close to clapping when the board shorts were pulled off and joined my pile of clothes on the floor. I was eager to feel him and wantonly opened my legs wider in welcome. Raff didn't hesitate as he angled himself and pushed in. My body quickly accommodated.

My momma used to say I'd know when I found *the one*. I always got a kick out of it. The woman was on her fifth husband. No one man was a perfect fit. The horizontal tango with Raff had me rethinking my dismissiveness. There wasn't that awkwardness of a first time. Our bodies moved in unison. Every thrust felt choreographed. I could feel my body cresting to achieve the ultimate climax. When I came, it was long and earth-shattering as if every molecule in my body vibrated with pleasure.

I could tell it was the same for him. He was still shaking for some time after. This was going to be a hard man to walk away from. I've had good sex before. This couldn't even compare. Raff set a new standard. As we were laying in a tangled heap of limbs, gasping for breath, a dreamlike haze settled over me and pulled me into true slumber.

****

I woke up in an empty bed. I stretched out like a cat enjoying the sun's warm morning rays before I curiously looked around. Raff's clothes were gone and I couldn't hear him in the bathroom. I found my bathrobe on the floor of my closet and slipped it on. Thinking Raff was most likely in the kitchen making coffee, I headed there. No lights were on, though, and the delicious aroma of coffee wasn't lingering in the air.

It never occurred to me he would leave without a word until I exhausted every other alternative. I hunted for a note perhaps left by the bed or fridge. I checked my phone for messages. I walked outside to see if his truck was truly gone. I waited over an hour thinking maybe he went out to buy us breakfast. Nope.

Well, fuck me.

I knew I rocked that man's word as much as he rocked mine. Every sign pointed to bedroom perfection, yet he hadn't even stayed around for seconds! I snatched my phone off the table and paced back and forth. Should I call him and give him a piece of my mind? Should I send a snotty text asking where's the fire? Should I— My thought was interrupted by the phone ringing.

Anger melted instantly to eagerness when I saw his name flash on the caller ID. "Hello," I answered trying to sound collected.

"Hey, darlin'." I could tell from the background noise he was driving. "I got a call about an emergency on the site and had to dash out."

"Oh?" I played it cool.

"Yeah, I would have woken you, but I believe I wore you out." His chuckle was flirty and my cheeks heated up.

"I did miss seeing you."

"About that…" There was a long pause that had me frantic about what he was going to say. "You won't be seeing me for a bit."

"Oh?" I repeated, not playing it cool.

"This emergency is a real mess, at least five days of cleanup and working around the clock. I will, however, be coming back for you on Saturday."

"No need to go to any trouble, besides, I think I'm working Saturday," I lied wanting to be a little hard to get for the lack of a proper goodbye.

"No, you're not." Raff called me out on my bullshit. "I saw your schedule on the fridge. I'll be at your place Saturday at eight."

"Maybe I have plans." Not sure why I was digging in my heels, except my desire to see him again was riding me so hard it scared me a little.

"Chloe?"

"Yes?"

"What are you doing? Why are you playing games?"

"Not sure what you mean."

"Okay, then…" Raff sighed heavily. "I'm coming for you Saturday."

"See ya Saturday," I replied. I ended the phone call and stared at the screen. The guy had an emergency and needed to leave. He called and made plans to see me again. None of this should be triggering my alarm bells, but they were. I was nervous he didn't want me as much as I wanted him. I felt like I had no control over my hormones around him. He said to jump and I said "how high?"

Shit! He was in charge.

Chapter Seven

The week was a total suck-fest. I couldn't focus on anything except wondering if Raff would call. I was scheduled to work Monday through Friday, but contemplated every day calling out sick. Mooning around the bar waiting for a dude to call was completely not me. Yet, I spent five days doing just that. He said he would be by to see me Saturday, but I still assumed some communication would happen. I'd sent him two texts and a voicemail and got back radio silence.

What the hell was wrong with me?

I missed him. Me! Missing a guy. After only one real date. Unbelievable. I even thought about the guys on his crew. I felt isolated and trapped in my life. Which was also strange. I liked being alone. I usually didn't mind ditching my friends to be solo. I wanted Raff to rub up against me like a starving man wants a cheeseburger, but I also wanted the comradery I felt with his crew the day at the lake. The easy acceptance they offered was like a balm to an open wound I hadn't known I carried. I missed the connection.

"I need a round of shots for my table." A plain-looking middle-aged man was staring at me. It was clear from his annoyed expression he might have repeated himself a bit before I took notice of him. Old me would be laying on the charm right now to get his frown turned upside down, but sappy-weak-needy me just shrugged sheepishly.

"Sorry, sir. What can I get ya?"

"Four shots of Fireball."

"You bet." I poured, I smiled, and I accepted his payment and shitty tip without comment. The routine kept me moving and was getting me through the week.

"Last call!" I shouted out ten minutes earlier then I should. Ray, the bouncer, gave me the thumbs-up. He had plans tonight after work in the form of a tall redhead, so he didn't mind if I sped up closing.

It was twenty past two when the last customer left and the place was cleaned up for Saturday. Ray walked me to my car before hustling over to his. I waved and smiled at his happy antics. That boy was about to get some, and I envied him something fierce. My mood lightened a bit on the drive home, technically it was Saturday. Raff said he would be by on Saturday. I just had to wait a mere eighteen more hours.

You are pathetic!

****

From the moment I woke up, I cleaned my apartment like a woman possessed. I fixated on every detail. New sheets were placed on the bed. Candles were pulled out for the nightstand and kitchen table. I changed my clothes four times before the outfit felt just right. I wasn't sure if Raff would be hungry, 8:00 was late for dinner, but just in case I put a chicken in the oven. I'm not a great cook, but I could manage that at least.

My man would need sustenance. I had every intention of keeping Raff trapped in my bedroom for as long as humanly possible. Sure, I was pissed he hadn't called, but he mentioned an emergency, so I gave him the benefit of the doubt. I'd be even more forgiving if he appeared with flowers and an inability to keep his hands off me. Just thinking about last weekend had my pulse racing and my mind conjuring new possibilities for tonight.

With no other details left to attend to, I sunk into the couch with a book in my hand, but mainly I watched the door. At 8:15, I tossed the book on the floor and glared at the door. At 8:30, I started checking my phone every minute. At 8:42, I began to worry he may not show at all. Rather than be my usual pissed-off self, I got a bit weepy and depressed. At 8:55, I started to worry maybe Raff had been hurt. That had me up and pacing the floor wondering what I could do. I didn't have any number but his, and I had a desperate need to discover if he was all right. At 9:12, a knock on the door had me running.

Flinging open the front door, I choked back a small sob seeing Raff towering in my threshold. I circled my arms around his waist and squeezed him tightly. "I was beginning to think you might be hurt."

He cleared his throat and patted my back lightly. "Sorry, darlin', I came as soon as I could."

I drew back hearing an odd edge to his voice and saw that Tate stood behind him. I wanted to immediately ask what the hell Tate was doing at my place, but realized I was looking mighty needy. It was a trait I scoffed at in other women. Instead, I drew back and stepped away allowing the boys to enter my apartment. "Hey, Tate," I acknowledged the giant.

"Ma'am." He nodded his head. "Mind if I use your bathroom? It was a heck of a long ride, and Raff hates to make stops."

"Sure thing. Down the hall." I watched the big guy stride past me and my spirits lifted. Perhaps they drove down together and Tate was going to leave as soon as his bladder was empty. Couldn't fault him. I turned my attention back to Raff. "How are things? Is your emergency fixed?"

There was a bit more stubble than usual on his face, and Raff scratched at it noisily while taking me in. "You're looking awful pretty tonight, Chloe."

As usual Raff answered my questions with another conversation, but a girl never minds being called pretty. "Thanks."

A crash and a curse echoed down the hallway. I turned my head in alarm wondering what the big lug might have broken, when Raff pinned me against the wall and kissed me senseless. His tongue danced wildly with mine, he nibbled and nuzzled against me, and all the while repeated, "So beautiful." I forgot about Tate. I forgot about the whole world for that matter. Only Raff existed for me.

"Something smells good. Did you cook, darlin'?"

I nodded dreamily. "Just a roast chicken. You hungry?"

"Starving." Raff clasped his hand in mine as we headed for the kitchen.

"Might be a bit cold now. I took it out of the oven at eight." I pulled back the foil over the baking dish and was pleased to see a bit of steam emerge when I inserted a knife into the bird. "There are plates behind you in the cupboard."

"Who needs plates?" Raff picked at the chicken with his fingers, ripping off a juicy piece and popping it into his mouth. I chuckled and joined him, pulling off more and playfully feeding him. We didn't talk. I watched his lips glide over my fingers and snatch my offerings. Occasionally he would nibble on the soft pad of my thumb, but I liked it best when he put an entire finger into his mouth and sucked. I felt it all the way down to my toes.

It was only when the bird was demolished that I wondered what the heck Tate was doing. He better not be funking up my bathroom. God only knows what kind of horrors come out of a man that big! "Should you be checking on your buddy? Making sure he didn't fall in?"

Raff pulled off a smile, yet unease lingered in his eyes. "I'm sure he's fine."

I didn't have a great view of the apartment from the kitchen. It was tucked away off to the side. "Maybe he left and we didn't hear him then?" I pushed off the counter ready to enter the living room. Raff stopped me.

"Got any beer in the fridge?" His finger circled around my wrists pulling me back to him.

"Yeah. There should be a few bottles. Help yourself." I sprung away eager to know if we were alone for certain.

"Chloe…" Raff's voice trailed off. I had made it to the living room and the jig was up. It was obvious Raff had been keeping me occupied and out of site while Tate raided my entire apartment. I stood frozen, my mouth hanging agape at the slew of boxes and suitcases stuffed with my things. I could clearly hear Tate from my bedroom still making a racket.

"What the fuck?" I turned to stare at Raff both terrified and immensely pissed. "Are you stealing from me?"

"I'm not stealing from you. Tate's packing you up. I told you I was coming for you tonight." There was a slight tinge of guilt in the way he licked his lips as he spoke.

"I'm not following you." I took a few steps backward.

"This chapter in your life is over now, Chloe. You are coming with me. Tonight."

"Like hell I am." My eyes darted around looking for anything I could use as a weapon. "I want you and the giant freak to leave. *Right now*!"

As if on cue, Tate entered the living room, effectively pinning me between the two men. His brow was furled and the lug looked like he was on the verge of tears himself. "I'm so sorry about this, ma'am." He fiddled with an envelope in his hands. An envelope with my sister's name on it that looked to be in my handwriting.

"What's that?"

"It's a letter to your sister," answered Raff.

"Why?" my voice cracked thinking about the possibilities. *Oh God, please don't be a suicide note.*

"It's a goodbye and don't look for me letter. You're not going to be able to see her again. This way your mom and your sister get a little closure and don't waste time looking for you." Raff took the letter from Tate and propped it on the kitchen table with the new candle I'd put out.

"None of this is making any sense. Why are you doing this?"

"I don't think you're ready to believe the truth yet." He smiled half-sheepishly. I wanted to slap him, but was afraid to move any closer.

"Try me," I dared.

"It's for the greater good," he replied solemnly.

Before I could ask another question or provide a derisive snort, Tate reached me. I struggled against his meaty paws. The man was made from iron. He placed a wadded wet cloth over my nose and mouth. I tried not to inhale initially, but the urge to fight had me panting. A sharp medicinal smell assaulted my senses before the room turned sideways and darkness rushed in.

Chapter Eight

My eyelids fluttered heavy with sleep. It was like my lashes had been glued together. I tried to rub my eyes to clear them, but the restraints around my wrist prevented me. Just like that, my situation rushed back.

Oh shit! What the fuck am I going to do?

"She's coming to," a soft voice alerted me I wasn't alone.

Tensing up, I struggled to take in air. Every breath felt like an uphill battle.

"Relax, Chloe. You're going to pass out. Take slow breaths to stop hyperventilating. That's it … in and out." As freaked out as I was, there was something nonthreatening and soothing about the voice. It wasn't Raff or Tate's.

"I can't see," I gulped through my breaths.

Pressure shifted near me, then footsteps faded away. I was on a bed with my hands tied above my head, yet my legs were free. The sound of running water had me straining toward my right. I was desperate to discover where I was, but not stupid enough to believe I could still be anywhere near my home.

"You've been out for a day. Tate gave you a dose for a man. Raff was hella pissed off at him for the slip. Your eyes are crusted over." A warm washcloth was applied to my shuttered eyes. After a few wipes, I managed to properly blink. My mouth felt as dry as cotton, and I had to lick my lips a few times to get them working.

"Lowe," I said once I could see him. "Who were you talking to when I woke up?"

"Raff."

My heart pounded in my ears as I inspected the room. It was empty save for us. It looked like a room in a cabin of sorts. It had paneled walls and beamed ceiling as well as a rough wood-planked floor. The only softness in the room came from the full-sized bed I was anchored to. "Where is he?"

"I called him when I saw you finally stirring. He's been worried about you." Lowe was perched on the end of the bed. Far enough away that I couldn't touch him. I was strangely grateful to see him. If any of Raff's crew had to be here, I would have picked Lowe. There was something unassuming about him, I had no fear he would harm me. Perhaps I could even play on his kindness.

"Raff is the one who did this to me. You have to untie me, Lowe. Now. Before he gets here. You have to let me go."

Lowe averted his eyes to my pleading stare and whined low in his throat. "I'm sorry, Chloe. I can't. We need you."

"If I can help you in any way, I will, Lowe. You need to untie me, though. I think Raff is going to hurt me. You don't want to see me hurt, do you?" The frenzied panic bubbled up clogging my throat and preventing air again.

Lowe reached in and patted my leg awkwardly. "There, there. You're getting yourself all riled up."

"Of course I'm riled up! I've been fucking drugged, abducted from my home, and kidnapped! Lowe, you *need* to untie me." I put the force of my conviction behind my words. I knew weak men, and Lowe was as passive and sweet as they came.

He noticeably paled at my tone, but mulishly shook his head. "Raff wouldn't like it."

"I don't give a shit what Raff likes," I hissed

between clenched teeth.

"Now, that wounds me, darlin'." A gravely baritone uttered from the doorway.

I slumped back on the bed and closed my eyes in defeat. My window to convince Lowe to do the right thing was too short. "Why am I here, Raff?"

"I can take it from here, Lowe." Raff jerked his thumb toward the door signaling the kid should beat it.

"She needs water and food. Can I bring her some?" Lowe shifted his weight from foot to foot while wringing his hands.

"Yeah, nothing too heavy. She won't be able to keep it down." Raff watched Lowe leave before he came to me. He didn't worry about keeping his distance. Not his style. Hopping on the bed like we were lovers, he angled his body over mine and set his hands beside each of my raised shoulders. I glared daggers at him while he quietly inspected me.

"How are you feeling? Headache? Nausea?"

"Are you for real?" I asked incredulously.

His answer was to raise his eyebrows in the classic *I'm waiting* gesture.

"I'm feeling great, Raff. Oh, except for being scared out of my mind, horribly uncomfortable, super confused about why you would do this to me, and ... I have to pee."

"I like the fight in you, darlin'. It's proper. I tell you what. I can make at least two of those things go away." He stretched above me and released the binding attaching my wrists to the bed. My hands were still tied together, but I could put my burning arms down. Pins and needles raced through my shoulders as I finally moved them.

Raff jutted his chin out at the bathroom door. "Go pee, but leave the door open."

I didn't wait for him to change his mind. I rolled to my side and struggled to my feet. Legs were a bit wobbly, but I angled away from Raff's offer to aid me. No way was I willingly touching him. I bolted for the door, not lying about having to go. I slammed the door closed behind me, but was crestfallen when I realized it had no lock. I went as quickly as I could, not wanting him to barge in while I was in a vulnerable position. It was difficult pulling my shorts up and down with my hands tied, but I managed. Raff hadn't pounded on the door, so I took the opportunity to explore the contents of the bathroom, hopeful I could find something useful. Damn thing was empty save a roll of toilet paper, a toothbrush, and toothpaste.

"Don't drink the water in there. Hasn't been treated this year and might get ya sick."

I had been two steps away from shoving my head under the faucet right before Raff's timely warning. Made me wonder if he could still see me with the door closed. I contemplated staying in the bathroom for as long as he would let me, but the aroma of something savory and the promise of water caused me to leave.

Lowe was back, and he brought a pitcher of water and a bowl of soup. He set the tray on the edge of the bed and made a quick retreat. "Untie me so I can eat?" I offered my bound hands to Raff.

He snorted and tugged at the rope causing me to step forward. "Sit on the bed with your back to the headrest."

I was tempted to flip him the bird, if I hadn't been so thirsty. I sat on the bed with my hands nestled in my lap and waited.

"So, you can follow instructions." He chuckled derisively. "I was beginning to wonder when you closed the bathroom door."

"Will you untie me now?"

Raff poured a glass of chilled water in a tall glass and held it to my lips. "Drink."

I held my lips firmly pressed together for ten seconds in silent resistance before I complied with his demand. The water ran down the sides of my mouth as I guzzled it. Raff pulled the glass away and wiped my face with the back of his hand. I jerked away from his touch, but he didn't comment on it. Grabbing the bowl of soup and a spoon, he sat close enough to my side to touch me. He dished up a spoonful and blew on the steam. It felt like an incredibly intimate action. I hated it.

"I can feed myself."

"Of course you can." He positioned the spoon in front of me encouraging me to take a bite. My stomach growled at the aroma. "My feeding you is an act of submission. It shows you I will provide for your needs. It builds trust."

"Why the heck would I trust you again?" *Dang it! I'll never be able to eat.*

"I can understand why you feel like that now, yet trusting me is something you want to do. It's part of who you are. You need to trust me, because I'll complete you."

"You know there are plenty of women out there totally into this kinky shit. Guy like you could have your pick of them. And they would want to be here. Unlike me." I moved my head farther away from the spoon even though my mouth was salivating and my stomach ached being so empty.

"Actually, the truth is quite the opposite. There are very few out there who could meet my needs." Raff attempted to feed me again, but I shook my head.

"Oh yah? And why is that? What makes me so special you abducted me out of the entire human population?"

"Well, for starters, Chloe, you're not human."

My mouth dropped open at that whack-a–doodle of an announcement providing Raff with the perfect opportunity to thrust a spoonful of soup in. I choked as it slid down my throat, but the small amount of nourishment made my stomach rumble like a hive full of bees.

"Quit being stubborn for once and eat, babe," Raff grumbled as he held another spoonful up to my mouth.

"Oh, I'm sorry. Is my captivity difficult for you? Why don't you just fuck off then and let me go? And what the fuck do you mean I'm not human?"

"Tsk, tsk, tsk." Raff gave a lopsided smile. "Such language."

I glared at him, refusing to let him rile me up anymore.

"Okay, Chloe, I tell you what. For every mouthful of soup you eat, I will honestly answer one of your questions. Tate gave you a large dose and you need food in your stomach."

"Why do you care?" I was so perplexed over my concerned abductor.

He held up the spoon again. "That sounds like a question."

I swallowed down the soup and willed him to speak.

"Because you're it for me, babe. You're my girl."

I snorted loudly in response. "I thought you were going to be honest. Are you insane? No, don't answer. You must be crazy if you think I'd believe that. Here's my real question. Why am I here?"

"Oh boy, there's more than one answer to that one." The spoon came up again and I slurped it down, hating him, but feeling better for the broth. "You're here because you're needed. Our species is on the verge of extinction and you could be part of the solution."

"Extinction? What the hell are you talking about?" I obligingly opened my mouth without being prompted.

"We are wa'ya, Canis Rufus to be exact, but red wolf is most commonly known."

"What about them?"

"Not them, *us*. It's what I am. It's what you are." Raff was serious. He set down the bowl of soup and huffed out a large breath. "I know you won't believe it until you have proof, but you are descended from the Aniwaya, the wolf clan. You are not truly human, you are part wolf."

I was glad he set the bowl down. There was no way I was taking another bite from the mental man. "Raff," I said as gently as I could, fearing I would set him off. "I think I would have noticed if I was part wolf."

"The gene is dormant in you. It's why our kind is going extinct. It's extremely rare for a female to be born that can shift these days, and the dormant females pass down only the dormant genes to their offspring. We are dying out. Fading into the human population to be gone forever." His forehead was creased, his eyes pinched, and his mouth set in a tight line. It was clear he believed every crazy word coming out of his mouth.

"Well." My mouth felt dry again as fear rose up accelerating my breathing. "Sounds like a lost cause. Maybe blending in with humans is what you're supposed to do."

"If you had cancer wouldn't you try to cure it? If there was a vaccine against HIV wouldn't you take it?" He stared at me intently, but I couldn't muster a response. I was afraid my answer would affirm his plan for me.

"We have found the key to unlocking the dormant gene. We can cure you. By doing so you can become a true female, able to breed. A pack needs a mated alpha pair to lead it, and you're my mate."

Oh boy! This was some crazy shit!

Reasoning with him was certainly out. The man was talking nonsense. I just needed to placate him until I could escape. "This is really sweet, Raff. I'm just not looking for that kind of commitment. I'm not even into any commitment."

"Chloe," he chuckled my name. "You've never been with your own kind before me. You move from guy to guy because they can't hold your interest. Admit I'm different. You felt a pull toward me you never experienced before."

His words were oddly unsettling. "Look. I'll admit you are a fantastic lay. Seriously, the best I've had, but that doesn't mean shit. I'm not what you think I am."

Because it's not real, you freak!

Raff huffed an exasperated sigh. "I'm not going to fight with you. Tate was supposed to get your dosage ready but after the last botch, I don't trust him to get it right. My brother should have it ready soon. I'll administer it, and then you'll see. We can talk more about what you are and what it means after."

He stood up to leave as panic gripped me. "Wait!" My cockiness vanished and I openly showed him how frightened I was. "What are you planning, Raff? What are you giving me? Some kind of drug?"

Showing him my weakness managed to break through to him. Raff sat back and stroked my hair. "Shhh, it's going to be all right."

"What are you going to give me?" My eyes watered but I maintained eye contact, allowing him to continue to comfort me.

"It's a serum. My father spent his life creating it to save our kind. Chloe, we need you." His eyes were pleading. My tears were affecting him.

"I'm scared. What if it hurts me? Has it been tested?"

His lips thinned warning me the truth would be unpleasant. "We have tested it."

"Successfully?" I truly wasn't sure I wanted to know.

His lips pinched even tighter. "No."

"What happened?" I breathed out the question.

"Doesn't matter. You are a better candidate. It won't happen to you."

He wasn't at all reassuring. "Are you going to hurt me?"

"I never want to hurt you."

"That isn't a real answer."

"Your new life is going to fit you so well. You've been aimless and floating. You're not happy. I'm going to change all that. Our pack will be your home. I'm going to fill all the things missing in your life. It will be worth a small amount of pain." He mussed up his thick black hair, letting his agitation slip out.

"Oh God! I'm going to die, aren't I?" I reached for him with my restrained hands. "Please! Please let me go."

"I'm sorry about all this, Chloe. I'm sorry you're scared. I'm sorry you hate me right now. I'm sorry this even has to be done in the first place. I promise I'll make it up to you."

He wasn't going to budge. My pleading fell on deaf ears. I ground my teeth and shoved him as well as I was able. "Yah, right after you kill me."

Raff stepped away, hands held in the air, showing

he wasn't going to push back. "You're an alpha female. It's in your blood to test me and fight me, but you should be resting up. I'll send Lowe back in. He'll have a more calming effect on you."

I glared at him until he opened the door and left the room.

Damn it! What the hell is going on? They're all fucking insane!

Chapter Nine

Raff was right about one thing—Lowe did calm me down. At least, I calmed outwardly. He came in, meek as a kitten, eyes cast down, wringing his hands like a guilty schoolboy. I could have ripped into him, made him cower in the wake of my anger, but I tried a lighter approach. Lowe was clearly the weakest link in this group, and if Raff was clueless enough to believe I wouldn't see it, then it was only Raff's fault if I exploited poor, sweet Lowe.

"I'm still hungry. Is there anything else to eat?" My voice sounded overly sugary to me, but the tone seemed to work its magic. Lowe smiled boyishly and nodded.

"I can grab you a bit more since you were able to keep the soup down. Be back in a jiff."

He hurried out the door eager to please. I launched myself out of the bed and scoured the room for something to help me remove the knotted cord around my wrists. Just like the bathroom, the bedroom was empty of anything useful. The dingy cabin room held one tiny window that I doubted I could fit through. The glass was filthy and covered in a layer of dirt, making it nearly impossible to see. I had to stand on my tiptoes to peer outside. No other buildings in sight. Looked like we were deep in the woods. Just as I was about to see if the latch would budge, Lowe walked in.

"I made you an English muffin, do you like…" he trailed off watching me. "It's nailed shut from the outside."

I spun around trying not to look guilty. "Can't blame a girl for trying." I smiled sweetly.

"I wouldn't ever blame you, Chloe." He shook his head, his expression sincere. "Our kind doesn't like small spaces. Your reaction is natural."

"Lowe," I maintained a gentle tone. "What is natural is a kidnapped woman trying to escape. It's a very real human reaction to being taken against one's will."

"Raff said you would never believe him until the proof was undeniable. Once you see what you are, you won't want to leave. Our pack will feel like home. Nothing in your experience will compare to the sense of belonging to something greater than just you."

"My momma used to say that about Sunday school, yet I haven't been inside a church in years. Not into the group thing so much." My stomach grumbled offering some proof to my statement of hunger. "Those for me?"

Lowe sighed at my rebuttal and handed over the plate. I took it awkwardly and just stared at it. It wasn't possible to hold it and eat with my hands tied. "Come on now, Lowe. I can't eat like this. I have no chance of getting out of the room, can I at least feed myself?"

"Promise to be good?" he asked hopefully.

"Cross my heart." *Not a chance!*

Lowe removed the plate from my hands and set it on the bed. He started on the knots, but the task proved too daunting to execute in any timely matter. He pulled out a large Swiss army knife from his pocket and fumbled around till he found the right blade to flip. Sawing at the cords took only a few moments until they blessedly fell away. I rubbed at my wrists and tried desperately not to look too longingly at his knife. Lowe was extra tense, watching me for any sign of duplicity. I decided to play it cool.

I scooped up the plate and sat on the large king-sized bed, tucking my feet under and getting cozy. The English muffin had cooled somewhat, but still had a good dollop of salty butter and a nice crunch. "This is perfect. Thanks."

Lowe visibly relaxed as I ate. He gingerly perched on the edge of the bed, checking all the while to see if I would object. He was the sweetest captor a girl could hope for.

"You don't have anything to worry about, Chloe. We're all going to be so good to you. You'll see."

The bread turned to cardboard in my mouth and I threw the remnants of the last piece onto my plate. "What the heck does that mean exactly? You guys planning some type of gang bang? I will fucking kill you."

With bulging eyes, Lowe turned beet red. "Oh, hell, no. You misunderstood me. We would never. It isn't like that at all," he protested. "Raff is alpha and only a mated pair … well … mate."

I snorted loudly but cooled down fractionally. "Are you telling me you guys are all abstinent?"

"Most of the guys fool around with humans, but never anything serious. Not possible. Humans can't hold our attention long, and the desire for more with them just isn't present. Not in the DNA."

I shift around uncomfortably. Lowe just described every so-called relationship I've ever had. If only I could write it off to not being broken, but chemically incompatible. These boys live in some serious denial.

"Where are we?"

"In the woods."

"I can see that," I scoffed. "I meant what city?"

"Sylva."

"Never heard of it."

Lowe shrugged. "Not much of a population here. Easy to get a cabin away from all living souls. We need large spaces when it's time for the change."

"When you turn into a wolf?" I clarified dubiously.

He just smiled causing innocent little dimples to form in his cheeks. Made me want to pat his head, when I should have considered smashing the plate over it. The idea of hurting him, however, was repulsive to me. I couldn't fathom why. I was a captive and needed to think clearly. He may be a sweet kid, but he was part of this. Oh, and don't forget crazy.

My eyes trailed the edges of the door. Unlike the window it wasn't locked from the outside. Lowe had come and gone with no issue. I wondered if Raff was far enough away. Could I make it out the front door? Then what? Trail an unknown wilderness or face a possible death sentence when they inject me with some home-cooked concoction. Probably a hallucinogenic. Make me believe I'm surrounded by wolves instead of men.

Wilderness hike it is! At least it was still early fall. Nights wouldn't get too cold. I might be able to forage for food. It could be days if it was as remote as Lowe implied. Then again, there could be a Stop n Shop a mile from here for all I know.

I stood and made a show of stretching. My muscles were plenty sore after being tied up and sleeping for so long. *Should I make a run for it while he's still in the room? Or did I need to try and knock him out somehow?* "Could I get another glass of water please?"

He jumped up as if happy to wait on me. "Sure thing!"

Lowe turned his back to me. Wincing, I forced myself to hit him over the head with the discarded plate. It shattered to pieces and caused Lowe to falter but not drop. I took advantage of his momentary confusion and tried to forget the look of hurt on his face. Shoving him with all I had, I yanked open the door and ran right into a brick wall, aka Tate. I bounced off the big man and landed flat on my ass. Scrambling to get back to my feet, I tried in vain to make it down the hallway. The Colossus scooped me up like a little kid, kicking and screaming. He didn't place me back in the room, however.

"Just settle down now, ma'am. I'd feel mighty awful if I hurt ya."

"Let me go! You asshole!" I screamed and beat at him with my fists. I might as well have punched a tank.

Instead of making a glorious escape out of the cabin, Tate carried me down the hall past another set of doors and into a communal living room/kitchen area. Raff and Rollin looked up as we entered. They were standing over a chewed-up, pine dining room table littered with small glass medicine bottles, the kind that use a syringe to draw out the liquid.

Shit! This was happening.

Raff's brows furled. "What happened?"

"She attacked Lowe and tried to make a run for it." Tate set me down as gently as a teacup in a saucer. I repaid him by turning around and kicking him in the shins with all my might. He grunted at the impact but didn't move an inch.

Raff handed his brother a roll of duct tape. "Wrap up her legs before she hurts herself and put her on the recliner."

Rollin approached me warily. I wanted to scratch his pretty-boy face. "Stay the hell away from me. I am not one of you freaks, nor do I want to be."

An exaggerated sigh from Raff was the response to my declaration. "Afraid it's too late for that, darlin'." Rollin looked uncomfortable, though, Tate would not make eye contact, and Lowe emerged from the room looking contrite as if he'd hit me.

"Don't let her get to you now, boys. Here," he snatched the tape back from his brother. "I'll do it."

Rollin held onto the tape a moment. "This is the…" he started but didn't finish.

"It's the right thing to do." Raff finished. "It's our only choice if we want to settle and be a pack." The other men nodded and any hope I had they would offer help died. "Y'all go and meet up with Weylin. Finish the supply run. We need enough for a week. I should do this myself."

"Okay, Boss," Tate tipped his head and headed out. Lowe chewed at his lip and waved a nervous goodbye at me. Rollin was the only one to hesitate.

"You sure you want to be alone?" He searched his brother's face. "You'll be okay?"

Rollin was worried about Raff being okay?

He clasped his brother's arm. "For the pack." Raff stated gruffly.

"For the pack." Rollin smiled faintly and trailed after the others. Raff unraveled some tape. It made a loud grating sound in the empty cabin room. "Come here, Chloe."

Chapter Ten

"Yeah, I'm good." Shakily I took a tentative step back, unsure if he would lunge after me when I didn't comply with his demand.

"I'm sorry it must be this way, Chloe. When it's all over, you'll see it's for the best. I'd have liked to give you more time with us first, but once I knew without a doubt you were my mate, time was up. I searched a long while for you." His lips were pressed in a tight, unhappy frown, and for the first time he seemed agitated.

"Let me go, Raff. I'd never tell a soul," I whispered my plea.

Slowly he moved in half steps. Unclear if bolting would bring him to me sooner, I hesitated and stood still. His eyes were a window of compassion. "I hate to see you frightened of me."

"Easily remedied. Take me home," my tone was clipped.

"Darlin', you are home."

Before I could blink, he was on me. I screamed and clawed at him like a wild thing. My nails left angry red welts down his face and neck. He didn't even blink. First he trapped one wrist then the other. Forcing my hands together, he wound the tape. The contents of my stomach plummeted and bile flooded my mouth. A sense of helplessness overwhelmed me, the damn broke, and fat hot tears scalded my cheeks as I sobbed loudly.

"Shhh," he attempted to console me. "I'm sorry to scare you. It'll be over soon. You need to calm down."

His words had the opposite effect. "I don't want it to be over soon," I wailed. I attempted to knee him in the groin, but he evaded. The action gave me some space, though, and I ran to the door. Raff tackled me before I could get two feet. I landed hard, banging my knee.

"Shit! Sorry!" Raff righted me while he inspected the damage.

Ignoring the pain, I kicked at him trying to break free of his hold.

"Damn it, Chloe! You are only going to hurt yourself. You need to keep calm and conserve your strength."

I kept up the kicks until the tape emerged again. "Please." The word escaped me in a shudder. "You don't have to do this." I watched in horror as he duct-taped my legs together. My wrists and hands were already bound all the way to the knuckles of my fingers, as if permanently fixed in prayer. *I will pray forever and a day if I get out of this.*

He chewed at his lip while staring at me. Those eyes, I had once thought seductive, were half-crazed and darting about the room. He took to frantically pacing the floor and running a hand through his disheveled hair.

"I'm sorry," he whispered for the hundredth time.

I wanted to scream, but was trying my best to survive. "You don't have to be sorry. Whatever this is, we can forget about it. Just let me go."

My begging made him wince, and made me hopeful I might be breaking through.

"I can't do that," he replied deflating me. "You have to understand, I don't want to hurt you."

"Then don't."

He looked outside the dirt-encrusted window. The sun was starting a slow descent into the horizon. He squeezed his eyes tight and scrubbed at his face. I could hear him blowing out a few deep breaths before he spoke. "I have to." It was as if he was trying to convince himself. I held my breath. His choice would seal my fate.

I trembled as he reached for the syringe on the nightstand. Panic set in. My stomach clenched and my skin grew hot and clammy. "No!" The tears fell heavily, temporarily obscuring my vision. "I don't want to die!"

He crouched back down beside me as I struggled to move away. I was no match for his large frame and strength. He kept me neatly in place as he injected burning hot liquid directly into my neck. His eyes bored into mine, remorseful yet determined. "You're not going to die, Chloe. You'll just wish you had."

"You fucking bastard! What have you done?" My reaction to the drug was immediate. Fire raced through my veins. I bowed my back as the heat consumed me.

"It's going to hurt like a bitch. You got too worked up and the adrenaline will make it move faster. You're going to feel like you have a fever for a day or two. You will be weak as a newborn. You might get sick, but you *will* survive." He huddled over me stroking the skin on my arms.

His touch was oddly soothing, keeping me grounded while my body was combusting. In the back of my mind I knew I should be repulsed by his nearness, instead, I panicked when he stood up.

"Where are you going?" I ground out through clenched teeth.

"I'm going to get some ice and a wet rag." His footfalls were hurried and he returned to my side swiftly. By now the burn was everywhere and I struggled against my bindings as a wild desire rode me to scratch off all my skin and set the fire free.

"Untie me!" I screamed.

"It's for your safety." He hoisted me in his arms and carried me back to the dingy room with the enormous bed. Settling me directly in the middle, he applied the cold damp cloth over my skin. It provided some measure of relief, but only where he touched me. Raff was tireless in his ministrations. He started at my forehead and worked his way to my feet. Repeating the process and refreshing the ice as it melted.

At some point I went numb to the onslaught of pain. My muscles were rigid, my toes and feet flexed, and my hands curled into claws. The painful fire living in my body was a constant companion, yet so was Raff. I focused solely on his movements. Imagining the small fleck of cold would grow and soon encompass me. I was able to slow my breathing to match his.

"Good, Chloe," he heaped on the praise. "Calm yourself. Don't fight it."

How, with the amount of pain I was enduring, I managed to be pleased with his praise, was beyond me. Yet, I did exactly what he asked. I let the heat wash over me. Thoughts became cloudy. My vision blurred. Raff hummed a sweet soft melody as he danced the towel over my body. Then, blessedly, I lost consciousness.

Chapter Eleven

The next two days were nothing more than a blur. I remembered Raff climbing into the big bed feeding me cool liquids, icy enough to make my teeth ache, but wonderful on my parched throat. I woke up once with Weylin sitting in a rocking chair reading a comic book. He embarrassingly escorted me to the bathroom since I was too weak to walk on my own. Occasionally, I would find Lowe curled up on the bed by my feet like a puppy, and Tate pacing the room while he sporadically checked my pulse and asked me if I was hungry.

When my fever broke, it was Rollin on guard duty. Just as Raff predicted, I felt like a rung-out dishrag, barely able to lift my arms. The pain and heat that had enveloped me was gone, along with the fuzzy head. I blinked my eyes repeatedly until my focus improved. Rollin was lounging on the bed next to me. He was prettier than his brother. Perfect cheekbones and a strong jaw to make any male model weep. I felt even more disgusting next to him. I could tell I smelled, and my long dark locks were tangled and greasy.

Rollin noticed me staring before I had a chance to move. He produced a megawatt million-dollar smile while pushing sweat-soaked hair out of my face. "Hey there," he cooed. "Welcome back to the land of the living."

I thought about shoving his hand away but my arms were made of lead. "No thanks to any of you," I sputtered.

"Are you one of those grumpy morning people? Although, it's actually early evening right now." He chuckled as he swung his legs off the bed. "I bet a nice warm shower will cheer you up."

"Don't fucking touch me," I glared, but there was little menace behind my words as I lay like a broken doll.

"I assure you, I would be a perfect gentleman, but it's Raff who has claimed the honor of nursing you. He's been a grump too. Seeing you fever free will set him right, though."

The thought of seeing Raff both terrified and excited me. Both feelings pissed me off. "Don't call him."

Rollin's eyebrows lifted high but then understanding replaced surprise. "You'll feel better being around him. He's our alpha. I know this is a lot to take in, but you belong with Raff. You just need to adjust."

"You have all drunk the Kool-Aid," I huffed. "This is kidnapping. Pure and simple. Anything else you imagine happening is all in your sick brains. The first chance I get, I'm out of here. I don't belong with you crazies."

"Tell that to me in three days." The bastard gave me a cheeky wink before shouting out the door. "Raff! Your girl is awake!"

"What's in three days?" I hated myself for taking the bait.

"The complete and utter shift of your reality." Rollin smugly wiggled his eyebrows.

Heavy footsteps echoed up the hallway. I actually smelled Raff before I saw him. The crisp scent of the forest mixed with citronella and cloves calmed me. I wanted to rage and scream when Raff replaced Rollin in the room, but my damn body betrayed me. If anything, I had the confounding desire to yip with excitement and bury my face against his chest.

Seriously! Get a grip!

Raff jumped on the bed, smiling like a damn fool

and jostling me while he touched me. His warm hands skated over my arms leaving a trail of goose bumps. He drew me close into a tight bear hug. With his nose and mouth buried into my hair he spoke, "I've missed you, darlin'."

"Go away," I replied. I was proud that I managed to sound gruff in spite of wanting to sigh in contentment. I sat up a bit and pushed him away.

Is it too soon to have Stockholm syndrome?

"I'm gonna get ya' cleaned up, put a proper meal in your belly, and get those muscles stretched out. You will feel right as rain by tomorrow morning." His huge goofy grin did not slip once. I'd never seen him so joyful.

"You doubted," I stated.

"Doubted what, darlin'?"

"There was a chance I could have died. You doubted I would make it. Admit it! You risked my life by injecting me with whatever that crap was."

"I didn't doubt you'd make it one bit," he stated emphatically. "Seeing you weak has been hard. Now the fever is gone, you'll be even stronger than you were before. The fever was just a cocoon."

"Bullshit. You injected something in me that almost killed me. Don't expect me to be grateful to you that I'm alive. I will always hate you for this."

The grin finally slipped from his face. "Well, you don't have to love me for this to work."

Before I could formulate a response, he scooped me up and carried me into the bathroom. I was unsteady on my feet. He wrangled the oversized t-shirt and plain cotton panties off me, not even registering my feeble attempts at slapping him away. I slumped against the sink and glowered when he turned on the shower and tested the water. He unbuckled his belt and snapped it off, followed by the button fly on his jeans.

"What are you doing?"

"Making sure you don't crack your head open. Weylin is better at stitches then he used to be, but he's still not great at it."

He tugged off his shirt and pulled down his pants. I averted my eyes and ground my teeth. My brain was telling me this was seriously fucked up. I should be screaming for help and fighting this man tooth and nail, yet my damn body was completely at ease. I was naked in a small room with my abductor and not a shred of panic.

Helping me into the shower, Raff anchored onto my waist so I could douse my head under the water. There was a few days' worth of sweat to scour off my skin before I even attempted to tame my hair. The familiar smell of cinnamon rolls alerted me to the bodywash being my brand from home. I remember Tate packed up most of my belongings. My shampoo and razor were also present in the shower caddy. "Where's all my stuff?"

"Only brought a bit of it here. Most of your things are in the trailer. We'll only stay here a few more days before we head out."

"Oh," I responded pondering if leaving would bring a chance at escape. I fumbled with the cap on the shampoo until Raff took it from me. He went to work massaging my scalp with one hand and keeping me balanced and upright with the other. Without even meaning to I leaned into him. The instant my breast hit his chest both of us stiffened. Desire darkened his eyes and the evidence of his arousal pressed against my thigh. Lust pooled in my stomach sending tendrils of heat down my legs, curling my toes.

"Don't," I pleaded in a breathy hiss.

"No need to worry, Chloe. I won't until you ask

me to." His eyes searched mine in silence.

"That is never going to happen." I swallowed the words hoping it wasn't a lie. "This is seriously messed up, you know? I'm not sure why you had to ruin everything by being batshit crazy."

He smirked but didn't respond. The tension between us was still set on level ten. Raff conditioned my hair, shut off the water, and toweled me off. All done while sporting an enormous erection. I would have been too weak to fight him if he was determined to have his way with me, yet I believed his promise. He made no move to initiate sex, and was cocky enough to believe I would. The memory of our one and only time haunted me. It was the best sex of my life. Hands down. Nothing else even came close. *Damn this man!*

Chapter Twelve

Blood pooled on my plate, the only remnant of the dinner I inhaled. Lowe had perfectly grilled the tastiest tri tip on the planet. He kept happily filling up my plate until I ate at least four servings and my stomach flew up the white flag.

"Is there anything you want, Chloe? Anything at all?" Lowe's warm brown eyes reminded me of a Labrador. They were loving and loyal. I wanted to be a bitch and shout out "my freedom," but those pleading-for-affection eyes halted the words.

"No, thanks, Lowe. I'm truly stuffed."

Dinner was spent in the cabin with Raff's entire crew. It was reminiscent of the day at the lake. They were attentive and sweet. I had to keep reminding myself this time I was a prisoner. Raff's demeanor, however, changed entirely from the bedroom to the living room. He was no longer delighted at simply seeing me fever free, nor was he smoldering and seductive. He was back to being a bit of an ass, barking at me when I didn't eat immediately, or remaining aloof during all the conversations. A strange desire to capture his attention and please him rode me hard. I simply couldn't understand why I continued to give a shit about him. Clearly, I was turning into a nutjob too.

"Is everything packed for the move?" Raff directed the question to his brother.

"Need a day or two to finish the foundation job and we should be all set."

"Good. Weylin, you go into town tomorrow and close out any credits we have. Pay in cash. Tate, go with Rollin and lend him a hand. I don't want to cut it too close. You all need to be back here with time to spare before the change starts. Gotta all spend enough time around Chloe so she imprints with the entire pack before the full moon."

"Full moon?" I couldn't help the giggle that erupted. "Wow, you guys go all out."

Raff's gaze settled on me, commanding and cold. Instantly I wanted to lower my eyes. "I know you probably won't listen to me yet, but this is important for your safety. If you don't feel a strong bond, there's a chance your wolf could go rouge. I don't want to lose you in the forest. Your instincts will help preserve you, but pack is safest. Over the next three days you need to spend time in close proximity with all of us."

My mouth dropped open. "Right," I drawled incredulous. "I'll add it to my to-do list. Spend quality one-on-one time with my captors. Check. I'll put it just slightly after finding a large shovel to bash your head in with."

"You must be feeling more like yourself. Sarcasm is sexy on you, darlin'." Raff leaned over and settled a hand on my thigh. I ignored the immediate tingles shooting into my groin. It's like the guy had a remote to my libido. "Come on. It's time for bed."

"I just spent two days in bed. Think I'll pass." I folded my arms over my chest and leaned back.

A slow sexy smirk was my only signal danger was coming. "I wasn't asking."

I gave a loud indignant squeal as he hoisted me up. I'm not a petite woman. I'm almost five foot ten. Damn if I didn't feel dainty cradled in Raff's arms. Sometimes you've got to pick your battles. I was full, still exhausted, and recognized the quicker I recovered the sooner I could try to get away. Even though I felt the need to kick and scream, I decided the smarter course would be to let Raff win this one.

He managed to carry me all the way back to the room without even breathing heavily. Raff was the perfect male specimen of athleticism. He set me down in the bathroom and we brushed our teeth standing side by side at the sink. It almost felt natural. Then he indulged me with some alone time, so I didn't have to pee in front of him. Exiting the bathroom, I had a tantalizing view of Raff undressing down to his boxers. Pajama bottoms and a tank top were laid out on the bed for me.

"You're planning to sleep with me? I don't recall asking for it." Being snarky was the thing I did most when feeling uncomfortable.

"I could chain you to the bed again and have Tate take up watch if you prefer." He pulled back the covers and sat down as if my acquiescence was a foregone conclusion.

I looked at the hooks anchored into the wall and shuddered. "Oh, fine!" I grumbled. "But stay on your own side." I performed the fastest quick change I could muster in my feeble state.

"My side, got it." The humor was clear in his voice.

"I mean it. Keep your hands to yourself." I tugged the sheets down and hopped in, immediately wrapping myself in a burrito of blankets.

"I'll only touch what's mine."

"Hmph!" I turned my back to him, not liking what his words implied.

****

Sure enough, I woke up with a heavy leg draped over me and a large hand clutching my left breast. As much as I'm loathe to admit it, it was nice. I felt all snuggly and strangely content. Raff's breath on the back of my neck was warm like a mini space heater. The mangy cabin was drafty. I used that as an excuse not to move away.

The hand around my breast started squeezing softly. "Mornin', darlin'."

"Not exactly keeping your hands away," I grumbled, trying to dislodge his fingers.

His deep chuckle caused goose bumps to dance up my arms. "These most lovely … no, *magnificent* breasts, are without a doubt my property."

That was enough to ruffle me. I threw his hand off and spun around to glare at him. He stretched slowly, exposing tan-skin and well-defined pectorals before looping his fingers behind his head and settling back. A mischievous smile tugged at his mouth.

"I could get used to this." His gaze was all sex as it slid over me. I squeezed my thighs tightly together in reaction.

"Get used to what?"

"Waking up next to you, babe." Raff rolled onto his side bringing him eye level with me.

"Don't bother. You can't keep me forever. I will find a way out of this."

"I have no doubt at some point the opportunity to run will present itself. But I also know when it comes, you probably won't. Very soon the only time you'll feel at home is with the pack."

I wanted to smash my pillow into his smug face. "Clearly you're delusional, so there's no point in arguing about it."

"There are better ways we could spend the morning," he leered.

"Ugh," I groaned as I threw back the covers and made my way out of bed. It was partly in disgust, but the other part I could barely imagine. I wanted him. Despite everything happening to me, I wanted the big jerk. I made a beeline right out of the room, wondering how much freedom I would be given. He didn't follow and my heart skipped a beat. The guys might all be off doing their jobs for today. Perhaps I could walk right out of here.

Or perhaps not.

Lowe and Weylin were seated out in the living area by the front door. Two steaming mugs of coffee were halted in mid-sip when I emerged. "Morning, Chloe. How are you feeling today?" Weylin inquired. His eyes were all crinkled as if he genuinely cared.

I was feeling more like myself than yesterday, but I kept my recovery private. No need to tell one's captors when you were back to full speed. "I'd be a great deal better in my own home and far away from all of you," I growled. It was driving me crazy how kind and caring these guys acted toward me. If they gave a shit, they would have stopped all this.

"I hate being cooped up too," Weylin replied smoothly, not reacting to the bite of my words. "How about we get some fresh air? I'll take you for a short walk while Lowe cooks up breakfast."

Lowe jumped up before I could answer. "Yah, Chloe. What do you like? Eggs? Pancakes? Both?" His big brown eyes were wide and searching while he waited for my answer.

Instead, I glared at Weylin. "You're really going to take me outside? I'm not on lockdown?" *I might actually get my chance to run sooner than expected!*

"It would build your strength up. The first change takes a chunk out of ya'."

"Well, let's go, then." I was halfway to the door when his chuckle stopped me. *Damn! Was he just kidding?*

"You should change first and put on some shoes.

The terrain is rocky, and while you look adorable in your pj's, they're not practical."

I looked down at the loose pajama bottoms and almost sheer tank. "Oh," my voice dropped. Needing clothes meant going back to the bedroom with Raff. "Will Raff let me out for a walk?"

"Excellent idea."

I knew that distinct rumbling voice behind me, and peered over my shoulder at the owner. Raff had sneakers dangling from two fingers and clothes in his other hand. Before anyone could think this through, I snatched the offering and ran to change.

"Thought you were going to pay off your open tabs in town?"

Weylin pointed out a path into the trees when we stepped outside the cabin. "Too early still. I'll head out after breakfast."

"So, we're not too far away, then?" I asked nonchalantly.

Weylin produced a secret smile. "Far enough, Chloe."

Far enough might have been an understatement. We walked for the better part of an hour. I don't have the best sense of direction, but Weylin's haphazard picking of paths had me hopelessly lost. The reality of the situation hit me like a ton of bricks. I would need food and water to make a proper escape. It could be days till I found my way to safety.

"Clever of you," I muttered under my breath.

Clearly not softly enough, though, since he heard me.

"Clever? How so?"

"This walk." I looked at him pointedly.

He grinned. "Making you feel better? Good.

Nature always settles me too."

"Don't play dumb. You took me out on an empty stomach. Got me completely turned around heading every direction but straight. This taste of the outside wasn't supposed to make me feel less cooped up. It was to show me how truly imprisoned I am." I stopped walking. "Take me back."

He halted too and leaned against a thick tree, regarding me for several moments. "Raff's mom is going to like you. She always fretted over Raff ending up with an empty-headed simple thing. You'll make a real alpha female, like her."

Why do they always resort to talking nonsense?

"Oh? He's planning on bringing me home to meet his ma? Do all your kidnapped girls get such special treatment?"

"She's sarcastic like you too," he chuckled. "I suppose you'll meet her soon enough. After the change, Raff can stake a claim on a territory for us to finally settle in. To do so, we need to head home first and talk with his father. Then of course, his family will want to have a ceremony for you."

I didn't like the sound of that. "Creepy cult ceremony?"

"Nah." He pushed off the tree and changed directions. "More like a wedding."

I ground my teeth to keep from screaming obscenities. "Perfect!" I shouted and threw up my hands.

"Knowing Raff, I'm sure it will be." He seemed to think that might please me.

"I'm not sure which of you is nuttier."

"You're right, it's time to head back. I'm hungry and the humidity will only get worse." To confuse me even more he switched directions again to where we had been walking. "Lowe will have a feast ready by now."

I yearned to pick up a rock and throw it at him, but the thought of a hearty breakfast and cup of coffee had me meekly trailing behind. He kept a brisk pace and we made it back in half the time it took to walk out. I tried to make sense of the trail, but I'm a city girl, and one tree looked exactly like the other.

I was sticky and my stomach was rumbling like a beehive by the time we made it back to the cabin. I wasn't sure which I wanted to do more, shower or eat. As soon as the door opened, the wonderful aroma of flapjacks and warm maple syrup settled the decision. Guess the appetite was back in full swing after the sickness.

"Chloe!" Lowe called out joyfully as if I was his favorite person. "Glad you're finally back. I was afraid everything would get cold." Lowe thrust a foil-wrapped tube at Weylin. "Here. It's a breakfast burrito for the road. Thermos by the door."

Weylin ruffled Lowe's hair. "Thanks, kid. Chloe…" He nodded at me and headed back out the door. I mainly ignored him and sat at the table.

Before I could even attempt to lift a fork, Lowe was at my side filling up my plate. "You don't have to wait on me."

Lowe smiled shyly while he poured me a cup of coffee and set down some cream and sugar. "I like to."

I could be horrible to all the other guys, but not Lowe. "Thanks. This looks great." I stuffed my face for a full ten minutes only managing to chew and swallow until the empty feeling in my stomach started to fade. I took a swig of coffee to wash it down. "Where's Raff?"

"I like how you're always thinking of me." The man himself emerged from the hallway still damp from a recent shower. He was shirtless and wearing only gym shorts slung low exposing cut hip bones. Suddenly I was hungry all over again. He sat down beside me and stroked his bottom lip with his thumb. A sly smile said he could read the dirty thoughts tantalizing my mind. Lowe filled his plate and poured him coffee, all the while Raff ignored the boy and stared at me. There was still a slight sheen of moisture coating his chest, as if he hadn't bothered with a towel and just shook himself dry. I wanted nothing more than to run my hand over the glistening skin.

"You just have to ask," he whispered tenderly.

I jerked back to reality. "Don't hold your breath." I stood up from the table needing some distance. "I'm taking a shower."

"You need some help?"

I blushed thinking about our shared shower yesterday. I was barely able to stand and still wanted him then. I wasn't sure I could even trust myself right now. "I can manage," I stated dryly as I skated from the room, berating myself for hoping he would follow.

Chapter Thirteen

My day could best be described as dull. I avoided Raff, which meant not watching the one TV in the old cabin, since he claimed the living room. Lowe checked on me constantly. His sad eyes and furrowed brows made it clear he didn't understand my desire to sulk in isolation. I needed an escape plan, but kept coming up empty. With nothing much to occupy me in the small room, I eventually dozed.

When the sound of the door opening around dusk woke me, I decided it was time to leave. *Maybe Raff left?*

Swinging my legs out of bed, I tiptoed out the door. A giant blocked my view down the hallway.

"Howdy, ma'am." Tate smiled sheepishly. "You look nice and refreshed."

"Hmm," I grunted in response.

"Bit bored?" he inquired.

I reluctantly nodded, but threw in a snarky comment for good measure. "Why'd you ask? Is it our special time together now?"

"Rollin, Weylin, and I usually play cards on Thursday night. But Weylin ain't gonna be back till late. Wanna be our third? It makes things more interesting."

Well, crap on toast! I love card games and I'm certainly bored as hell.

"Fine," I huffed.

I peered cautiously around the corner. Lowe was cooking again. It was nearing dinnertime. Raff was nowhere in sight, so I strolled over to the table where Rollin was shuffling cards like a Vegas dealer.

"What's your game, doll?" He winked as the cards floated from one hand to the other.

"Poker, but without money it's not the same."

"I could float you some, Miss Chloe." Tate dragged a heavy chair loudly across the floor and sat backward on it.

"Gambling with someone else's money makes it less exciting." I shrugged.

"Wanna play bridge?" asked Tate.

"She looks more like a gin girl to me." Rollin set the deck down.

"Bullshit," I said and smiled. "You guys know how to speak it for sure, but can you play the game?"

"Don't believe I know that one." Rollin quirked up an eyebrow at me.

"Deal out all the cards. The object is to get rid of them all. You get to discard the cards face-down so your opponent can't see what it is. It goes in order from aces, to twos, to threes and so on. If you don't have the number you should, you still need to play a card. Any player who suspects the discard is false can call bullshit. If it is false, the player picks up all the cards and if true the challenger gets them. Up for it?"

"Hell yah." Rollin grinned. "Sounds fun."

I thought Rollin would be the one to beat. His movie-star looks could distract from the truth of his actions, but it was Tate that fooled me every time. Usually shy and sweet, once the cards were down he was stone-faced. Tate gave away nothing. I almost had to resort to cheating to catch a break.

Not sure if it was the daylong isolation, the craziness of the situation, or the fact that around these guys I felt comfortable, but I had a blast. When Raff returned, I was giggling loudly while Rollin yelled "Bullshit" as my final card landed. I crowed when he flipped it over and it was the card I had declared it to be. Seeing Raff, though, deflated me. I should be fighting more. Making things difficult. Not making friends. *What is wrong with me?*

"Don't stop on my account," Raff said. He sauntered over and placed a hand on my shoulder.

I stood up abruptly, shrugging him off me. "I'll head back to my room."

"But," Lowe wined from the kitchen. "Dinner will be ready in five minutes. Don't hide out in there the rest of the night."

"Didn't peg you for a scaredy-cat." Raff inched in close enough for me to smell the cold air and pine scenting his skin. "You've been hiding under the bed all day."

"Yah, waiting for you to come by so I could scratch you."

"Oh, darlin'." His hand circled my waist. His fingers dipped as they held the top of my ass. "I have so many itches I would love for you to scratch."

Rollin's snort of amusement broke me out of the trance Raff's words evoked. I stepped away and proceeded to adjust my top. It felt like it was on too tight and chafed every inch of me. "I'll pass."

Lowe sidled up next to me. "Hope you like chicken and dumplings?" He wafted the plate before me. Steam spilled out carrying the savory aroma.

The kid can cook!

When it came to Lowe, I just had to be all sweetness. "It's one of my favs." I took the dish and sat back down, unable to make eye contact with Raff. I didn't want to see the bastard's smug face. I almost jumped when he sat right next to me, legs pushing against mine, and arm draped over the back of my chair. Lowe set a plate in front of Raff, but the man was hell-bent on getting a rise out of me. He speared a dumpling off my plate and slowly pushed it past his lips. The constant eye contact while he did it was almost an act of war. I had to sit on my hand. It wanted desperately to deliver the aforementioned scratch.

"Damn, Lowe." Raff grinned. "You never make it this good. Our girl must be a culinary muse."

The "our girl" comment should have made me uneasy. I didn't know what they intended to do with me. Yet, when all the guys nodded in agreement, offering winks and shy smiles, it felt like an endearment of family. I was more at home in that moment than I had ever been around my mother and sister.

Like every meal we have had together, the guys, save Raff, waited for me to start before they did. Almost as if my comfort was necessary for them to enjoy their food. The strangest shit made me feel safe. These guys drugged and kidnapped me. I should hate them. I should fear them. I should be trying a lot harder to get away from them.

"You gotta try 'em, Chloe." Raff held a plump dumpling to my lips, and without even the slightest hesitation I took it. That bite broke the silent waiting from the other guys. Forks scraped against plates, idle chatter about the weather forecast started, and Raff relaxed his posture next to me. Completely slouching in his chair, he ate with gusto. His gaze was a constant companion throughout the meal. He was as aware of my every action as I was aware of his.

I'm playing house with a bunch of crazies.

Chapter Fourteen

Two more days passed. I tried to keep my distance and remain aloof. I failed. My nights were spent curled up with Raff. My treacherous body was happier tucked against him than away from him. The crew continued to entertain and pamper me. If it wasn't for the forced captivity, I would admit to liking them, which was unfamiliar territory for me. I'm the girl that looks like she's popular, but in reality is alone in a room full of people. Yet, with the guys, I found moments of wanting to be with them. I think I was angriest then. How could a great group be this batshit crazy? Why is it that, when I was sitting down at a meal with said crazies, I could actually breathe? What the hell did that say about me?

The days formed a bit of a routine. Outside time with Weylin, Lowe was my personal chef, Tate was the game master, and Rollin kept me laughing. I almost forgot about the full moon deadline until late the final day.

I was out front, sitting on a stack of firewood with Weylin, while the sun started to set. It was the first time, since Raff stuck a needle in me, that fear engulfed me.

"What's going to happen tonight?" My hands shook as I tucked my hair behind my ears.

"Hey," his voice gentled as he rubbed small circles across my back. "You'll be fine. The change is a natural process. Once your body does it, it will come easier and easier."

"Is it drugs?" I shot him a pointed look. "Are we all going to hallucinate or something?"

"No drugs, Chloe."

"Seriously! What are you all planning?" The

uncertainty was clawing at me. I shivered uncontrollably, unsure if it was the crisp air or adrenaline riding me.

"I think you're starting to feel the effects now." Weylin stood and offered me his hand. "We should go inside and warm you up."

I slapped his hand away and bared my teeth at him. "I will fight you. I'm not going in there like a lamb to the slaughter. Whatever your sick plans are, I'm not just going to follow you!"

"I got this, Wey." Raff stood in the front doorway. Weylin looked relieved as he headed inside. I was glad he left and Raff took his place. I hadn't wanted to truly yell at Weylin. Raff's the one who deserved to get my ire. He's the ringleader of the bats in the belfry.

"Lowe made an early supper. Come inside and eat, darlin'."

"Not hungry." I folded my arms tightly across my chest and glared.

"Eating will calm you." Raff placed a warm hand on my neck. His thumb caressed my earlobe.

I shivered and stepped back "Why is that? Laced the food? Definite pass."

He closed the distance, this time resting both hands heavily on my shoulders. "No matter what you do, the outcome of tonight will be the same. Eat. Don't eat. Come inside. Freeze out here. Yell at Weylin. Make out with me."

"You wish," I muttered.

He shrugged, broadcasting a devilish grin. "You can't resist me forever."

"Like hell." The words sounded hollow even to me.

"No matter what you decide, tonight you stop pretending you're human."

My usual glib response failed to make an

appearance. "God, you scare me." Unwelcome tears spilled.

"Hey," concern pooled in his eyes as he shushed me. He kissed the top of my head and rubbed his hands up and down my arms. "I'm not going to let anything happen to you."

With trembling lips I gave my final plea. "Take me home, Raff. Forget all this weird wolf shit. I won't tell a soul. For some reason, beyond me, I don't want you all behind bars. But you have to let me go."

"I have taken you home. Don't you see? Haven't you felt it, Chloe? Haven't you felt part of this pack? Letting you go isn't an option. You'll see soon enough. It isn't just because you are it for me. You are my mate, but what's going on is bigger than that. This is about survival."

"Survival," the word dripped bitterly from my mouth. "I have a feeling I'll be the only one not surviving this."

Raff laced his fingers in my hand and tugged me closer to the door. The temperature was dropping as quickly as the sun. I could see my frosty breath hanging in the air with every nervous exhale. The dingy cabin spilled out welcome heat. Through the dirt-encrusted windows I could see the guys setting the table. Lowe was pulling something savory out of the oven. Damn, but if it didn't feel more like home than home did. Maybe the junk Raff shot me up with was enough to turn me crazy too.

I followed his lead. Head held high. I wouldn't beg again. It had no impact. I would play tame and keep searching for an escape. What other choice did I have?

Seeing my resistance wane, Raff draped his arm over my shoulders and escorted me to the table. Rollin jumped up to pull out a chair for me, and I thanked him absently. Lowe set a mound of food before me, along with a glass of wine. Like usual, Raff wasted no time. He sat down close to me and started shoveling in food. The others just waited.

What had felt so charming before now felt sinister. The guys collectively watched for me to take a bite before starting. They hadn't poisoned me before, but I didn't trust the food. This was a cult and the food could be the means of controlling my mental state. I speared a cooked carrot on my fork and delicately placed it in my mouth. It was enough to appease the natives. They dug in, attention, for now, diverted from me. I pressed a napkin to my lips and spit out what was in my mouth as discreetly as possible. I pushed and played with my food, repeating the napkin trick when necessary. I even attempted to join the chatter, completely unaware of what I was saying as my nerves rose and dusk settled outside.

The meal was fast. The guys, save Raff, hustled to clean up. Lowe frowned as he reached to grab my plate. "You didn't eat much."

"I wasn't very hungry."

"She thinks you spiked the food." Raff shoved the last bit of cornbread in his mouth.

Lowe's eyes grew as big as saucers. His lips pinched up and I swear he looked about ready to cry. "Chloe, I would never."

Why am I feeling guilty here? "Too nervous to eat." I glared at Raff daring him to contradict me again.

"You should have eaten," Lowe admonished. "Who knows over the next few days if we will eat? It's winter and prey can be scarce. Always fill your belly before a change."

"Good to know." I smiled at Lowe as he shook his head and scrambled to clean up with the others.

"He's right," Raff said looking pensive. "There

are a few unopened things in the cabinets. If you don't trust the cooked food, open a can of beans or the peanut butter. Something high in protein. You, more than any of us, will need it."

I covered my face in my hands and huffed. "For the last time. You are delusional. People do not change into wolves."

The frenzied activity of the group coupled with Raff's gruff concern, unnerved me. I stood and started pacing. My skin was on too tight. I scratched as if loose hairs dangled off me. *Oh crap. Have they managed to drug me after all?*

"It's time." Raff was quiet in his approach, as if he could sense how close to snapping I was.

I rung my hands repeatedly and shook my head. Perspiration beaded off my temple. Raff was still. Watching. Waiting. The others turned off the lights and filed outside. I had taken two steps to follow before I realized what I was doing.

"Follow your instincts," Raff advised. "It will get you through this."

"Then I should run away as fast as I can."

"Well, darlin', I can promise you there will be running." He chuckled.

"Is that some sick joke? Why are you playing these games? What is wrong with you?" I shoved him farther away from me.

"The only thing that's wrong with us will be fixed tonight. We are just a bunch of lone wolves making our way through this world. Tonight, we become a family. A true pack." He shrugged off his fleece hoodie and tossed it on the couch. "We need to be outside."

I chose not to fight him. I had a better chance of running outside than I did if I was trapped in the cabin. Raff locked the cabin behind us, jamming the key in a hidey-hole under the windowsill. Turning, I froze. Rollin, Lowe, Weylin, and Tate were all lined up in nothing but boxer shorts. Raff was similarly undressing and stashing his stuff in the pickup truck. I clutched the chunky sweater I wore tightly, ready to come out fighting if any of them made a move toward me.

A light emerged. The full moon was pulling itself from the horizon, arching to achieve its supremacy over the sky. I couldn't take my eyes off it. It was luminous. Cold. Uncaring as it observed my strange fate. I dimly registered the guys turning as one to stare at it too. The moon was all I could focus on. Time slowed. I grew smaller as the moon grew larger.

Breathe in.

My vision narrowed to just the point of light.

Breathe out.

Nothingness.

Chapter Fifteen

Wet dirt.
Dark.
Run.
Hunger.
Sunlight.
Wind.
Trees rustle.
Dark.
Safe.
Pack.
Hunger.
Chase.
Bite.
I
Am
Chloe.

Chapter Sixteen

It was the smell more than anything that woke me. A pungent mixture of unwashed bodies, decayed leaves, and the coppery tang of blood. Light penetrated my eyelids, but I felt no warmth. The ground below me was muddy, as if it had just rained. Shivering, I opened my eyes.

Dead glassy eyes stared back at me. I clamped my hands over my mouth instinctively stifling my scream. It was a deer, mutilated and torn open, lying beside me. The scent of blood became even more powerful. I looked at the hands I had drawn over my face in horror. My skin was stained red up to my elbows. My nails were jagged, raw things littered with clumps of deer meat and fur. I sat up causing the chilled metal of Raff's pendant to slide across my skin. It was the only thing I was wearing.

I'm fucking naked in the mud. What the hell?

The only part of me that felt any heat was my back. A warm body was tucked close beside me. Lifting to my elbows, I turned to stare. Raff was still deeply asleep, along with four other naked men that circled me. The pragmatist in me urged me to move. Get as far away from these men as I could and assess the situation.

The last days of my life were a blur. My mind, a primal thing, poorly cataloged events. My last clear memory was the fight I had with Raff at the cabin.

"Shit," I breathed out. Running bloody fingers through the tangles in my hair, I looked around for anything familiar. What was there for me to do? Where could I possibly go for help? Who in their right mind would believe this? Despite being so careful, did I just go on a drug-fueled hallucination, or did I just seriously change into a fucking animal?

The only people I knew who would have answers were my captors, but I couldn't trust them. Worse yet, I couldn't trust myself. A small voice in my head screamed at me to move. To run. It wasn't as loud as the sense of belonging I felt, which kept me crazy calm. Heedless of my nudity around five men, I decided to wake them up.

"Raff." I shook him roughly. He sat up quickly, instantly vigilant. Like me, blood stained his skin. His face was a gory version of a toddler eating birthday cake. He relaxed after taking me in and stretched lasciviously. His gaze roamed over my body.

"Seriously!" I hissed at him, sweeping my arms out indicating the situation.

The bastard chuckled, incredibly pleased with himself. The laugh caused the others to wake. I crossed my arms over my chest, attempting coverage. The men came to and scrambled to their feet. I averted my eyes and stared sullenly at the ground.

"Anyone able to pinpoint where we are?" Raff's voiced rumbled, increasing the shivers coursing over my flesh.

"Best guess?" Weylin surveyed the landscape. "Pisgah National Forest. Looks like we ranged farther than normal. It's gonna be a bit of a hike to get to our first hidey-hole." Weylin's inquisitive eyes landed on me, but never strayed south of my shoulders. "How are you holding up, Chloe? We'll need you able to walk."

"Let me get this straight. The plan is to walk naked, no shoes, no supplies, through a dense forest? You boys sure know how to treat a girl."

The guys laughed. Rollin, still managing to look like a movie star, albeit a grubby one, gave a sheepish grin. "It's all part of the lifestyle."

Bitterness spiked. "One I never chose," my voice cracked.

Lowe looked like I slapped him with my words. "You'll get accustomed to it, Chloe. We'll make sure of it."

If anyone else had spoken, I would have started biting heads off. Lowe was a weakness for me. "Yeah, yeah, yeah," I griped. I stood and gave up trying to hide my lady parts. If we were going on a long hike, I couldn't possibly cover it up the entire time.

Raff angled closer, invading my personal space. His hands were hot as he briskly rubbed them up and down my arms in an attempt to warm me. I was numb with cold, otherwise I'm sure I would have shoved him away, despite the delicious tingles his touch inspired. Yep. I still would have shoved him. I was simply using him to get warm. Nothing else.

"I hear water nearby," he spoke softly, as if just to me. "Would you like to get cleaned up a bit?"

I knew the water would be freezing cold, but I wanted to wash all the blood off me something fierce. I nodded mutely. He gathered me by his side and headed off. The others trailed behind. Some part of Raff was touching me at all times. His hand rubbed the nape of my neck. His pinky laced with mine for a few steps. He gently picked leaves from my tangled tresses.

It felt more than normal, it felt necessary. A true sign of the deep emotional and physical shock I was in. I should have clawed his eyes out, yet his reassuring gestures kept me calm. His voice was low and compassionate, his pace considerate to my shorter legs and sore bare feet. I didn't even object when we crossed a field filled with nettles and he slung me into his arms. I even rested my head against his chest and listened contentedly to the steady beat of his heart.

Once we reached a small lake, he set me down as if I was made of glass. The frigid water had me shivering as soon as one foot plunged in. Raff tended to me before washing himself. Again he heated up his hands and rubbed me down briskly, sloughing the blood off with the water as quickly as he could. When I was "clean-ish," he found a flat bolder, warmed by the sun, for me to sit on. The crew all jumped in the lake then. While they yelped at the cold, splashed each other, and laughed, Raff washed methodically. He kept his eyes trained on me the entire time. He actually shook himself off, much like a dog. An action that was demanding a snappy retort, but I stayed mute. It hurt too much to think.

What in all hell is happening to me?

When he scooped me up and angled us so I was cradled in his lap, the desire to nuzzle against him rode me hard, I couldn't deny it. He didn't spout out any false platitudes that everything would be okay. He didn't cajole me into talking. He didn't make any lewd comments, even though I was naked and pliable in his arms. He just held me … and I let him. I was stranded, without a stitch of clothes, in the forest with five men. Perhaps I could have been stronger, but I decided to give myself a break instead.

My world had just ended. My reality was forever altered. Something happened. Something I couldn't explain. I wanted to believe there was a reasonable explanation for waking up in the middle of nowhere covered in deer blood, an explanation other than the one the boys kept feeding me. I couldn't have turned into a wolf. It just wasn't possible. Was it?

Chapter Seventeen

It was a solid hour of a nature hike to end all nature hikes, before we found the stash Weylin referred to. The guys tore into a pack of protein bars like wild animals, no pun intended. I opted for clothes. Donning a pair of simple grey sweatpants and a black t-shirt made me feel human again. It was like leaving behind the fantasy realm and entering back into reality. They didn't have tennis shoes exactly my size, only a pair of flip-flops stayed on reasonably well. Not much support for my feet, but I would take the trade-up. Those tiny rocks hurt like a bitch when stepped on.

"You should eat." Raff handed me a bar.

I nodded while tearing off the wrapping and taking a bite. I needed the calories, I could feel how diminished my body was. Each chew and swallow would get me closer back to civilization. I'm not sure I would ever feel normal again, but I was starting to at least feel more like me.

"There you are," Raff whispered. His eyes were intent on my face.

"What is that supposed to mean?" I snapped.

A full-blown smile was his reaction to my anger. "Sometimes it takes a while to come back fully. Like a little of you exists still while the wolf is in control. When we come back, the wolf can sometimes hover in our mind." His hand skated over my shoulder and I swatted it away.

"Don't," I warned.

"You don't need me to touch you?" he inquired calmly.

"Why the hell would I need you at all?" I snarled.

"Your wolf wants its mate."

"Stop talking nonsense." I crammed another huge bite in my mouth and glared.

"The truth, Chloe," his voice was pure seduction. The hairs at the nape of my neck tingled. "You want me too."

"Bullshit!" I spit bits of bar out with my expletive.

"You can deny it all you like. This thing," he continued to whisper as he pointed between us. "It's not imaginary. We are bound. Fight it if you want. Fight it if you must. I'm not worried. The pull of the pack is stronger than any emotion you believed yourself to have felt before."

The guys had finished dressing. We had an audience. I wanted to curse them all and storm off, but I was scared, confused, and terribly lost. I would not admit it out loud, but I could sense Raff was telling me a truth. It might have been only his truth, but he wasn't completely wrong. The terror I had as their captive was gone. I should be freaking out , yet I felt bizarrely safe. Clearly, I was no longer sane and most likely would end up in some horrible mental ward after this was finally over. At the very, very least, I should be in hysterics.

Being in Raff's presence was like coming home after a week away and climbing into your own bed. It was a contented sigh. It was familiar when nothing else ever felt that way. I wanted to be with him.

That realization pissed me off to no end.

"I hate you." I meant to scream it at him, but instead it came out like a mangled sob.

Raff's eyes narrowed. He looked about ready to speak when his brother broke the tension. Rollin looped his arm around my shoulders, obscuring my view of Raff. His half-hug was all comfort. It was the warm blanket of family I didn't even feel when hugging my perfect sister or my catastrophe of a mother.

"I find," Rollin's tone was kind, "after a shift, emotions can be a jumble. You just had your first shift and the world is a different place now. It's a lot to take in." He glanced back over his shoulder during the last sentence, as if his words were for his brother as well as me.

"I wish you guys would just cut the crap!" I snapped. "I'm not sure exactly what happened, but I don't believe people can turn into wolves."

"But, Chloe," Lowe practically whined. "You must remember some of it? The hunt? Our runs?"

I clenched my jaw refusing to admit to any insanity-induced memories.

"What about the feeling of pack?" Tate asked looking concerned. "That feeling stays with you after a change. You must still sense it. It isn't fully formed yet, but I can feel the beginnings of the bond now."

"She's just too stubborn to admit it." Raff rolled his eyes, and I took a step toward him with the intent to shove him as hard as I could.

His brother intercepted me. "Come on." Rollin prodded me to walk as Weylin took up position on my other side.

"What's your favorite movie?" Inquisitive Weylin asked.

"Why?" I huffed.

He shrugged his sinewy shoulders. "I find talking about the normal mundane things helps when I feel like the world is spinning."

"The world *is* spinning," I responded dryly.

"That it is, girl!" Rollin laughed.

"When I was a kid," Weylin continued not missing a beat, "I was obsessed with *The Matrix*. The first time the camera stopped, the action froze, the camera circled around and then everything sped up again, I was hooked. It was so impactful to my young brain. I imagined everything I did could be bending the possible to obtain the impossible."

"You mean like turning from a human to a dog?"

Rollin cracked up. Weylin offered an impish grin. "Something like that."

"Mine," Rollin jumped in. "Was *Shaun of the Dead*. I was scared shitless of zombie movies. If there were shifters in the world, who's to say a zombie apocalypse isn't a real possibility? When my brothers all went to watch this film, I tried to figure how to get out of it."

Despite my best efforts to stay withdrawn, the boys managed to keep me moving and engaged. It made me wonder what Raff and Rollin's other brothers would be like. Does his entire family believe they are wolves too? Or is it just this group?

"I don't know if Raff told you, but he and I are the oldest." Rollin raised his eyebrows in question.

"He did tell me," I confirmed. Part of me wanted to look back and see if Raff was listening, but I refused to act on it.

"Well, then, you can see my dilemma? I mean, big brothers cannot admit to being afraid of anything. So, I kept my mouth shut and went into the theatre. Then the movie plays. It's hysterical! I can't stop laughing. Even though those dead bastards rip people apart and jump out at them, the main characters are epically funny. It made me even find some hilarity in the truly scary zombie films. Now I'm a zombie film junkie."

"Let's get this straight," I shudder. "You don't also believe in zombies?"

Rollin squeezed me tighter. "No, little sister, I

know they're pretend."

The endearment wasn't lost on me. As Raff's supposed mate, I guess it would make Rollin my brother. I didn't correct the oversight. The guys were right. The inane banter was keeping my mind from freaking out. I liked these guys. They were truly the best kidnappers a girl could hope for.

We continued to chat for almost two hours. The conversation never exhausted. We went from movies, to books, to travel, to favorite foods and things we never should have eaten. It was light. It made me feel like I was still Chloe. It was exactly what I needed.

Raff stayed back, trailing in the rear behind Tate and Lowe. I never lost track of him. His eyes were heavy on me. When I would glance back, he met my stare every time. I was the one forced to look away. My little bubble of calm was a fragile thing. While the guys were easy company, Raff was a sharp need.

Right about the time I was about to toss the large flip-flops off my feet to avoid aggravating the blisters I had forming between my toes, the shabby cabin came into view. I never thought I would be happy to see that damn place again, but the thought of a hot shower quickened my pace.

"Ten minutes, gentlemen," Raff bellowed. "Get your shit and make yourself scarce. You all have jobs to do before we roll out tonight."

The guys collectively groaned. Rollin's quick tightening of his lips showed he was about to argue. Raff pulled my back against his chest and circled his arms around me, staring pointedly. "You got a problem with it, little bro?"

Rollin took a long look at me and smiled before he shook his head. "No, man. I just wasn't thinking."

What the hell does that mean? If Raff thinks some

alone time with me is a good idea, he has another thing coming.

Chapter Eighteen

Raff made me wait outside on the porch while the guys ran into the cabin to shower and change. I tried just barreling past him twice, but he gently restrained me and told me to please wait.

"I want a hot shower," I griped. "I don't even feel human right now under all this dirt."

Raff lifted an eyebrow. "You aren't."

"Is that what this is about?" I hissed. "You want me to agree to your fairy tale story before I can go inside?"

"No, darlin'. I just want the place to ourselves for a bit."

"Why?" I dared him to proposition me. I was going to spit in his face. Or claw and spit. Or maybe go for a punch.

"You're still restless. You're scared and you need to be reassured. I'm going to take care of you now. I need to show you. It will help you settle."

If the world could be a color, mine would be red. The desire for physical violence took control. I didn't jokingly think hitting him would make me feel better, I believed it with all my being. *If that man lays one hand on me, I will show him how much I want his reassurance!*

"You've been a lone wolf too long. It has made you antisocial at times, downright bitchy other times. But it isn't who you really are. The presence of your mate and your pack should be settling you, making you content. Instead, you're feeling aggressive."

"I *am* feeling aggressive." I rounded on him, my hands clenched into fists. "I think it has more to do with you drugging me, kidnapping me, taking me out into the woods, and ruining my fucking life!"

"Your life was shit and a lie. You never had a relationship that lasted more than a few months. You lost your job because your wolf was restless and acted out on a night when you were born to be wild. You were meant to be in a pack. And you would have been, if your mother had not abandoned your father."

"What is that supposed to mean?" My jaw dropped. "Do you know my father? Did you know about me before we met?"

Raff ground his teeth showing he gave away a bit more than planned. "I knew your father. He died last year."

I sat down on the porch rail without looking, my legs not working properly.

"I know who your mother is too," his voice was grim as he regarded me. The truth finally spilled out. "She was born a shiftless wolf. We didn't have the cure then. She wanted to leave the pack and my father let her. Your father chased her for a while, but he couldn't live outside the pack. The pull was too strong. Your mother, even though she can't shift, still shows all the signs of a lone wolf. Restless. Moves around a great deal. Different partners. Never feeling content or satisfied. Sound familiar?"

His raised brow made me feel the question was more directed toward me than about my mother. It was a lot to process. He was still batshit crazy, but was he lying too?

"Just last year, he died?"

"I'm sorry. It may not have been the best time to tell you."

He took a step and I held my arms out warding him off. "The time to tell me was when you walked into my bar. It could have been really simple. 'Hey, I know your dad. I'm insane and believe you're a dog. Want to come home and live with me in the wild?' Then I could have told you to fuck off and saved both of us the time."

Raff scrubbed at his face and sighed loudly. "You want a fight? Fine. If that's what you need, then I'll give you that too."

I was saved from having to come up with another biting reply by the crew exiting the cabin. They were freshly washed, dressed, and packed up. They filed out one at a time. Lowe looked at me with sad puppy eyes. I'm sure they all heard me screaming. He loaded up the back of a car with crates of food and a duffle bag of clothes. Tate accompanied him, carrying the biggest load. Weylin and Rollin walked out together.

Rollin wiggled his eyes. "You two have fun, now."

I swatted at him, but he was faster and moved away.

Weylin laughed as I fumed. How could they all be happy at a time like this?

"All clear, Boss." Weylin nodded at Raff. "Your room is the only one left."

"Thanks." Raff jutted out his chin. "Leave me the pickup. I'll meet you at Lou's in three hours."

"We'll have the trailer hitched up and ready," Tate yelled from the car.

Raff kept me standing outside till the guys drove away.

"Just you and me now, darlin'. Let's get started. Shall we?" He held out his arm signaling I should walk into the cabin.

I stormed in, planning to hightail it to the bathroom and lock myself in. Raff had other plans. He grabbed my wrist and spun me around. My chest bumped against his. I jerked backed and slapped him across the face.

"Don't," I panted. "Don't even touch me."

He held out his hands palms-down and approached me like a cowboy with a wild horse. "Shhh, everything is going to be fine."

I shoved him when he invaded my space again. Rage pushed me to continue the assault. I shoved and shoved, but he was a brick wall. He stayed calm and continued to try to soothe me. It pissed me off even more. I started slapping him continuously. I scratched at his arm, drawing blood.

Through the entire ordeal Raff kept still. He didn't block my blows or protect himself in any way. He took every injury I could inflict on him. I screamed at the top of my lungs and banged my fist against his chest till I was exhausted and panting.

"Is it enough?"

I glared at him perplexed by the question.

"It's natural to want to show your mate strength before you submit. To show me that it's your choice, not mine. Your wolf is ridding you. Has she had enough?"

I dropped down on my knees, the energy leaving my body in a wave. A loud sob escaped me. "Please. I want to go home."

"Chloe," his warm breath brushed against my cheek as he kneeled down next to me. "We have been through this. This pack is your home. Nothing else will ever feel like home after you are pack, and you are pack now."

He scooped me into his arms and rocked me while I cried. My arms were made of lead and my teeth chattered. I was unaware if it was from the cold or the shock of it all hitting me. Something was different. In his arms, I felt safe. In his arms, I wanted to curl up and stay. In his arms, I felt content. My brain told me it didn't add up. But, God, did my body want him.

As if sensing my change in mood, Raff picked me up and carried me like a new bride to the bathroom. He sat me on the counter and I stared at him, mute, as he turned on the water and waited for it to get hot. When tendrils of steam started forming he turned to face me. His hands were sure as he undressed me. I didn't fight him. The fight was gone.

He kissed the top of my head, trailed a kiss on my brow, and a peck on my nose before he scooped me up again and placed me in the shower. The hot water startled me out of my stupor. Mechanically, I reached for the soap and started scrubbing my hands where the dirt and blood remained. Raff reached for the shampoo and lathered my hair. His fingers in my scalp released the last bit of tension from my shoulders. I fixated on cleaning my hands, having my own Lady Macbeth moment. Raff tipped back my head and washed out the shampoo. He stole the soap, forcing me to stop my excessive scrubbing. My eyes flew up meeting his. He was busy attending to his own body, his movements quick, a sharp contrast to the gentle care he showed me. Wordlessly I stepped aside, giving him access to the water.

The soap bubbled, sliding down his muscular frame and toned legs before circling the drain. I watched mesmerized. Raff opened his eyes after being directly under the spray and regarded me. His hand snaked out, capturing mine. He pressed my fingers to his lips and slid my hand down till it settled on his pectoral muscle. I could feel his heart beat a steady thump. His skin felt like satin, slick from the water. I took a step closer.

With his other hand, he circled the back of my neck and rubbed his thumb across my cheek. He leaned toward me slowly, gauging my reaction. I held still. Encouraged, he closed the gap and his warm mouth covered mine. His tongue lapping at my lips till I opened for him. I felt his body shudder slightly with my acceptance. He kissed me till the water started to cool.

Shutting off the shower, Raff stepped out and grabbed two towels. He wrapped one around his waist before using the other to dry me off gently. Soft kisses accompanied his movements. I closed my eyes, lost in the sensation of his warm mouth followed by the nip of cold air. My body was humming. Clean. Dry. Relaxed. An unimaginable state after waking up naked and covered in blood.

I gasped when his lips pressed against my intimate folds. My hand clutched his head, fingers buried in his hair. He continued to kiss me there till my knees went weak and I was leaning on him heavily for support. My body shook as an orgasm hit me suddenly. Heat coursed through me and erupted in a million tingles, causing my spine to bow and my nails to bite into his shoulders.

Raff stood and lifted me in one smooth motion. Still recovering, I barely noticed he was walking till my back was pressed against the bed and he was lying on top of me.

He brushed the hair away from my face. His eyes were smoldering. "No one will love you as completely as me. We are your family. You will feel connected on a level you never thought possible. You don't have to be lonely ever again. You just need to let me love you."

I could have rejected him. I should have. This was all so fucked up. He had me second-guessing everything. My outlook on life. My sense of family. My sanity. Instead, I pulled him closer, offering a tentative kiss. That was all he needed. He slid inside me in one quick move. I was more than ready for him after his attentions in the bathroom.

The magic from our first time wasn't a fluke. With Raff it was simply a perfect fit, our bodies completely in sync. Each thrust chasing the ultimate ending. I came much harder the second time, just seconds before Raff. He rolled me over till I was draped on him. My wet hair drying in a tangle of curls over his chest. My limbs nimble and sated. His steady heartbeat a lullaby.

Blissfully I passed out.

Chapter Nineteen

Happy humming soothed. Feet shuffled on the uneven wood floor. Zippers closed on a duffle bag. A cocoon of blankets surrounded me.

I blinked to clear my blurry vision. Pushing myself up, I watched Raff before he noticed me. He was packing. Shirt off. All tanned skin and too many muscles. Sweatpants slung low on his hips and swagger in his step. He was a walking add for Photoshop. Completely unreal.

He's happy, and I'm a total cluster.

I chewed at my bottom lip as he chuckled and jumped on the bed. "None of that now, darlin'. You get trapped in that pretty head of yours too easily. Come on and get dressed. We're late."

I held the blanket tightly to me, covering my naked body. I suddenly felt shy. He nuzzled my neck leaving loud sloppy wet kisses. I squeaked in this girly super-adorable way instead of gagging or shoving him. This man had me utterly confused.

He bounced off the bed and tossed a sports bra and panties at me. His grin split his face from ear to ear. I could almost feel his contentment and joy seeping into my skin.

Maybe I'm hypnotized? Programmed to lust after him, whenever he gets near me.

There was a moment I almost convinced myself, but if I was brainwashed, I would believe in this wolf nonsense hook, line, and sinker. Instead, I'm questioning everything I believed I'd experienced. Wondering if drugs could have been involved. Or if it could be a lingering illness making me hallucinate. Anything had to be a more plausible reality than I can turn into an animal.

"Why don't I remember more?"

Raff scrutinized a miniskirt of mine before tossing it into the bag and selecting leggings for me instead. "You mean of the change? Or did I just blow your mind in the literal sense with some utterly amazing sex?" He was in a joking mood. Daring me with the mischievous glint in his eye, to remain sullen.

While the sex was otherworldly, I needed to stay on topic. "I remember the moon and then waking up this morning naked."

"The wolf was in control. Not you. Your dreams for the next few nights will be a little wild. Your wolf will still want to play, but she will not take front and center until the cycle starts again." He added a tank top and a full-zip fleece hoodie to the pile of clothes in front of me. "But I can tell by your expression you still don't believe me."

My chin jutted our proudly. "Why should I?"

I expected to rile him up. Get him good and angry. Yet, his eyes were soft as he gazed at me. Gently he brushed the bangs away from my eyes. My pulse jumped and my skin thrummed under his touch. "Chloe, I know it's a lot to digest. You take your time. Ask your questions. I'm your mate. I'll give you everything you need."

"Except my freedom?" The question hung for a beat before he sighed.

"I gave freedom to your wolf. In time you will realize the gift for what it is. Until then, I hope you can at least give your new life a chance. You will find the balm to your restless soul within the pack." He pointed at the neglected pile of clothes. "Speaking of pack, the boys have been waiting for a few hours. We need to get going before they worry."

I was up and dressed before it truly hit me. I missed the guys. I wanted to speed up my movements so we could be with them. All this talk about pack was nonsense. Right? Yet, every fiber of my being felt slightly incomplete without the others. The thought of escaping from my kidnappers made my stomach turn, a sense of dread buried deep in my belly like a child's irrational fear of the dark. I had asked to go home, but the thought of entering my apartment, heading back to my life, going to work at the bar, sounded horribly unpleasant. Lonely.

I had just been surviving. I wasn't living.

Raff went back and forth carrying our things out while I changed. He leaned against the doorframe as I put on my shoes. "You ready, darlin'?"

I nodded wordlessly. Followed him to his truck. Buckled up. "Where are we going?"

"To my family's home."

"You're taking me to meet your folks?" I clarified.

His lips quirked up on the side. "Yup. And a few brothers too."

"Is that usual practice after a kidnapping?" The sex was good all right, but I wasn't ready to accept everything.

"I'm a selfish prick, Chloe. I know this. I took without asking." His right hand grazed my leg. I didn't move away. "And you still don't believe me, but I did it for more than just myself. I have so much to show you. Another world entirely."

"What do…" I started to ask a question when the phone rang.

"Hey, bro," Raff answered and I could hear the other guys loud and clear through the speakers.

"Mad props, my man. You are epically thorough

in your duties. But we are starving," Rollin shouted out while the boys made lurid noises.

I simultaneously scowled and blushed a deep shade of red.

"We are about thirty minutes away from Lou's, we can grab a bite at the diner next door."

"Shit. Thirty minutes? I don't know, man. Tate is starting to look at me funny. I might have a large piece missing if I wait that long."

"Fine," Raff said and chuckled. "You have my permission to start without us. We'll catch up."

The boys whistled and cheered on their end of the line, making such a ruckus Rollin had to holler to be heard. "Cool! See ya, bro. Thanks."

The phone disconnected. "What the hell is that about?"

Raff looked perplexed before my question clicked. "Pack stuff. I eat first. I'm the alpha."

"Are you for real?" I laughed. Memories of every meal threaded through my mind. "I'll be damned. They have been doing exactly that since the first time we ate."

Raff shrugged. "It's a wolf thing."

"Hold up! I have to wait till you start eating before I can eat?" I crossed my arms over my chest to stave off the desire to shove him. He was driving after all.

"You?" He shook his head. "Nope, you get to eat whenever you want. You are my mate. We are the alpha pair. But the guys do have to wait on you. So, it's best to be polite and not always keep them hungry."

"That is the craziest." I rolled my eyes.

"Crazier than being a wolf?" he teased.

"Nope," I admitted. "It's all loony-bin shit."

"Yeah." His lips curved up in a half-grin. "I would recommend not mentioning it to strangers if you wish to avoid a straitjacket or a government testing facility."

He said it in a playful tone, but his words held the ominous ring of truth. People would find elements of my story insane. The missing time after the moon, waking up covered in deer blood, and running through the forest naked were not things I would willingly share. Then the other nightmarish option that wormed its way in my thoughts—if I was a shifter, then I was no longer human. I would be something to be hunted and experimented on. Sobering thoughts.

Does this mean I'm only safe if I stay with Raff now?

****

The gang was still eating when we walked in. I liked seeing them. My soul was calm, comforted by their presence. Lowe jumped up and gave me a grateful hug. He was as exuberant as a puppy. My heart melted a little at the adoration in his eyes.

"We thought you'd never get here," Lowe fidgeted as he talked. "It's good to see you."

I ruffled his hair. "You too, kid," I said and actually meant it.

We took the booth next to theirs, Raff sliding beside me rather than sitting across. I used to be annoyed when I saw couples do that in places, but damn if I didn't enjoy his warm body beside mine. My eyes roved over the menu. I was ravenous. When the elderly waitress waddled over, I ordered an appetizer, a salad, and an entree. I might have had a moment of embarrassment until Raff ordered even more.

"Is someone else joining you?" she asked frankly.

"Naw," Raff produced his sweetest smile. "Long road trip."

She nodded sagely. Turning to the guys she held

up the bill. "Can I get ya'll anything else?"

A chorus of "no, ma'ams" followed. Raff held up a card. "I'll get that for them."

"Ah, gee! Thanks, Dad," Rollin exaggeratingly gushed, and I couldn't help but giggle.

I really do like these guys. It was a staggering revelation.

"Raff?" Tate stood up first. "Thinking about shooting some pool at the bar."

Raff waved the group off. "I'll text when we're done."

I was quiet as the guys sauntered over to the bar across the street. I watched them playfully shove and laugh—at what I could only guess. It was at that precise moment that I took in my situation. I was in a public place with my kidnappers, and it had not even occurred to me to yell for help.

"I can feel you stiffening up," his whispered words were a caress over my skin.

I had difficulty swallowing. "God, what have you done to me?" He angled even closer. His forehead almost touching mine. I was all atingle from our proximity in the booth, but shouldn't I have felt it was more of a way to keep me trapped?

"You're thinking too hard. Can't you trust your feelings?"

"My feelings," I parroted dumbly.

"Yah, babe." His eyes were earnest and searching. "How do you feel when you're with me? With all of us?"

"Confused."

Raff huffed out loudly. "Elaborate."

"I should hate you, but I'm drawn to you. I should be running right now. Yet, I'm sitting here quietly whispering to my captor."

Grabbing my hand, Raff placed it over his heart. I could feel the steady, soothing beats. "Do you feel that?"

I nodded.

"It beats for you now."

I rolled my eyes.

"Cheesy. I know. But truthful. You give this pack meaning. A true purpose. More than that, though, is what I feel for you. Human emotions are not strong enough to describe the bond between mates. It's instinctual. I am meant to be with you. I feel it. What do you feel?"

Either I was too stubborn to admit I felt the same or too scared to believe in what I felt. "I'm not sure."

My words caused him pain. I fervently wished I could take it away, but I wasn't ready to commit to this insanity.

The food came just in time. Despite the awkwardness of the situation, my appetite demanded immediate attention. We ate in silence, devouring everything on the table in under twenty minutes. I was shoveling the last of the fries into my mouth when the sweet aroma of fresh-baked cookies wafted by.

"Hmm," I breathed in deeply. "We should totally get some for the guys."

Raff's eyes warmed visibly at my suggestion. "You bringing them hot-out-of-the-oven cookies? They will worship at your feet."

"As all men should." I tried to play it off lightly.

Raff didn't laugh, instead, he leaned in and buried his hands in my hair, cradling my head. "I can live with that, as long as you're all mine." His kiss was unexpectedly passionate for a public display. I didn't care. I was hungrier for him than I ever was for food.

I broke the kiss before I could do something truly terrible, like straddle his lap and ride him in public. "I need the restroom."

He released me and stood up. I slid out of the booth and edged past him. His hands trailed down my arm leaving goose bumps. "I'll order some cookies to go."

I stood in front of the bathroom mirror an inordinately long time, even for me. I looked different. Not a dramatic different, as if I grew a foot or my eyes changed colors. It was a subtle different. I looked happy. My eyes weren't crinkled in the corners from disdain, they sparkled. My skin was flushed. A genuine smile emerged without any effort on my part.

Strangest thing.

I spotted Raff as I emerged from the bathroom. He was at the counter getting a pastry box I could only assume was filled with cookies. The waitress was chatting him up, making a big production of wrapping the box with twine and taking her sweet time. Chimes rang, signaling new customers at the door, but she didn't glance up. I did. My heart stopped.

Police.

Two officers strolled in, passing Raff at the register, and taking seats at the counter closer to me. Time slowed. The older one glanced my way briefly before studying the menu. The younger cop's eyes held a spark of interest at my frozen form.

"Howdy, Miss." He nodded his head at me.

I managed a fraction of a nod in return. My tongue was tied and my eyes frantically searched for Raff's reaction.

He leaned on the counter, not a care in the world. No sign of worry etched into his forehead. No hesitation in his smile. So certain I would not scream for help and run to the officer. Why? He kidnapped me. He should be terrified. He drugged me. He should be looking utterly guilty.

I took a few wooden steps closer to both the police and Raff. My head and my heart warred.

It wouldn't even matter if I could prove this crazy story. The moment I screamed I would be free and Raff would get arrested. But … what if? That wonderful feeling of home. The urge to care when I never had. The desire to please someone other than myself. The sense I would never be alone again. Raff called it pack.

What if?

Raff headed to me, balancing the box in one hand, and held out his other to me. "Are you ready to go, Chloe?"

I placed my hand in his.

"Yes."

The End

DEDICATION

This book is dedicated to my best friend, my biggest cheerleader, my personal stalker, the person I turn to first if I hit an emotional low or a personal high—my husband.

We have known each other as kids, faced down life's obstacles side by side, and shared in so many heart-squeezing moments of joy. There is no one else I want to go on this crazy adventure-filled ride with.

MARIA MERCURIO

PACK FOR A LIFETIME

Survival, 2

Maria Mercurio

Copyright © 2023

Chapter One

I robotically buckled my seat belt, awash in a sea of disbelief. I willingly walked past two uniformed officers and got back into a vehicle with my kidnapper. Why? It's not like I didn't have a choice. I consciously chose Raff over my freedom. My Stockholm syndrome had obviously reached epic proportions.

I settled a pink pastry box filled with fresh-baked cookies on the floor by my feet. Cookies I had suggested we buy my other kidnappers. Because that was what you did when kidnapped, right? Buy the guys cookies and stroll past friendly policemen without a care in the world.

Raff started the engine, jolting my attention to his face. There was a glimmer in his eyes. Smugness over my acceptance of things, or happiness I was still with him? I didn't know. He looked over at me quite frequently as he sped away from the diner with the squad car parked in front. *Is he wondering if I'll change my mind? Should I be changing my mind?*

Once Lou's Diner was no more than a speck in the rearview mirror, Raff tapped the hands-free to dial his brother. I could hear the rowdy crowd at the pool hall in the background when Rollin answered. Weylin was shouting at someone to, "just take the shot," while country music played.

"Hey, man. Change of plans. Got back on the road. Go ahead and finish your game and beers. Meet you at the usual motel in a few."

"Saw a black-and-white in the parking lot," Rollin's voice trailed off as if he would say more.

"No worries. Chloe bought ya'll some cookies." Raff gave me a wink and squeezed my thigh.

"Did she now? Huh, that was awful kind of her."

"Yes. Yes, it was." Raff continued to smile warmly.

"So, no need to hurry? Weylin's got a hustle in the works." Rollin chuckled.

"Take your time. See ya." Raff disconnected the call. "Guess it's just the two of us for a bit more. I don't mind having you to myself."

I didn't answer. The shock of my actions settled over me. I wasn't second-guessing my decision, rather, I was trying to come to terms with it. *Have I just accepted this is my life? Will I try to run if given another chance?*

"Do you want to talk about it?" he asked gently.

"Talk about what?" The words came out a little snappier than I intended.

"Why you didn't turn me in to the police."

"Not really," I said in all honesty.

"It's okay."

I snorted. "Sure. For you."

"Better than just okay. For me, it's a dream come true."

I moaned. "Spare me the flowery words. Something happened. I can tell I'm different. I'm not saying I'm buying into your crazy stories, but I feel the need to stick around until I figure it out. That's all." I was emphatic.

"It's the beginning of the pack bond." He rubbed my leg again.

How could his touch be both incredibly annoying and wonderfully soothing at the same time? I felt weak for giving in and allowing my captivity to become self-enforced, yet I experienced such a sense of completeness when I was with the guys. "Stop trying to brainwash me."

He removed his hand from my leg and placed it back on the steering wheel. I immediately felt the loss. A tortured sigh escaped his lips. "Even seeing isn't believing with you."

"I believe I woke up covered in blood and naked. That doesn't prove I turned into an animal. The simplest solution is I hallucinated because you drugged me."

"Does it feel different with me then it has with other men?" he prodded.

"What?" I snorted. "You need an ego boost?"

"Our connection is more than physical. Admit it."

I crossed my arms over my chest, hugging tightly. My gaze strayed outside the window. I was finding it increasingly difficult to make eye contact.

"You're embarrassed," he accused.

I shook my head, more to chastise myself then to deny his words. I refused to rise to the bait and hand away any more of my soul than I had in the diner. Raff jerked the car to the side of the road and threw it in "park." It appeared he wasn't going to leave me with any dignity.

"Do you feel how deep our connection is?" He faced me and leaned in. His presence in the car grew, and I was like a caged animal.

"What do you want from me?" I screamed in his face.

"For once? How about the fucking truth, Chloe?" He reached for my hand and placed it over his heart. I could feel it beating wildly. My own traitorous heart raced to match the flutter. "This heart beats for you. I'm not a true alpha without you. This is not a pack without you. You are my mate. I will never feel complete without you. Please stop pretending this thing between us isn't real. You're just hurting us both. Admit you feel the same things."

"You don't get it!" I yanked my hand back. "I do feel it. I'm not just embarrassed. The better word would be *ashamed*. I just walked away from my freedom! You took my life away from me. You changed me without my permission. God help me, but I do feel complete with you, and it is pissing me off! How dare you be everything I want! Any woman with an ounce of pride would have run. I stayed because the thought of leaving you and the guys was unbearable." A dam of tears burst. "I'm ashamed of myself. I should be stronger. I should be fighting harder. I shouldn't be a willing captive."

My sobs turned ugly. I struggled to breathe as I buried my face in my hands. The sound of my seat belt unclicking was followed by strong arms engulfing me. Raff drew me across the bench seat till my head rested on his chest. I continued to gulp in air during my soul-shattering keening. Raff made soothing noises and stroked my hair. The deep sense of mourning vanished as his body warmth seeped into me.

"I'm sorry," his voice shook with emotion. "It was a shit thing to do to you. I couldn't see past the survival of our kind. It's not fair to expect you to embrace it all. I don't want you broken, darlin'. I love your fire. I wish I could give you the choice, but what I did can't be undone. We are part of each other now. It's only gonna' get stronger."

The confession of my shame was at least cathartic. I was able to pull myself together and lean back. "Where does that leave us then? A part of me still wants to hate you."

Raff flinched but nodded his understanding. "Your resentment is warranted. I'm hopeful it will lessen in time. Hate and love are the most powerful emotions, yet in our case the line between them is blurry. Our mate bond and the pack bonds are going to make you want to love."

"You see how messed up this is, don't you?"

"I do."

I slid back over and refastened my seat belt. "Then you'll understand why I will need to make you work for it."

A strangled sound between a laugh and groan echoed in the truck cab. "I'd expect nothing less."

I nodded as he fired up the engine. It was a huge concession on my part. I admitted he was what I wanted, and I agreed to stick around. I doubt it escaped his notice, considering the silly grin that remained on his face for the duration of our drive.

****

"You're gonna' get on well with my mom. My dad is a hard-ass alpha. He manages one of the largest packs of our kind. The guys and I have not been back as a group in quite some time."

He was taking me deeper into "crazy town." So deep, I might not find my way back to normal. "Why is that?"

He swallowed, struggling to formulate his words. "My father and I have a biological dilemma. As men there are no issues. I respect him. He's a good man, fighting for the salvation of our kind. My wolf, though— too dominant. I can only visit in-between changes. If I'm ever there when the change happens, there's a chance my wolf might take his out."

My face scrunched up, surely he meant it differently than I understood it. "What does that mean?"

"No two male alphas can exist in the same pack. We would try to kill the other for control. As you can imagine, we are talking about my dad, so as soon as it was clear I was becoming an alpha, I left."

"That's terrible." My heart warred with my head. I could feel the grief in his words even if I wasn't ready to believe it all.

"A lone wolf doesn't do well, so my dad sent my brother to join me. Lowe and Tate followed. We picked up Weylin on the road looking to join a pack about five years ago. Only problem is, a pack doesn't function properly without an alpha female. That being said, we were lucky. Our wolves strayed at first going their own ways. When we were human, we would meet back up. Eventually our wolves took the hint, yet it always felt forced until this last change. With you around, the pack has a purpose. The pack has a real future."

"So help me, God, if you talk about knocking me up again, I'm jumping out of this moving vehicle. I'm just getting my head around the kidnapping." I forced out the joke, despite the heavy weight of destiny's grip on my thoughts.

"Are you?"

"Am I what?"

"Getting over the kidnapping?"

My mind flashed back to the diner and the cops. That was my chance, and instead I willingly left with Raff. Pride kept my lips pressed firmly together. Raff didn't seem to mind. His hand settled on my knee, and as he squeezed gently a rush of heat pooled in my core. I swallowed and looked out the window, trying to manage my quickened breathing. A distraction was necessary, otherwise I might find myself making him pull over and straddling him on the side of the road. "What's your mom like?" Surely talking about his mother would calm down the libido!

"She's a witty fast-talker. Usually, the pack goes to her for advice and to solve arguments. She takes crap from no one, not surprising considering all the boys she raised." He chuckled fondly.

"You really have six brothers?"

"Yep. You will be meeting the other five in a day or so."

"Why so many? Are big families a thing with you guys?" I couldn't bring myself to say *shifters*.

"We are a bigger group than most. My parents kept trying for a girl."

"To help continue the survival of the line?" I pursed my lips.

"Nah," he snorted. "Mom just always dreamed of having a daughter."

I warmed up to his mom a bit hearing that. I could understand the desire to have a special mother-daughter bond, even though I had never experienced one with my absentee mother. "I imagine there are things you say and share with a daughter that a woman just wouldn't with her son."

"I imagine so." He winced. "But spare me what

those topics might be, not sure I'll want to know everything the two of you will chat about."

"The two of us?"

"Mom's splitting at the seams to meet you."

"Huh." I slouched back in my seat and chewed my lip.

"What is the 'huh' about?" he asked sounding a little worried.

"One moment I'm having a normal conversation with you talking about family relationships and the next we're back in crazy town. Discussing your mother being excited to meet your kidnapping victim definitely falls firmly on the weird side."

"Don't say that." Raff's lips pressed firmly together and his grip on the steering wheel tightened significantly.

"What?" I asked baffled. "It's weird."

"Don't call yourself a victim! I don't see you as a victim! You. Are. Not. A. Victim."

His anger made me clam up. I'd never seen him so offended and annoyed. Considering my constant jabs, it was saying a lot. An uneasy silence settled in the car. His rage at my words was a palpable thing. I'll admit to a slight fear. I huddled in on myself, clasping my arms, and frowning. *If I want to address myself as a victim, I should be able to! I'm talking about myself, for Pete's sake! Why does he get to be mad? I was kidnapped!*

By the time twenty minutes passed, I had properly worked up enough self-righteous indignation to turn and glare at him. I just wasn't sure what I should say. I walked past my chance at freedom. Does that remove my victim status completely now in his eyes? Yet, did I truly want to see myself as a victim? My lip curled at the thought.

Raff pulled the truck into the parking lot of an

oddly whimsical motel. The half-lit neon sign by the roadside read, RAPUNZEL'S. The motel looked like it was made from ten mini-water towers. Each guest room was freestanding with a carport below and the room above. The staircases had thick ropelike sides, which upon closer inspection were meant to look like hair braids. The bungalows were shaped like round castle turrets, and the windows were covered by wood shutters shaped like mini-drawbridges.

The place was so startling in its uniqueness, I forgot I'd given up speaking. "Fancy," I muttered while taking it in. "This the usual place you mentioned to the guys?"

Raff rubbed the back of his neck. "Yep," he replied sheepishly. "It's clean and the restaurant across the street makes a mean chicken-fried steak." He put the truck in "park."

"Wait here. I'll get the keys."

He ran to the only building not hoisted in the air. The office was situated in a perfectly square building with a faux boulder façade. He left me alone. I wondered briefly if he'd done it to prove his earlier point. Once again, I was able to walk away, yet I didn't.

Raff strolled back with three brass door-knocker key chains dangling from his fingers. *This place goes all out.* Opening my car door, he offered a hand to help me out. I reached back for the box of cookies and balanced them on my open palm while yanking my duffle bag from behind the seat. Raff promptly took it from my shoulders and gathered up the rest of our things.

"Head to number eight." He pointed. "The guys can take four and five."

It wasn't until I was halfway up the stairs when the angry woman in me resurfaced. I should have asked him where he was planning to sleep, in a haughty and pissed-off tone. Instead, the idea of not sleeping curled up next to him was physically painful. My chest hurt just thinking about turning him away. I took the keys from him to open the door, left it open wide behind me, set the cookies down on the nightstand, and plopped on the bed.

I absentmindedly rubbed at my chest as I watched him stash our things away in the closet. The corners of his eyes crinkled as he observed me. "You look tired."

I nodded mutely. It was just turning dark out, but it felt like the longest day of my life. Sliding on the bed beside me, Raff pulled me down, angling my head to rest on his chest. Once his arms were around me, I could breathe. I was almost immediately lulled to sleep. An admonishing thought had my eyes springing open.

"You said hate and love," I whispered.

"Hmmm?" his response was sleepy.

"I'm mad, yet all I want is to be with you. The thought of not being with you actually hurts. This is what you meant earlier. The bond."

I could feel him swallow his first response. He grasped me tighter as he sighed. "Pack bonds are a powerful thing. They affect us both." I stiffened and he hastily added more. "That doesn't mean what we feel is forced. It just makes our feelings more intense, deeper."

I attempted to move away but he continued to hold me firmly. "You're beat. Rest a bit. We'll get dinner once the guys arrive. Being close like this will make both of us feel better."

"I don't care about making you feel better," I mumbled into his chest. We both knew it was a lie, as I made no further moves to leave his side. It was where I wanted to be.

Chapter Two

Pounding on the door startled me. The room was dark and my vision fuzzy, waking from a deep sleep.

"Yo, bro!" Rollin's voiced was muffled by the door. "The chick at the counter said you picked up our keys. We're freezing our balls off out here. Open up."

Raff's chest rumbled beneath me as he groaned. I untangled my legs from his and rolled away so he could get up. With an elongated stretch he walked toward the door.

"For the love of God!" Rollin pounded on the door again for good measure. "Open up."

"Hold your damn horses," Raff's voice was feral as he swung the door open and flipped on the lights.

The guys didn't wait for an invitation. They barged in. Rollin folded his arms and acted all put out for having been kept waiting. Weylin gave me an evil smirk as I rubbed sleep from my eyes. "And what have you kids been up to?" he asked with exaggerated cheer.

"I remember a mention of cookies," Tate huffed while peering around. "I'm starving."

I ignored Weylin's innuendo and answered Tate by pointing to the nightstand. Rollin grabbed the box first and took a long time deciding on which cookie to take, deliberately driving Tate mad. The big guy had enough and snatched the box from Rollin's hands. He shoved at least three cookies into his mouth before Rollin was able to put his hand back into the box.

Lowe bounced on the bed beside me. "How about this place, huh?" he asked. His eyes sparkled with mirth. "Crack up, right?"

His giddiness was infectious. I couldn't have stifled a grin if my life depended on it. "Yeah. They went all out."

"Are you hungry, darlin'?" Raff closed the door and leaned against it, taking in the scene.

"I could eat," I said and shrugged.

Weylin joined Lowe and I on the bed. He slung his arm over my shoulders and whispered to me like fellow conspirators. "Always the safest answer when Tate gets in a feeding frenzy."

"Why are we yapping about it then when we could be eating?" Tate sputtered out a few crumbs while he talked with a full mouth.

"You're spitting cookies at me!" Rollin griped. "We have a lady present, close your damn mouth."

Tate's shoulders dropped and he hung his head. "Sorry, Chloe."

Not that the big man needed rescuing from me, but seeing him dejected brought out protective urges. "Back off, Rollin! Tate, I just need a bathroom pit stop and I'll be ready to go."

"All right, mongrels," Raff raised his voice. The others stilled instantly. "Throw all your shit in your rooms, and we will meet you outside."

The guys all turned and left in unison. "Was that you being alpha?"

A throaty chuckle was my only response. I crossed my arms over my chest waiting for an answer.

"Why don't you get yourself ready, darlin'? Gotta keep the troops fed."

I huffed at the evasiveness, but decided to do as he asked. It had been a day of fighting and drawing lines in the sand. I was exhausted and chicken-fried steak was sounding pretty darn good. After freshening up we joined the others and walked across the street. Raff's warm hand was clasped tightly in mine. I didn't pull away.

Dinner was a boisterous, noisy affair. The guys were exuberant, talking over each other nonstop and groaning in happiness over their food. Tate was a bottomless pit and kept ordering new things every twenty minutes, running our poor waitress ragged. He would make sure to offer me a bite of each new thing before wolfing it down. Rollin and Weylin vied for my attention by telling stories to see who could make me laugh more. Raff's hand lingered on my thigh, sending a constant stream of shivers down my back. Lowe kept looking at the two of us and smiling brightly. I guess they all must have appreciated we weren't fighting. Hell, even I appreciated a break from the constant need to escape. I'd been living totally amped up. I decided to just roll with it for the evening. I was going to turn off the part of my brain that persisted in screaming at me to get back to reality. I resolved to live in the moment and just enjoy the comfort food and the connection. Of course tomorrow was another day.

****

The room was cold when we returned. I could see my breath misting in the air. Shivering, I rubbed my arms.

"Dang it, we left the window open," Raff cursed as he shut it and drew the curtains. "Come here, darlin', I'll warm you up."

Raff reached for me and I stumbled into his chest. He circled his arms around me while peppering kisses along my neck. The warmth from his mouth was heavenly against my goose bump-riddled skin. He walked me backward till I felt my legs hit the edge of the bed. I sank into the lumpy mattress as he covered me with his body. Raff didn't rush. He continued his slow seductive kisses. I arched into him, pressing my chest against his and twining my fingers into his hair. His groan encouraged my hands to flutter down and explore his broad shoulders, muscular back, and finally settle on his tight ass. That action put the throttle down to full.

Suddenly I'm being quickly divested of clothes and tucked under the covers. Raff jumped away and entered the *Guinness World Records* book for fastest stripping of apparel. I didn't even have a chance to make a snarky comment before his flesh was pressed against mine and I lost the ability to string together coherent thoughts.

As soon as we were together under a cocoon of covers, Raff slowed back down again. His hand settled between my legs in a lazy exploration while his mouth sucked hard on my erect nipple. He bit down playfully, causing me to jump. His laughter sent vibrations flooding my core. I closed my eyes and just let myself feel. The few days' growth of his beard heated my skin. His clever fingers drove my hips to buck.

He positioned himself over me, asking me with his eyes. I lifted my hips in response and he sighed as he slid into me. Despite my best efforts, he kept the pace slow. With his weight on his elbows, his nose was only a few inches from mine. Our eye contact was intense. I couldn't look away. He was conveying many things to me in that moment. This was nothing like the crazy fight-and-make-up sex at the cabin. This wasn't rage mixed with pent-up lust. I was willingly here. I was a part of this. Raff's lips ghosted above mine, breathing in as I breathed out. He watched me for all my cues as to what felt best, kept me there with him, rather than escaping in pure feeling. The heavy weight of his body pinning mine felt comforting. My limbs tensed as pleasure consumed me. He took me over the edge one, two, three times before finding his own release.

I had never felt as connected to another human being in my entire life. *Maybe because he wasn't human, after all?*

Chapter Three

I was quiet in the morning, lost in my head. Raff told me we would reach his family by the afternoon. A sense of curiosity buzzed though me, but it was often accompanied by bouts of fear. Each day brought me deeper into the rabbit hole. Would I ever climb out? Would I want to?

My continued denial of what had taken place grated on the guys. They were incredulous when I didn't immediately agree to being a wolf shifter, a fellow wa'ya. It sounded insane, yet they acted as if I was the crazy one for not accepting their reality. Maybe I was? Something I couldn't explain definitely happened. I admitted that. I just needed to experience it again. Maybe I would remember more than short blurry fragments next time.

"Penny for your thoughts, darlin'." Raff's hand squeezed my knee diverting my attention from the passenger window back to him. "Care to tell me what's going through that beautiful head of yours?"

I cleared my throat. I wanted answers, but dreaded asking the questions. "The next time…" I trailed off not sure how to phrase it.

Raff was more in tune than I gave him credit for. "The next time we shift?"

"The next time things happen." No way was I going to just go along with it all. "Will my memories still be fuzzy?"

Raff sucked on his teeth a few minutes before forming an answer. "When we shift, our other half is in control. We think and react animalistically. When we shift back, it's only ever flashes of memory."

"So, I'll never be able to truly confirm this turning-into-a-wolf thing?" I couldn't help glaring while I folded my arms over my chest.

"Man, I gotta respect your tenacity. It will turn me prematurely grey, but I am humbled by your stubbornness." Raff alternated between chuckling and grimacing.

"Don't be an ass!" I hissed. "You have to admit it's all sorts of convenient that you can't offer hard proof."

"I'm pretty sure I did," he mumbled.

"What's that now?" My voice rose an octave.

"My father has recorded wa'ya shifts as part of his research. They are heavily guarded, on film only, no digital evidence allowed, but I'm sure he'll let you watch one."

His statement was like a bombshell detonating. A nervous energy surged from my stomach out to my limbs.

"Would that finally put this to rest?" he pressed.

"I suppose it would." My mouth was dry. I licked my lips thinking about what this would mean. "Why would you want your animal side to take over? Why would you be okay with the loss of control?"

"It's a part of who we are. Control is a human illusion."

I snorted. "How do you figure?"

"Well, you get mad, right? When you're pissed off you find yourself doing stuff you regret, wish you could take back? Same thing." He shrugged.

"It's a huge difference! I wouldn't willingly make myself do terrible things I regret."

"Our wolves don't do terrible things. They're simple in their thoughts and desires." He tried to placate me, but I didn't want any of it.

"They can kill."

"That is part of nature," he reasoned.

"You said once you showed signs of being an alpha, you left your old pack so neither you nor your father would hurt each other. Not because you wanted to, but because you could not control your wolf."

"We manage it. It's who we are. No sense in fighting against it." Raff was so calm it made me want to slap him silly.

"It wasn't part of who I was. At least not until you injected that crap into me!"

He visibly cringed at my words and miraculously looked contrite. "I know." He sighed. "My actions were selfish. When I walked into that bar and realized you could be my mate, my instincts made me laser-focused. Save our species. Make you mine. I didn't care about changing your life or how you might feel about it. It was wrong of me."

My jaw dropped open at his admission. "Wow. Finally."

"But I don't regret it, and I won't apologize for it. Both our lives will be better now."

"And the arrogant bastard is back," I growled.

"The benefits of our lives outweigh any cons. Being part of a pack is a sense of completion humans never feel. There is no uncertainty in our unity. We belong together. All lives have hardships, but our burdens are less since we share them with our pack."

This was the root of why I stayed. I felt the connection. It was everything he described. I'd be damned to admit it, though. I angled my body back toward the window. "How much longer? I have to pee."

I hate gas station bathrooms. I imagine only a truly messed-up soul with a gross fetish would admit to liking them. Usually I find a fast-food joint on road trips when nature calls, but we were truly in the middle of nowhere. It was either gas station or pee on the side of the road.

"No paper towels. Figures," I muttered to myself. Shaking my hands to dry them, I gingerly lifted the two-by-four attached to the bathroom key. I would need to sanitize again after returning it.

Raff and Weylin were leaning against the cars while the tanks filled up. I spotted the three other guys inside getting snacks and opted to join them. Lowe grinned as I walked in. "Chloe, come help me choose." He was standing in front of what I can only describe as a monument to jerky. There were six rows of shelves about five feet wide packed with clear bags of meat. Flavors I had never heard of before were handwritten on signs above each one.

My eyes trailed over the different types. "Wow, I've never seen kangaroo before."

"This place has the best jerky," Lowe exclaimed eagerly showing me his picks. "Venison is my favorite, but I can't decide to go spicy or teriyaki. Raff always wants just plain old beef original flavor. He's old-school that way. What should I get? Its buy two and get one free."

"Then there should be no problem. Get Raff his, then get the spicy and teriyaki."

"The third bag is for you, of course. I wanted to get what you liked." Lowe was just too adorable. He even blushed when I smiled at him.

"What about the other guys? I'm sure they will want some too. If it's as good as you say."

Rollin heard me and waved his bags at me. "I got the rest of us covered."

"How about we share then?" I turned back to Lowe. "Get both your flavors and we can split."

"Really?" His voice jumped up in excitement before he schooled his features. "I thought you might like something fancier. They have alligator and ostrich too."

"That's sweet of you to think of me. Venison is fancy enough for this girl. You said it's your favorite, so I'm game."

Lowe jumped and gave me a tight and unexpected squeeze. "Thanks, Chloe!" He beamed as if I bought him a present.

I shook my head at his antics and ruffled his hair. "Don't mention it, kid."

"Chloe," Tate called out. He was standing by the soda machines. "Want a drink?'

I nodded. "Root beer, please."

He held up two different cup sizes and I pointed to the smaller of the two enormous cups. "Lots or little ice?"

If a girl could just get over being abducted, these guys were extremely considerate. "Lots. Thanks."

Rollin waited at the register to pay while the others gathered the stuff to bring over. "Want anything else, Chloe?"

That's a loaded question.

"Nah, I'm good." I scrunched up my lips. "How much farther till we reach your folks?"

"Little less than an hour." Rollin's eyes sparkled. "We're excited to show you off. You and Raff getting hitched! This is going to be big news."

"I want to be clear. I did not agree to a wedding."

"What?" Rollin looked stunned. He spent a few minutes looking at the necklace around my neck and then back at me. "I thought you guys worked it all out?"

"Wrong." I crossed my arms and leaned against the counter. The clerk was standing there curbing my desire to elaborate. Tate handed me my drink. He had unwrapped the straw and stuck it in for me. I nodded my thanks to the big guy.

"Well…" Raff hesitated while he paid the clerk and accepted a bag. We were heading out the door when he spoke again. "The serum works. You being part of our pack is life-changing for our family, believe me, but you becoming a full shifter is species-changing for our entire community."

"Oh." My head filled with hundreds of kidnapped women tied up and screaming as they were being injected with that burning poison. The warm and fuzzy I was feeling in the store vanished. It was one thing seeing where this journey was going to take me. It was another to subject innocents to this. I walked outside in a zombie-like state and headed toward the truck.

"What's wrong?" Raff's voice was filled with concern. "What did those asshats do in there?"

"Are there going to be others?"

"Other what?" he asked puzzled.

"Other women?" I pressed.

"Not for me," he spoke solemnly shaking his head in denial.

I could tell he missed my point.

"I mean other women you plan to inject to trigger their genes?"

"Ah." He nodded sagely, took my drink, placed it in the cupholder, and got me buckled in.

"Is that an answer?"

"I don't want to fight." He closed the door on my response and walked over to his side.

"Not an answer either," I groused when he climbed in.

"The truth is, most likely, yes."

"Not acceptable. You just admitted what you did was wrong!"

"True. I also said I have no regrets." He shrugged.

"You can't go around kidnapping women!" My voice went slightly past shrill causing Raff to wince.

"I will not be kidnapping any women. You are my one and only, darling." Jerk had the nerve to wink at me.

"It's wrong, Raff."

"We have women who will try willingly now that they see it works. Your case is rare. You had no idea what you were. Only a handful of our females are clueless and live outside the pack. Even though most females are born not able to shift, they still stay with their pack. Without shifting, their ability to sense pack bonds is also dormant. You'll be bringing them hope. The dream of truly belonging."

"Because they are bummed they don't turn into mindless animals once a month?" The idea was incredulous.

"Not mindless, just not human. And yes. They want to experience being part of the pack. They are living a half-life."

"I find it hard to believe."

"Is it?" he challenged.

"I know I'm the picture of health now. But that crap was bad. I thought I was going to die. It felt awful."

"I hated seeing you in pain, darlin'. I promise you." Raff held steady eye contact with me and I could sense his sincerity. "People often endure pain if there's a promise of something better on the other end. Having a pack and never feeling alone in this world is a strong incentive to try. Better than some crap plastic surgery procedure causing tons of pain for something as superficial as a wrinkle."

I didn't have much to say in response. Even when

I didn't want him to, Raff made sense. "Whatever," I grumbled.

"Well, you'll be able to see for yourself soon enough. My dad will call in all the packs with this news. Saving our species has been his life objective."

"Why try on me then? Why not on women from your own pack?" My gut clenched to hear his response. His lips pressed tight and he white-knuckled the steering wheel before he spoke.

"We did try on one girl from each of the allied packs." His Adam's apple bobbed a few times. "We picked the toughest and physically strongest of the dormant shifters. They didn't make it."

Dread settled in my stomach at how close I had come to dying. "Why the hell did you inject me then?"

"We realized we were looking at it too scientifically. We are mythical creatures. We needed to find the spiritual link. Combine two elements to form the solution. A mate bond is more powerful than a pack bond. Some women with the dormant shifter gene can still feel the mate bond even though the pack bond isn't noticed. We reasoned that those women would have the strongest chance of survival since they had a bond connecting them to this world. I was tasked with finding my mate and testing the theory."

I winced. "Glad to know. I guess you didn't want to kill off anyone in your pack, so you stumble across me in a dive bar and think what the heck?"

"First, I'm related to most of my pack in some way. Second, the mate bond is mystical. Alpha females can sense if a mate bond exists. My mother told me where to find you, there wasn't any stumbling." He looked at me then and I could sense a pouring out of emotion cocooning me. "Love at first sight is of course a cliché, but with wa'ya we can sense a true mate the first time we meet them. My mother was right, you were the one. I also knew you felt the connection. The way your eyes would dilate. Your body language so in tune with mine. Then we spent the night together and I felt our souls connect, I knew I couldn't wait any longer. It would hurt both of us if we were apart."

"That doesn't make sense. You bolted before I even woke up."

"I left the next morning and headed out to speak with my father."

"To ask for the serum? So you could test your theory?" I couldn't hold back the bitterness that bubbled over.

"No." He scrubbed his face with his free hand. "I actually freaked out. I told you I was coming back, but my first thought was it might be best to leave you alone."

"What?" My stomach clenched and my heart stuttered at the thought.

"The leaving you part lasted all of one hour and I knew I couldn't manage it. Problem was my father. He knew I'd found you and was pressing me to move things along. Get back in time to secure things before the moon forced the change. He's obsessive in his drive. Very Alpha. What if he was wrong? I couldn't picture a world where you weren't in it. The chance was too great to take. I begged him not to pursue this. To allow me the choice of not connecting the pack bonds and just be with you. Never telling you the truth about what we were. He lectured me about obligations to our pack. The greater good had to be served. I called bullshit and stormed off."

"How did I end up here then?" I asked mystified.

"My mother. She said I wouldn't live a complete life. That you wouldn't live a complete life. I was already aching being away from you. I thought about you obsessively."

I shifted in my seat remembering my zombie-like state the week I waited for him to return.

"So many of our kind suffer with this illness plaguing us. The inability to shift in many of our females has made forming new packs such a rare thing. We are miserable. We are lonely. We are not true pack mates. She told me to believe in the bond. Never doubt your survival, because our survival counted on it. Going back for you was a leap of faith, but the moment I left her side and returned to yours, I felt complete certainty it would work. I stood a real chance of you hating me, but it would work. The idea of leaving you alone then left me completely. It was agonizing being away from you. I told you it was selfish, but I didn't do it just for me. I believed it was the right choice for this pack, and for you. We can become a family now. Share life's burdens and its joys."

We were both silent after Raff's admission. It was a great deal to process. I'm not sure how I felt about the risk he was willing to take with my life. The real issue, for me, was not having a choice. It played havoc with my sense of right and wrong. I could appreciate the idea of sacrifice for a greater good, but the sacrifice was me. I should have been informed and allowed to choose. My life had been on the line. Raff would have still been alive at the end of it all. He might have been a wreck for what he did, he might have never shaken off the guilt for his actions, but he wouldn't have been dead.

His dad was a hard-ass alpha willing to care for the whole over the individual, and his mom was a spiritual cult leader waving a wand to see who was up next for the sacrificial altar. Not really the in-laws of my dreams. I fretted over meeting them as the miles were eaten away and we finally pulled off Highway 64 onto Wolf Creek Road.

"Seriously? Not very subtle."

Raff had the grace to look sheepish as he took a few more turns and drove the truck up a windy dirt road, past a worn farmhouse and newly built horse stable, into hillier terrain. The trees were dense and the air smelled crisp with the tang of dying leaves. The tires crunched and then rolled to a stop in front of a massive forest-green metal security gate. Raff sat back and waited as the boys in the car behind us hopped out to open it. Lowe waved at me wildly as we passed him driving in. He looked excited. I wished I could share his enthusiasm.

I had a bunch of crazy thoughts on what this pack would look like, ranging from mud huts along the roadside to one gigantic mansion they all lived in. Reality was more mundane. It looked more like a gated community, a typical suburb. Eight wood-paneled two-story white houses lined up neatly in a row along one side of a cul-de-sac.

The other side of the street was a field. It was after harvest time, no crops still lingered, and the soil had been freshly tilled and prepped for winter. At the end of the cul-de-sac was a slightly bigger house, painted to look more like a red country barn. It had a huge wraparound porch accessorized with a wooden bench swing. On that impressive porch waited what appeared to be all of Raff's family. I counted eighteen men and five women.

"Looks like you're getting quite the turnout. Everyone's here." Raff put the truck in "park."

Guess pickings were pretty slim for Raff then. The moment I thought it, I felt sad. He mentioned one from each pack had died. That one loss was almost twenty percent of the pack's female population. That must have been a devastating blow.

My palms were slick when I reached for the door handle. Raff affectionately squeezed my knee and jumped out of the truck's cab. I stood up a little stiff from the long drive. I fisted the small of my back working on the muscles while I watched what could only be Raff's parents walk down the stairs to greet us. They looked to be in their late thirties even though I knew they were late fifties. Raff favored his father in looks, tall and rugged. He would be sexy late in life. His mother was stunning. Flawless skin, sun-touched golden tresses, and a perfect figure. The couple was smiling from ear to ear, making them far less threatening to approach.

Raff jogged around the truck and captured my hand. "Darlin', I'd like you to meet my folks. This is my dad, Austin, and my mother, Valentina." Raff beamed at me. "And this is my Chloe."

Valentina clapped her hands like an excited child and did a happy screech as she pulled me in for a bear of a hug. My eyes teared from the pressure. I was so shocked that I barely lifted my arms to return her embrace. She pulled back and placed both of her palms against my cheeks. "We are delighted to have you with us, my dear." Tears of joy spilled down her face while she chewed on her lip and regarded me. "You are a breath of life. We are so grateful to meet you."

"Don't overwhelm her, babe." Austin chuckled as he disengaged his wife's arms and pulled me into a gentler hug. "Raff's told us a great deal about you. Welcome to the family."

Again, if I could just overlook how odd my life was right now, this might have been a sweet moment. "Hello," I replied awkwardly not sure if the usual "pleased to meet you" would be genuine.

The rest of the boys from the other car had parked and rushed up. While they were being greeted by Raff's parents, I was passed along to the other brothers I had yet to meet. "Chloe, these are my little bros." He pointed at each in turn. "Baree, Canim, Nash, Lark, and that hulk over there goes by Runt." Runt was almost as big as Tate. I wondered if the nickname irked him or humored him.

A slew of more names was thrown at me. Austin's pack consisted of his brother Lucas and his wife with their two boys, his sister Marta, and her husband. They had a daughter, Akela, who was in her early twenties. She was as stunning as Rollin. Standing next to her appeared to be her brothers, twins in the midst of their awkward teen years. Out of the remaining six males, four were Austin's cousins and two were childhood friends that left their packs to join his. One of the cousins had a daughter named Lupa, a quiet little thing, but never stopped staring at me and shook my hand for so long that Raff had to remind her to let go. "Sorry…" She blushed. "This is just very exciting!"

Valentina's arm settled over my shoulder as the sun began its decent. "Let's get you all fed."

Chapter Four

The backyard barbeque was a carnivore's dream. The boys, of course, made sure to fill my plate and get me situated before sitting and digging in. Wolf thing or not, a girl could get used to being doted on by *almost* all the men in her life. Raff continued to be another story. It was clear from the get-go that Valentina had a favorite. I'd say the sun rose and set around her eldest. He sat apart from us with her at the next table. They were talking quietly and she hung onto his every word. I would have never thought of Raff as a momma's boy, but he was sweeter to her than he ever was to me. I had a girlfriend once that preached if a man was good to his momma, he was a keeper. There was such a thing as *too good*, though. I mean, this is the woman who convinced him to abduct me in the first place.

As if Valentina knew my thoughts centered on her, her eyes snapped to me and a sly smile spread across her face. "Son, I do believe your beauty is feeling like she is playing second fiddle. Come on now." She gestured for him to move to my table. "Go sit beside her and make her feel less lonely."

"That isn't necessary," I protested, but damn if I didn't feel immediately better when he sat beside me and rested his arm around my shoulders. "How could I feel lonely when surrounded by people?" I laughed weakly.

Valentina shooed Tate out of the chair across from me. No small matter considering the giant struggled extricating himself from the folding chair and had to perch on the end of the bench Lowe and Rollin were sharing. Spinning the chair around, she straddled it and leaned forward on her elbows. "I'm sure some of the loneliest times in your life were when you were around people. Makes it more apparent when you don't belong." She tilted her head to the side, her golden curls bouncing in the wind. "But now that you have a pack, those kinds of feelings will never be acutely felt again."

I shifted in my seat, not sure I liked the direction of the conversation. "Well, if that's the case . . . no need to ply me with attention." My smile felt brittle, but I still attempted it.

Her blue eyes clouded with compassion. "Nonsense! You're an alpha female in another alpha's territory. That alone would and should make you uneasy, but couple it with the bizarre change in your life and being here among strangers, I'd say you need a great deal of positive attention."

All the guys were looking at me affectionately, including Raff. He placed a gentle kiss on my forehead that sent tingles down my spine. Lowe gave me a heart-melting look of pure joy. Weylin wiggled his eyebrows making me smile. Tate shyly slid his dessert from his plate over to mine, and Rollin reached over mussing my hair while grinning. A warm hug surrounded me, yet no one touched me. The warmth settled in my core and I almost sighed as every tense muscle I had relaxed. It was like the dopey drunk feeling you get after a hot stone massage.

"There it is," Valentina crowed triumphantly. "Your pack bonds have settled in. You're all connected. Now, I don't have to worry about my boys!" She slapped her forehead playfully. "Correction, *your* boys."

My forehead scrunched up. "What do you mean?"

"What my wonderful wife is trying to say..." Austin sauntered over with a beer. Placing his free hand on Valentina's shoulder, he beamed at me. "It took you to make the pack bond form for the boys. When they left my pack, our bonds dissolved. It's a hard life to live without them when you've only ever known the feeling of being connected in such a way. Closer than family, that is what pack means. I can see you all have the glow of new bonds completing. It's indeed a cause for celebration." He lifted his beer in toast. "Let us welcome the new pack!"

"To the new pack!" a group of voices called out in unison.

"To our pack," Raff spoke. He held out his glass and all the boys joined. Every one of them looking at me expectantly. My hand circled around my glass as if it had a mind of its own. The hopeful look in Raff's eyes sparked by my movements was my undoing. I clinked my glass against all of theirs and downed my drink. Not sure if it was the influx of alcohol, but that warm and fuzzy feeling spread through my entire body.

Valentina squealed happily and clasped her hands in thanks. "Well, now it's all settled, what date are we setting for the wedding?" She looked at me eagerly.

Even with my new happy glow, her words provoked outrage and horror. I was left speechless.

"Geeze, Mom! Give her a moment to process." Raff pulled me up from the chair and snaked his arm around my waist. "You'll have her running into the woods with talk like that!"

"Well," his dad chuckled. "Not for another three weeks at least."

"A wedding!" I sputtered incredulously.

"No," he clarified. "The running through the woods." He pointed up at the sky. "When the moon will be full." Austin had the gall to wink at me, as if I should see just as much humor in his jokes as apparently everyone else did. My ears rung with his pack's laughter.

"Okay," Raff said while pulling me away. "Long drive. Time for bed. We'll see you all in the morning."

"Oh, honey," Valentina called out as we walked toward the house. "I made up the guest room for you two. More privacy on that side." A slew of whistles accompanied her statement.

"Thanks, Mom." Raff waved his hand to indicate he got the message without turning around. After years of bartending, I should be immune, but I flared red at the catcalls behind us. Raff closed the porch door and looked at me nervously. "You okay?" He tucked some loose hair behind my ear and grazed his thumb across my cheek.

His touch was incredibly comforting, like a balm over dry skin. Immediately I was soothed. "Honestly?" I licked my lips. "I think I'm going crazy."

"Well, you'll be in excellent company." He offered me a crooked grin.

I crossed my arms across my chest. "There will *not* be a wedding."

Raff shook his head, laughing silently. "We'll see."

****

"Your mom said this was the guest room. Does that mean you have a bedroom still here too?" I perched at the threshold of the room as Raff strolled past me.

"I shared a room with Rollin when I lived here. Still has double beds with trundles. Tate normally takes the couch in the living room since it folds out to a king, but the other guys will all bunk together."

"Sounds cozy." I watched Raff place my suitcase on the dresser. He opened it and handed me my toiletry bag, a tank top, and shorts. "Thanks." I tucked them all under my arm, not quite settled enough to get ready for bed.

Raff noticed. He noticed everything I felt. "Come here." He patted the bed beside him.

Twisting my mouth to one side, I eyed him warily. "Why?"

"You're all wound up." He shrugged and continued to pat the bed until I made my way over. I settled next to him and placed my things down. His hands massaged me working out the tension in my neck and shoulders. "I think everyone really liked you."

"Always happy to impress my captors," I muttered.

Raff didn't respond with his usual growl of frustration. He let me have my pout. His hands continued to knead my stiff muscles. I dropped my shoulders and sighed. I could feel the others with me. The guys were not in the room, but I could feel them. They were happy. A warm happy little hum fluttered in my heart.

"Thank you," he whispered so softly, I wondered if I was supposed to hear it.

"For what?"

"You could have rejected us and continued to fight it."

"The bond?"

Raff's eyes lit up. "It feels wonderful to have it back. After our last shift we all felt it awaken, but now it feels settled. I can feel them with us. My dad was right. These last eight years on the road were tough. The constant search for a home, when we knew we wouldn't feel at home until we found you. Now we can put down roots. As long as we're together, anyplace can feel like home. A permanent home and set territory. Safer for the pack." His right hand rested solidly over my heart. "This is where the pack lives. You've accepted us. Thank you."

"I've never been the warm and fuzzy type." I nervously licked my lips.

"You were a lone wolf. Aggressive. Selfish. A pack will settle you too."

I tried to take umbrage at his words, but they had the ring of truth. I thought I was the shit and everyone else should make way. Only my wild anger would ruin anything good I had going on in my life. "How long are we staying here?"

"Not too long. Two weeks at most. We need to find our territory and mark it before the next moon."

"And please tell me that does not involve watching you all pee in the woods?" I snarked.

"Ha, you're hilarious." He bopped my nose. "We have to search a spot out that calls to our other nature."

A million questions sprouted from that seed of a sentence, but I declined to ask any. It was too close to admitting I believed in all this if I did. I still wanted more proof. This could just be some crazy cult with powerful "knock you on your ass and make you wake up covered in deer's blood" drugs. "Two weeks with the folks then. What will we do?"

Raff smiled lasciviously but answered forthrightly. "The other packs will be here soon. My dad sent out a call. It will get kinda crazy around here. We're not all friends. Some packs actively work against us. It will mainly be other packs we are closely allied with that will join us."

"You fight with the other packs?" That was worrisome.

"Well, wolves are territorial by nature. We don't share land well. For us, it breaks down into species groups. We are from the original red wolf pack, most packs are grey wolves. They are bigger and more aggressive than reds, but reds tend to be faster and cleverer, so it evens out. My family is a mix of reds native to the Americas and Norwegian reds. Tate is actually a grey wolf. He was the runt of his pack and was therefore abandoned. He showed up at our doorstep one night, a little boy all alone, and my mother took him in."

"Tate was a runt? And they just left him?" Both thoughts felt ludicrous.

"Well, he grew into his own. A show of strength with the greys is more important than overall survival. To them a pack is only as strong as the weakest member. Reds don't subscribe to that. We play the long game of numbers. Family first."

"Poor Tate!"

"His old pack still gives him shit if we cross paths. It's as if they'd rather he died than joined us. Another humiliation for them."

I had a strong urge to punch the asshole who would abandon a small child. "Will they be coming here?"

"God, I hope not. The truce we have with packs allows them to, but my father will not try to invite them. They see the shiftless females as a weakness and often cast them out of packs. I doubt they would think highly on a cure. My father says feelings must be put aside for the greater good. But I don't think they deserve to cure their females if they cannot see all lives are precious to us."

I scooped up my things and headed to the bathroom. I wasn't sure what to make of all this. Even more people would be coming here soon, and not all of them friendly. What kind of life did I have ahead of me?

****

"You haven't touched your breakfast, dear. Do you not like eggs?" Valentina grabbed a pot of coffee and refilled her mug.

I woke up before the sun, confused about where I was. Then realizing it was Raff's childhood home, I was even less at ease. After pacing around the room, I decided a bit of air was needed. Valentina stopped me on the way out the door and lured me into the kitchen with the promise of coffee.

"Eggs are great. It's just earlier than I normally eat."

"My husband is the scientist, but I'll always be a farm girl. Wake up before the roosters. I usually have the boys up and out the door by now, but I told them today would be a holiday from chores. More coffee?"

"Yes, please." I held out my mug and observed her while she poured. Her skin was beautiful. Not a freckle or blemish could be seen, even though she was tan from being outdoors. The only wrinkles on her face were from smile lines around her mouth and a slight crease in her brows. I imagined that occurred while giving boys stern lectures. What must it be like to literally be raising a pack of wolves? Or people that acted like wolves. "Do you like this life?" The question spilled from my mouth.

She set the coffeepot back on the warmer and got comfy in the seat beside me before speaking. "Truly, I haven't known another. Not like you. I've always lived in the world where pack exists. I imagine for you this feels unreal."

I nodded my agreement and she smiled at me over the rim of her coffee mug.

"But, to answer your question, I love my life. It's quieter than some might like, but it pleases me. How are you feeling about your life?" Her perfectly formed eyebrows rose as she addressed me.

"I'm not truly sure what's real." I scrubbed my face with my hands and rested my chin on my knuckles.

"Yea, Raff told me you want to see the tapes."

I perked up. "There really are tapes?"

She nodded. "Austin can take you to the lab today, if it will set you at ease."

A rush of air escaped me like a deflating balloon. "I'm not sure it would. There's a lot of comfort in denial."

That set off Valentina. Her laugh was deep and throaty. "Ain't there a barrel of truth to that!"

Lowe puttered into the kitchen, stifling a yawn. "Am I interrupting girl time?" He smiled sleepily, but his eyes perked up at seeing coffee was made.

"You are indeed," Valentina mock-scolded. "But for you, sweet boy, we can make concessions."

Lowe looked at our plates of eggs and the clean kitchen. "Would you like me to make cinnamon rolls and bacon?" He didn't wait for a response before sticking his head in the fridge and pulling out ingredients. He looked comfortable, like he cooked here often.

"This boy knows all the paths to my heart." Valentina sipped her coffee, watching Lowe get to work. "I taught him all my best recipes and then he goes and makes them even better than me!"

"Not true at all," Lowe denied. "No one can touch your chicken and dumplings."

"He's also incredibly honest and forthright." She nodded sagely forcing me to chuckle with her.

My stomach was waking up and cinnamon rolls sounded better than cold eggs, but not to be rude, I started digging into my plate.

"You will need to find a special woman deserving of him." Valentina was smiling at Lowe warmly, he was blushing furiously, and the eggs turned quickly to sawdust.

My difficulty swallowing was duly noted. Lowe looked at me wide-eyed and horrified. "Don't worry about me, Chloe. I'm just fine."

"Of course there's no rush, dear. You just became a real pack only last night. When the time is right for you to bring in others, you'll just know."

"I think you're getting ahead of yourself. I'm still taking you up on that ride into the lab today to view the tapes." I was in this woman's home, so I tried to keep my tone respectful.

Valentina didn't bat an eye at my brittle nerves. "You are one hundred percent right. You need reassurances to get settled. When you're ready to embrace your roll in the pack, I'll be here to answer any questions you have." She patted my hand to emphasize her statement.

Normally the certainty in her tone would have made me bristle, but her words were said with such kindness, that I simply nodded in response. Lowe went back to cooking. I rinsed off my plate and placed it in the dishwasher. "Do you need help?" I never offered to help Lowe before, but I was antsy and needed a task.

Lowe's warm smile made his eyes sparkle. "Sure! Can you open the bacon and lay the strips on those cookie sheets I lined with foil?"

"Yep." I saluted him. "I can manage that." *Just don't ask me to find you a life partner and make huge decisions for everyone.*

Valentina readied another pot of coffee when she heard the house starting to stir. "Stampede should be here soon."

I tossed the four sheets of bacon into the double ovens and set the timer. Lowe had the dough rising and was busy making the filling. I'd never seen someone make cinnamon rolls from scratch before. It was a lot of work.

"Nuts?" He looked at me expectantly.

"Huh? You're all nuts if you ask me."

"In the cinnamon rolls," he clarified.

"Only if they're pecans."

"Amen to that!" Valentina seconded. It was hard not to like the woman. A part of me wanted to confront her about what her decisions did to derail my life, yet it felt wrong to challenge her. The instinct was so strong, I stayed silent.

Raff's younger brothers made it downstairs before our crew. They looked a great deal like Raff and Rollin, but I didn't feel any connection to them. They seemed nice enough. The one named Runt was so sweet to Lowe, thanking and praising him for pitching in to cook and help their mom. I confirmed he did get a kick out of his nickname too, which made me like him all the more. Nash and Lark might be twins they looked so much alike, I was still puzzling it out, but I could tell they were the youngest. Baree was the only one of the men with completely different coloring, almost a ginger, and Canim looked the most like Rollin, hot blond movie star, just not as jaw-dropping.

I wondered if Rollin regretted leaving his family to join his older brother's gang. Not fully ready to commit to the word *pack* quite yet. Rollin slid down the stairs almost magically appearing by my side, as if my thoughts summoned him. Tate and Weylin were close on his heels, most likely lured awake by the smell of bacon. Raff was absent. I wondered if I should wake him since the food was done.

Lowe was loading up the table with piping-hot cinnamon rolls dripping in sticky white icing and covered with caramelized pecans. He served Valentina one and waited for her to bite in with gusto and give a thumbs-up, before he brought out the plates. Nash and Lark shoved each other to get at them.

Rollin smacked both his brothers on the back of

the head before they dared touch the rolls. "Ladies first, boys. Chloe?"

I should let them tuck in since I had my eggs and wasn't particularly hungry, but the siren's call of gooey baked goods was too hard to resist. "I'll take the smallest one. Your mom was kind enough to make me food earlier. Should I go wake Raff?"

"Oh, he's up," Valentina managed to speak daintily between mouthfuls. "When you were prepping the bacon he waved and headed to meet his father in the study."

"I already sent them a tray." Lowe sidled up next to me. "They like to talk alpha stuff in the mornings."

I felt a tad bit slighted he hadn't said good morning. It was a needy ugly feeling and I didn't like it. I wasn't a needy girl. I was the cool aloof girl. Weylin slung his arm around me and I felt the hum of the invisible connection between us. It was like aloe on a sunburn.

"He must have been tickled to see you getting along with his mom. Probably didn't want to interrupt your quality time." Weylin stroked my arm and spoke softly enough that the others wouldn't hear.

It was exactly what I needed. It made sense. Raff wanted me to bond and spend time with the guys without him, hence his mother would be no different. Now it didn't feel like a slight, but more like silent encouragement to embrace my new life. Weylin smiled down at me and Rollin held out another roll for me to take.

That was the signal for the brothers to dive in. "Go get some!" I laughed at Weylin.

What took Lowe an hour to make was consumed in less than five minutes. I shook my head in wonder.

Bunch of animals.

Chapter Five

Adjusting the clasp on the beautiful artifact necklace Raff gave me, I studied myself in the mirror. My finger rubbed at the lingering condensation over my reflection, a remnant of my shower. Austin agreed to take me to his lab and show me the film. Proof that men can turn into wolves. Resolution to walk downstairs and get in the car waned slightly. I had demanded to see the tapes, but did I truly want to?

"Chloe," Raff's deep voice trailed down the hallway to reach me. "You coming, darlin'?"

Breathing deep, I closed my eyes and counted to three. *Don't be such a wuss!*

I sailed down the stairs and almost barreled into Raff. He steadied me and drew me in tight. "We can do it another time."

He knew, without me uttering one word about my reluctance, he knew. "I want to go," I spoke almost convincingly.

"Then, after you." He gestured outside. I could see his father sitting on the porch waiting. I strode purposefully to the car, hopped in, and buckled up without further hesitation.

Austin drove and Raff sat up front with his dad. I was quiet on the drive, listening to them talk about the neighbors and local news. My head rested on the window while I catalogued the landmarks we passed. All the guys wanted to come with us, but Raff said it was only for me. I was grateful. Depending on what Austin showed me, I would see the guys in a new light. Either this thing was legit and this was my pack, my reality, or I've been making nice with my kidnappers and cult followers for far too long.

The car sped up to a security fence that swung open as we neared, and soon after, a guard gate loomed ahead. Austin came to a stop but didn't roll down his window. The man at the gate peered at him, gave a sharp nod, and lifted the bar blocking the road.

"Is this a government building?" I asked.

"No," Austin answered. "This is all private sector. I rent out this facility with the help of a few grants for genetic research. I'm working on reversing the effects of aging at the cellular level. Lots of money in that arena. That covers the cost of the pack's needs, and I get a secure place to work."

I'm not sure why I was expecting a place more like a kennel and less a state-of-the-art facility. Raff held my hand as we walked inside. It was all sleek metal and glass. Two security guards were seated inside at the reception desk with three shiny mirrorlike elevator doors behind them. Once again Austin did not need to speak, only nodded as we strolled by. We turned the corner to find a fourth elevator door. It was matte metal and looked like a service elevator. He punched in a pass code for the door to open.

"Upstairs are my research scientists. They're conducting experiments for our benefactors," he stated as he pressed the button for the basement.

"Your fountain of youth project?"

He chuckled appreciatively. "We are making some great strides. Our research on mice is quite promising. Slowing aging on the cellular level and expanding life expectancy. It's quite remarkable stuff."

"Sounds like it."

Elevator doors pinged to announce the commencement of our descent. I gulped.

"You going to be okay?" Raff rubbed at the goose

bumps appearing on my arms.

"That is the question, isn't it?"

"How will I know it's real and not movie magic?"

Austin held a film reel from a locked safe while Raff set up the projector and screen. "I'm going to show you Tate. You know him, it'll be more believable to you that way."

Austin readied the film. Raff dimmed the lights. I held my breath.

The camera showed a plain white room, much like the ones we passed on our way to the safe. A young Tate was seated in a chair. He looked antsy. Tiny Lupa was in the room with him.

"It's almost time now," she cooed.

"Maybe you shouldn't be here? It might not be safe." He was sweating a bit. *"I feel the need to be outside."*

"That is a good sign. The shift will happen in or out. Your wolf would just prefer outside."

"That's just it. What if I attack you?" He looked extremely concerned.

"Your wolf will sense I'm an omega. An attack would be rare. Don't stress. I have a tranq gun just in case. This isn't the first shift I've recorded. I need to be in the room to get all the readouts, but I have a safe spot to run to as well." Lupa stuck monitoring equipment on Tate's temples, tested his blood pressure, and took his temperature.

"I think you need to step back now," Tate implored.

Lupa simply nodded and stood a reasonably safe distance away. Tate started undressing but before he could remove his boxers he froze. He looked up, as if he could see the sky outside. His eyes showed only the whites for a heartbeat before they darkened to almost black. Then it happened. His body twisted and contorted. Clothing shredded or fell off. It looked incredibly painful, but Tate never made a sound and continued to stare transfixed at the ceiling until his face morphed too.

Faster than I could have imagined possible, Tate disappeared and an incredibly large grey wolf took his place.

My mouth went dry and I fell to the floor in a boneless heap. Tears sprinkled down my cheeks as I struggled to take in air. Raff was by my side in an instant, rubbing my back and instructing me to breathe.

"That's it, darlin', nice and slow. "

Either Austin deserved an Academy Award for special visual effects or Tate just turned into a wolf on camera. "Fuck!" I pounded at the floor more scared now than when I woke up covered in blood. "I'm going to keep turning into an animal every month! What if I get shot! What if I get separated and wake up in a zoo? What if I get lost in the woods and die when I turn back?" I cradled my head in my hands and rocked slightly. "Oh my God, oh my God, oh my God."

Out of the corner of my eye I saw Austin exit the room and leave comforting a hysterical woman to his son.

I was a bit catatonic on the ride back to the main house. Austin drove, but Raff stayed in the back holding me tightly to his side and whispering what he imagined to be soothing words. "Everything is fine. You're safe. You're with your pack. Can you feel them supporting you? This is how we are meant to live."

The last line got me to shift away in my seat. "If we were meant to be this way, then why was my wolf side dormant until you injected me with your crap cocktail? I was meant to be human. You took that from me."

I could see Austin's frown from the rearview mirror as he regarded me. He started to speak but Raff stopped him. "No, she's right, Dad. I did take away the life you had, pretending to be simply human." He leveled me with an intense stare. "But we've been over this, Chloe. It was a half-life. You were wasting away in some dive bar. This is your true purpose. When you get over your shock and let go of all your denials, you'll see I'm right."

I rested my head on the cool glass window looking anywhere but at him. "Don't hold your breath," I muttered softly.

Raff, not tolerating the distance between us, slid closer, pushed his fingers into my hair, and massaged my scalp. His gentleness undid me. Silent tears I refused to acknowledge ran freely down my face. A whirlwind of emotion resided in me. How could I hate and want someone as much as I did this infuriating man? It defied all logic.

A caravan of new cars greeted us as we pulled up. "Fuck," Raff cursed. "How the hell did the other packs know to be here so soon? Jesus, Dad! I wanted Chloe to have a little time to adjust."

"This is news that can't be contained, son." Austin used his no-nonsense tone. "You dry up your face, Chloe. When I stop this car, you walk out proudly. Show no fear or emotion to those other packs. You are an alpha. Raff's pack was never officially acknowledged before. The way you act will determine how you will be treated by our society."

Many snarky remarks were on the tip of my tongue, as well as several genetically creative insults.

"You may be pissed at Raff right now. I can see you have the temper of an alpha. You think of your other pack mates. Those boys need you. The bonds have settled, so you can't tell me you don't feel compelled to protect them."

And just like that, he had me. My anger deflated and I worried about my guys. There was a corner of my mind screaming at me to not give a crap, these freaks brought it on themselves, but the new me was stronger. She snarled at the idea of these strange packs treating my pack as anything but equals.

Dammit! I have a fucking pack!

Chapter Six

Five other packs were present to witness the miracle that was me. In a strange way it felt like I was a celebrity exiting the car to a field of paparazzi. Questions were being yelled, random people I didn't know were calling my name, trying to get me to look in their direction, all while Raff was steering me quickly into the main house, repeating, "No questions just yet. We will answer them all at the meeting tonight." The door closed behind us, but Austin stayed outside with the other packs.

"Sorry about that, darlin'," Raff whispered in my ear before he placed a kiss on my temple. "Runt! Nash!" He shouted for his two largest brothers. "Dad needs a bit of crowd control." All his brothers emerged at the summons.

"We got ya, bro!" Runt grunted as he hurried past. The brothers all filed outside except Rollin. He saw my pale expression and pulled me in for a hug. God, it felt like hot cocoa on a cold night. I buried my face against his chest and breathed deeply until I didn't want to cry. Both the brothers proceeded to guide me into the living room where I found Tate and Weylin. I couldn't settle until I hugged each of them. Lowe walked in with a whiskey on the rocks that I knew he made for me.

Unbelievably, it made me laugh. "I might need a bottle."

"Anything for you, Chloe," he said in all honesty. His eyes brimmed with unshed tears. "You don't know how much it means to have you."

I pulled the kid in for a tight hug, sloshing the whiskey on the floor in the process. "Hey there, darlin'," Raff protested taking the glass. "This is the good stuff."

He offered me the drink, but not before taking a long sip and slowly licking his lips. Damn if it didn't give me the shivers to be the recipient of that heated stare. I chugged the rest of the whiskey and as it burned my insides, I started to feel less numb. Standing there, surrounded by my pack, I felt cherished and loved. None of us have used the *L* word, yet I felt it in the bond that tied them to me.

"What do all those people want?" I'm proud of how normal and disinterested I made my voice sound.

"They mainly want to interrogate my dad, I suppose," Raff answered. "But they also want to see you, see us with you, and believe there's hope."

"Not sure I'm ready to be stared at." Even from thirty feet, the clatter outside was loud.

"No need to return out there just yet." Tate jerked his head at the TV. "We got that cooking show on that you like. Let's just chill for a bit."

I nodded my head to signal how perfect it sounded. Lowe ran out and then back into the room with a fine bottle of whiskey, making us all laugh. Raff tucked me into his side on the couch, and I nestled in, resting my legs over Tate's massive thighs, and waited to see which chef would be victorious.

My chill session lasted through three episodes. The house was bustling, getting ready for a huge bonfire meeting tonight, but we didn't lift a finger. I felt guilty and started to get up after about ten minutes but Weylin threw a pillow at me and growled to relax. Valentina popped her head in, gave me a conspirator's wink, and discreetly closed the door to the den leaving me alone with my guys. I needed it. I wanted them right beside me while I adjusted to this being real. The wonderful warm happy glow from the pack bond buzzed all around me.

With a luxurious stretch, I sat up. "Okay, I'm

ready to tackle this." That got everyone's attention in the room. "I have a few questions."

Tate smiled kindly and switched off the TV. "What do you want to know?"

"How is this going to work with us?" I chewed on my lip feeling nervous. "I feel this soul-deep connection to all of you. I can go years without seeing my sister, but I feel it would tear me in two to try that with you."

I watched in amazement as all the guys, sans Raff of course, blushed and looked pleased. Lowe was beaming more than most. "We stay together," he spoke. "Now that we're pack, we can stop living like nomads and find a place to live. Put down roots. Have a place like this for us." His eyes traveled longingly around the room.

"We all just live together in one house?" They nodded at my question. "Don't you guys want space? Want lives of your own?"

Rollin smiled devilishly. "Only Raff wanted a mate. The rest of us are quite content sampling the human population for now."

Tate placed my slender hand in his meaty one. "You're the alpha female. You will know when it's time to increase our pack. That could be with your kids or selected mates for us. Until then, we are happy as long as you are."

My mouth dropped open and I looked at Raff. "Your mom was not messing with me? I'm actually in charge of choosing mates for the pack?"

Raff's fingers played with a tendril of my hair as he assessed me. "It's an alpha thing." He shrugged. "You will know instantly if it's right. Just like I did with you."

I swatted his hand aside. "Just because I started drinking the Kool Aid does not mean I'm prepared to make the next poisonous batch for a poor unsuspecting woman."

"Whatever you feel is right, Chloe," Lowe's voice wrung with cultlike dedication.

"No." I shook my head. "That's just messed up. What if you find someone you love and want to spend the rest of your life with? What if I say no? You're going to just accept it?"

"Sometimes individuals leave a pack. We did to follow Raff." Weylin motioned to the group. "Sometimes it's over love, but those instances are rare. It's usually when an alpha emerges and a pack has grown too large to sustain itself. The point is, we are content right now. All you need to worry about is when it doesn't feel like enough. You will know before us. The females always do."

The guys all laughed at that, but I was still mystified how they could pass over such huge decisions to me, a virtual stranger.

"It's a wolf thing," Raff once again answered my unspoken thoughts.

"What's the deal with all the packs tonight then?" I looked at the window as the sun started setting. I knew preparations for the bonfire were well underway.

"Information sharing mostly," Raff continued to speak. "And it's also a chance to meet each other. We usually keep to ourselves, but with our survival on the line, my father is encouraging a large gathering. Usually we only meet once a year during the end of summer, hoping for future mates to recognize each other. My dad thinks it would be good to meet up more."

"And what do you think?" I pressed.

"I think it will be a lot of alphas in one place. Four more packs have arrived since we've been in here. I'm hoping a few will not show up. Some of us have been at war for generations. Not likely a love match will spring from that."

"Should I be worried then? Will there be packs not happy to see me?"

Raff shifted closer till I could feel the delicious heat radiating from his body. "You're completely safe with us. Don't wander alone, though."

Tate grimaced. "What we need to worry about are the greys. They may reject this serum outright as unnatural or see it as a mandate to inject all the females. We know without the mate bond the results are deadly, greys may not care about that. Or worse, they may now feel it would be fine to start stealing the few females left that can shift and leave the formula to the rest of us. They have a thing about purity and weakness."

Knowing Tate's story makes his words all the more frightening. If this beast of a man was considered weak and left to die, what would strong look like? Seeing his sad expression made me want to change topics. "What should I wear then? What reads 'badass alpha, don't mess with me'?"

Raff's deep chuckle sent tingles down my arms. "I might have bought you just the thing."

Chapter Seven

"When you said my outfit would scream don't touch, I thought you meant it would be intimidating, not, 'I'm so hideous, you wouldn't want to touch me'," I griped at Raff, adjusting the long baggy sweater that was swallowing up my figure.

"Trust me, darlin'. You go to them dressed like you used to when tending bar, and those unbonded males are gonna think you're putting out an offer." Raff cupped the back of his neck as he inspected me.

"Ugh!" I spun around on him. "I feel like a dithery old maid. Not the bolt of confidence I want when meeting a large group of strangers."

"I wish! Yet there's no way to hide how hot you are." He gestured to my face.

"What?" I raised my eyebrows. "You want me to cover my head as well?"

Raff looked sheepish. "Would you?"

"Get serious!" I huffed.

He settled his warm hands on my shoulders. "I'm deadly serious. It's gonna be hard as hell for me, having other packs looking at you."

"You haven't been the jealous type yet. You leave me with the guys alone all the time."

"Different. They're family. I absolutely hated walking into that dive bar and seeing what you had on display. It took everything I had not to bash in a few drunken skulls."

It was wrong that his misogynistic ways gave me the warm and fuzzy, but they did. No way, no how would I tolerate it, though. This wasn't the Dark Ages. "You are insane. I'm not wearing this wool muumuu." He started to argue, but I held my finger over his lips. "I'm not planning to dress like I'm clubbing in Vegas either. Full coverage, but jeans and a top of my choosing."

"Too sexy." He shook his head.

A grin broke out over my face. "You haven't even seen it yet."

He did not smile back. "I mean it."

"And I don't care." I stuck out my tongue. "Don't go caveman on me. I won't accept it."

I pulled off the giant monstrosity Raff had demanded I wear and tossed it violently to the floor. My eyes blazed and I dared him to refute me. Maybe giving challenge while I stood in front of him in only my bra and panties wasn't the smartest option—it visibly excited him.

He lunged for me. I squealed in surprise when his hot mouth covered my collarbone. His tongue traced a line from my shoulder to my earlobe. My knees buckled slightly when he nibbled. Hands grabbed at my ass. Instantly, I was plastered tight against him. His erection pressed into my stomach through his jeans. Instead of shoving him out the door and getting ready, as there were like a hundred people outside, I found myself cupping him with one hand and fumbling under his shirt with the other to touch those amazing abs. Raff didn't require any other encouragement. His pants were shoved down while he spun me around and set me on the bed. Ass in the air, I glared at him over my shoulder. With his dick in his hand, he leered back and snapped my little thong clean off. Before I could formulate a coherent sentence, his hands were all over me. I could not hold back the moan of pleasure that his touch incited. With a deft few fingers rubbing my clit and some expertly placed nipple pinches, he was sliding in with little to no resistance. My breath caught as he hit just the perfect bundle of nerves. Raff was relentless in his discovery, jerking my pelvis up even higher so I felt him more deeply.

Setting a demanding pace, I could only gasp in response. A rumbling chuckle was all I heard from him. He held the power in this moment and was damn pleased about it. This act was on his terms. A punishment of sorts since I overrode his wardrobe selection. He had me squirming as oversensitivity warred with an emerging climax. As the intense and draining orgasm built, I felt no complaints. I welcomed this form of torture. I muffled my scream into the pillows, aware that we were in a house filled with people. My clenching walls pushed Raff over the edge, and he spiraled down with me.

After, I lay spent and in a daze, jaw slack and eyes slightly glazed over. I was panting and sweaty from our quick romp. Raff moved the hair out of my eyes to look directly at me. His words penetrated through the fog of contentment. "Cover up however you like. Just remember I covered the inside of you up to my liking." He winked when I swore and threw a pillow at his head. He swatted my butt, rolled out of bed, and did a shuffling hop into his jeans. "Meet you out there in ten, darlin'."

Asshole! That man will never let me just have it my way!

I was half-tempted to dress as slutty as I could just to prove the point I wouldn't be controlled. It was near-freezing out, though, and I'm not a masochist. Instead, I settled for a slim-fitting sweater and a puffer jacket that still showed I had a figure. I did take extra care with my makeup, wanting my face to be memorable. It was kind of a thrill to see Raff jealous. He was an aloof ass when I tended bar, making me work extra hard for a flicker of his attention. In hindsight, he sensed I was his mate and played it cool not to spook me. Damn if it didn't work too. I should have been ashamed I fell for it, but the thing was, he was the first man in my life that had presented any sort of challenge. Even now, as I prepped for the party, I was thinking more of his reaction at seeing me, than meeting hundreds of strangers—strangers that were not human. I pursed my lips, smoothing my lip gloss, and gave my reflection a hard stare.

The video of Tate was still playing on repeat in the back of my mind. Not human, just like me. It took three deep breaths to steady myself, adjust to my permanently altered reality, grab my coat, and head outside.

The party was in full swing. Spits were being turned with roasted boar. Drinks were flowing from two different makeshift bar stations manned by Raff's younger brothers. Outside heat lamps kept the worst of the chill away, along with a massive firepit with flames at least five feet tall at the edge of the property. The crowd was fairly rowdy. The mood was festive and drinks were flowing.

I was noticed immediately. A silence settled around me as I passed groups of people. Whispers followed in my wake. Austin and Rollin approached me before I could catch sight of Raff. His dad was smiling at me, probably sensing my unease. Rollin loosely draped an arm over my shoulder, a slight thrum pulsed between us. Confidence and comfort enveloped me. This bond stuff was seriously amazing. Living without it had felt like existing in a world without color. These guys were quickly taking up residence in my heart. A wave of warm and fuzzy feelings expanded inside me.

Rollin gave me his megawatt movie star smile. "I felt that," he teased. "You're like a little purring kitten."

"I have no idea what you're talking about." I shrugged his arm off my shoulders.

He annoyingly bopped my nose with his finger then leaned in conspiratorially. "You're starting to love us just a little. Don't lie. You sent the emotion straight to me just now."

"Getting ahead of yourself, man." I crossed my arms over my chest. Austin just watched our exchange with only a hint of a grin.

Rollin was like a dog with a bone "I like the bond too. Closer than family. Endless support." He slung his arm over my shoulder again and it was back full force. Contentment. In life, that bliss was always short-lived, but I could feel it whenever I opened myself up to the bond. My insecurities, doubts, and fears were still present, but faded. They were simply not as important.

I gave up trying to pretend I wasn't affected. "How does it work?"

"I like to think it's our wolf," Austin answered the question I directed to his son. "They have simpler needs. As long as there's no immediate danger and they're with the pack, they're happy. The bond syncs our human side to our animal side."

"I suppose it makes turning into a beast each month slightly, and I mean *slightly*, more palatable." I was not about to let them think I was suddenly willing to be the poster child for their shifter cure. Not when the chance of death was high.

Austin chuckled. "Come, my soon-to-be daughter, let me introduce you while we find your husband."

"Yikes," I grimaced. "Please tell me that will not be part of the introductions? I have not agreed to a wedding."

The alpha looked puzzled. "You wear our traditional betrothal necklace on display."

My hand settled on the necklace Raff gave me

from his work trailer, before we had even kissed. He was in such deep shit! "He never mentioned it," I breathed out.

"When you wear it, does it feel like it belongs to you?"

From the very moment I put it on. "Maybe."

A knowing smile spread across his face. "By our standards, that equates as a yes." He scratched at the bristle on his chin. "But you give my son hell for not doing it proper." He nodded at the necklace. "It's up to you to make an honest man out of him."

Rollin laughed so hard he teared up. "Man, your face!" He wiped at this eyes. "I cannot wait to see you tear my big bro a new one."

"Son!" There was a growl to Austin's tone. "Raff is your alpha."

The cat that ate the canary could not have grinned any bigger. "Chloe's my alpha too. She is woman, I'm ready to hear her roar." He winked at me. "I'm here for total support. I got your back. Who's your favorite pack mate? Huh?"

I crossed my arms and pulled back to scowl at him. "Lowe."

Rollin put his hand over his heart wincing in pain. "Ouch! Not fair. Everyone picks him."

Austin playfully cuffed his son on the back of the head. "I wonder why, smart-ass."

"They are intimidated by my good looks." He shook his head sadly in response.

Even though he was joking, I sort of agreed. Rollin could pass for a Nordic god. He was possibly the most attractive man I had ever met. "It's because Lowe is sweet, unassuming, and caring," I scolded.

"Weakest of the pack is always chosen by the alpha female to protect." Austin smiled down at me.

"Lowe is not weak! He is wonderful," I snapped before I could stop myself.

Both Rollin and Austin chuckled. "I rest my case." The older alpha put both hands up in surrender.

Before Austin could introduce me, a few young women muscled up the courage to approach us. I could see them edging closer and egging each other on. I'm not really a girl's girl. It never occurred to me that the nervous stares and excited whispers were about me. I assumed it was Rollin, aka Movie-Star Hotness, the girls wanted to talk to.

"Excuse us," a tall brunette about my height spoke first. She shot her hand out almost touching me. "We all want to say what an honor it is to meet you."

By reflex only I shook her hand, not comprehending her words. "Excuse me?"

The bubbly and adorable auburn beauty beside her captured my hand next. "You are the bridge to our future. Hope!"

I pulled back my hand before the three others could reach for me. "Does that mean you're like I was? Human only?"

Tall Brunette seemed to be the leader. "Well, you were never human only, and neither are we. But we are shiftless. The gene is dormant in us."

The bubbly one gushed. "But that can all change now!"

"I almost died. It was agony," I cautioned, but the words fell on deaf ears.

"And to think," a slim dark-haired girl in the back spoke. "The secret all along was to find your true mate."

Bubbly squealed. "Just like a fairy tale!"

"Yeah," I snorted. "But not the Disney kind, this was more like the Brothers Grimm."

"To go from feeling alone your entire life, to

finally feeling part of a pack must have been magical."
The tall brunette's eyes glazed over.

"You mean, you grew up in a pack but didn't feel
the connection?"

"No," the slim girl answered sadly. "Only the
girls that can shift feel it. It's how our mothers knew we
wouldn't be able to."

"Wait." I held up my hand at a horrible thought.
"What happened each month when your mothers shifted
and you were just babies?"

The women looked surprised at my question.
Rollin came to my rescue. "Chloe didn't grow up in a
pack," he explained. The ladies gave me varying degrees
of sympathetic gazes and pity. "When one of our females
gets pregnant, the shifts halt and do not start again until
she stops nursing, usually around a year. Children start to
shift around five. All packs have an omega. When there
are children in a pack, the omega shifter will cease to
shift completely until all children are of age."

"And when there are children who do not shift
ever?"

"The omegas will go back to shifting again after
the children are older than five." Austin took over
explaining. "It's what prompted many of us to form
larger packs, with more children, so an omega would be
available. Or in some cases, a trusted human friend, who
becomes honorary pack. These last four generations have
been a tough adjustment for our kind. Each new
generation has less natural shifters than the one before.
Any girl born able to shift now is a celebrated rarity. It
equates to about one in five."

"So you see," the bubbly one said and smiled
wistfully. "You bring hope to our continued survival."

"Survival," I repeated the word. "You're not
dying, though. My mother couldn't shift, but she had me.

You're not dying out. Just changing. Maybe there's a reason for it."

A collective gasp met my words. "There can be no reason we are forced to feel this emptiness, when others can feel complete. It's a sickness, and Alpha Austin found the cure." The tall brunette was not pleased with my lack of exuberance. "Some women have issues conceiving, would you tell them they are not meant to be mothers? Some people are born with poor eyesight, would you tell them not to get surgery so they could see?"

I held up my hand trying to pacify her. "I get it. It's not as simple, though. You can die from this cure."

"Some of us have died." A bit of light washed out of the bubbly one. "It was a risk many were willing to take before, it's much less of a risk now. Our future mates will know if the bond is forming even if we will not. Then and only then will we take the serum."

"One success does not guarantee another," I stated solemnly.

"Yes," Austin agreed, surprising me. "The next woman will need to be incredibly brave to try."

His words chilled me, but roused his audience. Shoulders straightened and pursed lips decreed the women's determination. I couldn't stop them from risking their lives no matter what I said.

I tried my best not to cringe when Austin smiled at the women's bravado. "If you will excuse us, ladies, I need to introduce Chloe to the other pack alphas."

"Of course, Alpha. Thank you for all you do for us." Hero worship shined from the tall brunette's eyes.

I was happy to be steered away. Their hope was a tangible thing, and I didn't want to be responsible for their deaths.

Chapter Eight

Austin paraded me around for over forty minutes meeting more people than I could possibly remember the names of. I saw Raff only twice out of the corner of my eye. He was greeting newcomers and seemed to be in a debate with Tate at one point. I was a bit miffed he ignored me and allowed his father to escort me through the party. All that talk upstairs about being jealous of other alphas was clearly just that—talk. Since he sure as shit wasn't here glaring daggers at anyone who leered at me. I'm not saying I wanted the caveman vibe right this minute, but my man acting aloof didn't sit right. I wasn't interested in making small talk with anyone, or worse, earning frantic fandom by misguided women.

As soon as I deemed it enough time with my latest introduction, an alpha from Texas, I excused myself to the restroom. I hid out for a bit, readjusting makeup, and wondering if I should put on something outrageous to rile Raff up a bit. I realized how pathetic the idea sounded before I zipped up my jacket and headed downstairs. Lights flashed through the main entrance windows as a monster truck tore up the driveway. Instead of heading out the back, I opened the front door to see who would be rude enough to park halfway in Valentina's rosebushes.

Running for safety would have been the wisest action the minute two figures emerged from the vehicle. These were not men, they were behemoths. Grease-stained clothes strained to cover barrel-shaped chests and tree-trunk arms. They felt wild, feral even. The hairs on the back of my neck lifted when their eyes caught sight of me. The bigger one sauntered lazily over, dark eyes constantly appraising and finding me lacking. He scowled when he spoke. "You must be Raff's."

Usually, I would reject a statement like that. No one owned me, but this thug was as intimidating as fuck. "I am." I straightened my spine knowing my guys were only a shout away. "Can I help you?"

Dark and Dangerous scoffed. "I greatly doubt it."

"Ah, come on now, Miles," the other giant taunted beside his leader. "She looks like she could be at least good for something."

I inadvertently took a step back. It was the wrong move. I could see the predatory interest shine in his eyes. My fear was a sweet dessert. The one named Miles remained unimpressed. "Cool it, Dex." He patted his lackey's shoulder. "I hardly think this science experiment is worth the trouble."

The front door banged open. I expected my guys to swarm around me, instead, a young woman stormed out. She had hair like spun gold falling in waves past her shoulders, a tall willowy frame like a European runway model, and deep-blue eyes that were spitting fire. It took me a moment to recognize Raff's cousin. I'd only met Akela briefly when I first arrived. We'd not spoken a word since.

"What the hell are you assholes doing here?" she hissed. "Leave before Tate catches sight of you."

"You planning to make me, little girl?" Miles puffed out his chest, making himself unbelievably bigger. Even though Akela was built like a warrior goddess, Miles still dwarfed her with his sheer size. I liked her immediately when she gave zero shits about his intimidation tactic.

She rolled her eyes looking disgusted. "You're not welcome here."

"That's funny," Miles played at acting confused.

"I heard all packs were welcome to behold the manufactured miracle." His tone was derisive. His look of utter contempt told me all I needed to know. These were shifters that didn't see me as the beacon of hope I was paraded around as all night.

Akela folded her arms across her chest and did that perfect "fuck off and die" head tilt that only a woman can execute flawlessly. "Leave before someone sees you."

Miles appraised the woman challenging him. There was definitely more heat and less hatred when he stared at her. "Maybe I want to be seen."

Akela huffed. "Careful what you wish for, Miles. You two ass-clowns might be the size of woolly mammoths, but there are still only two of you."

Like magic, Raff and all the guys came spilling out from the side of the house, thankfully accompanied by Raff's five other brothers too. Ten against two behemoths felt like more than promising odds. Raff tore up the porch stairs and placed himself between me and the two interlopers. "What are you doing here, Miles?"

Miles ignored Raff completely and oddly singled out Tate. "Started my own pack, Tate. If you're done playing house with these rejects, you should come join me. We have seven pack members now, soon-to-be eight, better than Raff's little pack of five."

I was slightly offended. "You mean six." I crossed my arms and scowled. If Akela wasn't acting like these tools were planning on murdering us, I wasn't going to roll over. It also didn't hurt that we had them clearly outnumbered.

Miles snorted. "You aren't a real shifter."

"Not this crap!" Akela hissed. "You are just like your family! Always looking for a weakness to stamp out. Throwing away Tate like he was garbage!" Akela's face mottled red. She dropped her arms and clenched her hands into fists.

Miles ground his teeth and made a disgusted noise at her comment. The realization that this man was one of the people responsible for leaving Tate as a little kid, had me seeing red.

Tate might have been weak as a child, but he was only a few inches shorter than Miles now. My gentle giant was breathing heavy and looking fierce as he stared his brother down. "I don't understand you at all, Miles. If this piece of shit represents your pack,"—he pointed at Dex—"it doesn't speak very well of you, brother."

If I hadn't been looking at Miles so closely, I might have missed him flinch before his face became stone as he glared back at Tate.

"Look at that!" crowed Dex. "Lil Tate thinks he finally grew himself some balls. You a real man now, boy?"

Tate ignored the comment and returned his brother's stare. "I believe my alpha asked you what you were doing here."

A brief glimpse of disappointment flitted across Miles's face before his lips twisted with scorn. He dismissed Tate with a shake of his head and faced off against Raff. "Since your pack has decided to create its own women, I came to see if any of the true she-wolves left would finally stop pitying you all and leave with some real shifters?" A barely audible breath escaped Akela, but I could see how Miles's words left her pale and shaking.

The tick in Raff's jaw was working overtime. It contrasted with his bored demeanor and slow breathing. "Sticks and stones, man. It's sad how your family won't evolve from the bullies on the playground. Our kind is dying out and you treat it like it's a race to the finish."

It might be horrible timing, but I was feeling my man was mad sexy right now. The lady bits were all atwitter watching him square off against a bigger alpha.

"Well, Dex," Miles drawled. "I guess we're not invited to the barbeque."

Dex grabbed at his heart and winced. "That hurts," he mocked.

Raff was about to speak again, but Miles cut him off. "Don't bother." His glare flew past me and settled on Akela. "I've seen all I need."

He nodded at Dex to follow him, but not before his sidekick licked his lips and blew me a disgusting kiss. Raff's hands immediately clenched into fists, and I jumped in front of him before he lunged. They were leaving, better it ended now than with broken bones later.

"He doesn't bother me, babe," I crooned, hoping to calm him. His eyes flew to mine and a devilish smile perched on his lips. He liked the pet name. I could tell instantly from the amount of heat he poured into his gaze.

"Of course not, darlin'. He's less than dirt compared to you."

Miles and Dex were halfway to the truck, but I knew they heard. Miles stiffened and glared over his shoulder, but Dex turned and gave a cocky wave.

Akela released a breath we all might have been collectively holding. "God! I hate that man," she stated emphatically as they drove away.

Raff tried to pull me against him, but I pushed back. I needed to make sure Tate was okay. "Tate?" I placed my hand on his arm. He smiled down at me. "I hope he didn't get in your head. Family has a way of doing that."

"Naw, Chloe." He shrugged. "Dex isn't my family, and he has no power over me anymore. Miles wasn't always like you saw him today. I was lucky enough not to be raised by my parents, he can't say the same." He placed his hand over mine and we shared the feeling of contentment that flowed from each of us. "This bond heals any old hurts."

"You still deserved better," grumbled Akela. "They never appreciated a man as kind as you."

Tate looked down at his feet, not acknowledging the praise. "Smells like the meat is all done, who's hungry?"

"You're always hungry!" Rollin laughed, patting his friend vigorously on the back.

Raff held out his hand, something indescribable twinkled in his eyes. "You look beautiful, by the way." His compliment gave my stomach flutters and I forgot all about being annoyed at him for ignoring me earlier.

"I could eat!" Akela agreed wholeheartedly. She playfully nudged Tate in the ribs as she passed him. "And I better get in line ahead of y'all, otherwise there won't be any ribs left."

I grabbed Raff's hand and followed him to the backyard where the party was in full swing and no one seemed the wiser about our unwanted guests. I watched Akela a few times that night and wondered if she could be sweet on Tate. I recalled Raff mentioned she was one of the few girls who did shift. I could welcome her to the pack with a clear conscience since she wouldn't die from the shifter cocktail injection.

Tate would be a closed book about his feelings, but if I learned anything as a bartender, it was to get people to open up and spill their life stories. I knew I could get Tate to talk, but I was curious to learn more about Akela. My new mission tomorrow would be girl time. Surrounded by boys twenty-four-seven, I was completely out of practice.

Chapter Nine

Before breakfast the next morning, I quietly exited the house and made my way over to where Raff said Akela lived. I wanted to catch her early in case she had to leave for work. I only had to wait a minute before my tentative knock on the door was answered. Akela had a purse strapped over her arm and car keys in hand.

"Oh, Chloe…" Akela startled when she opened the door and then looked behind me to see if I had someone with me.

"Morning!" I started cheery. "I hope I didn't catch you on your way to work?"

"Did Aunt Valentina send you over for coffee? I told her I would bring it by."

"No." I tilted my head trying to understand why she was acting nervous.

"Phew," she breathed out. "That's a relief. I kinda forgot it yesterday and Auntie V said 'first thing tomorrow, girly'." She mimics the pack female alpha. "Then I got up and realized we're out too. I'm just on my way to the store."

"Oh, it can wait then." I shrugged trying not to show my disappointment.

She shut the front door while assessing me. "Wanna come? Just a quick five-minute drive and back, but the place has killer scones and they're always best hot."

Internally I fretted if Raff would allow me to go, but then balked at the idea.

"Do you need to talk with Raff?"

"Are you a mind reader?" I huffed out an uneasy laugh.

"Come on." She winked. "We'll be back before they even notice."

A grin much wider than I'm used to split my face. I liked the idea of having my freedom back. "I'm a sucker for any hot carbohydrate."

"So," Akela drew out the word like a conspirator. "What did you want to talk about?"

"Pack stuff," I blurted out. "I feel like I had a peek at an unreal world and now I'm expected to navigate through it with blinders on. Valentina throws weird things out at me like I'm supposed to find mates for the guys, but that's just crazy. Why do some packs get along and others don't? How do I know who is trustworthy and who is not? I'm so confused."

"It's hard to imagine what you're experiencing. To find out what you are this late in life. I'd love to help. I mean, we will be cousins soon."

"See!" my voice jumps. "Stuff like that. Why do people believe any day now Raff and I will be getting married? I'm just waiting for Valentina to ask when she can expect grandkids!"

"Well, she knows the answer to that one. Most likely not this January but the next one." Akela bit her lip and grimaced as she delivered the news.

I scrubbed my hands over my face and groaned. "I'm not sure I should even ask."

"Well, Chloe. I never thought I'd be having a birds-and-bees talk shifter-style with a female alpha, but I promise to start at the beginning and go slow."

We both break from talking as we get in her car and buckle up. It's early but a few of Raff's younger brothers are out cleaning the back yard from last night's party. I slouch in my seat as we drive past, not wanting Raff to stop me from leaving before I can get some solid answers.

Akela doesn't keep me in suspense too long. It's like she senses I need directness right now and no more vague answers. "I'm not sure what Raff told you, so if I repeat things, you know, just tell me."

"Highly doubtful," I grumbled.

"Okay, this is strange, but I'm going to start with the lesson we teach the children when they reach age five or six."

"As long as we get to the advanced lessons before we return." I folded my arms over my chest and settled down in the seat.

She giggled and nodded. "Deal." Blowing out a full breath she began. "The earliest accounting of our people dates back to eight hundred years ago. The story is, a harsh winter ravaged the lands, and many were dying. A human tribe entered a village inhabited solely by wolves. They fled, terrified of being eaten in the harsh climate, but agreed to return during the day to pillage what they could from the abandoned huts. When the sun was high and nocturnal creatures slept, they returned and found that people occupied the places only wolves were in the night before. Instead of fear, the humans approached the village with awe and hope. The villagers did not seem ravaged by the cold, they were well fed, and the children were healthy. Perhaps this magic could save them as well.

"The villagers were welcoming and offered the human tribe shelter in exchange for their agreement to never mention the existence of the village to outsiders. It was this human tribe that recorded the first history of our kind, teaching our people primitive writings and how to craft stories to pass down to generations. They lived in harmony for a few hundred years.

"A hunting party from the human tribe set out one day and was swept down the river by a flash flood. Only two men survived but were terribly lost. On their journey to find their home they came across a nomad tribe that appeared to be like their wolf-shifter brethren. One night they saw all wolves, the next day men. They didn't keep the secret their elders had preached to them. Perhaps they thought these nomads would know the location of their village and help them, or that there was no real danger to fear, so they spoke of the wolf village to the nomads. What the young hunters did not know, is that there are two kinds of wolf shifters."

"Raff told me we are red wolves and Tate and his brother are greys. But do you mean something more?"

"Yes and no." She grimaced realizing she was doing the vague thing I hated. "Back then, the differences were far greater. More than just red and grey wolves exist in the world. The two types of shifters are feral or adaptive. The greys the humans encountered barely passed for men. They were wild and savage. The reds had been living seamlessly with humans for generations. They had become more civilized and used higher reasoning over brute force. Migrating packs from Europe, the Arctic, and South America brought more feral shifters to these lands. Over time we all had to become adaptive to survive, but a few packs prefer the feral ways. Humans are seen as the enemy and weakness is to be stamped out from any pack mates."

I sighed knowing where the story was going. "So I take it the greys did not happily return them to the village and go on their merry way?"

"They did return the men to the village, curious to see if others like them were near. The greys were disgusted with how domestic the scene was and challenged the reds to return to the old ways. They even offered to help them kill the humans in the tribe and bring their animal side to the forefront to regain dominance. As you can imagine, a brutal fight ensued. Most of the humans, despite the reds' best efforts, were killed. The greys took many of our young men and women with them, the ones they considered strong enough, and merged them with their own. Yet they were never treated as equals and even today if a grey wolf shows weakness they say he or she has a red stain—referring to the mixing of bloodlines producing inferior wolves. They are such elitist assholes. Much of our troubles with packs stems from the kind of wolves we associate with."

Remembering the way Miles looked at me like I was less than dirt, made her story easy to believe. "I guess no one is truly able to escape stupid prejudices."

Akela's lost in thought as she drives. "True," she added in such a sad quiet voice I almost missed it.

"While I appreciate the history lesson…" I hold up my hands. "And I do. I truly want to know about current shifter society."

"Right." Her sadness is wiped away by a side smirk. "Birds-and-bees talk now."

"Oh, come on! Help a girl out here. What the hell did you mean about a next January bundle of joy?"

"Okay, I'll get there, I promise. First, I have to tell you about pack dynamic and alpha pairs. I know Raff has told you that a pack cannot truly form until an alpha pair is established. It's the alpha pair bond that fixes the other pack bonds into place."

I nod to show I'm following so far.

"After the pack alphas, there's either a beta male as second or a beta pair, then gammas to protect the pack, and omegas to serve and care for a pack's needs. The bigger the pack the more powerful the bonds and the stronger chance for survival. When an alpha pair bond is established a baby usually follows by the next year."

My brain was spinning thinking about my guys. Instinctively I just knew Rollin was Raff's beta. Tate and Weylin were gammas and Lowe had to be the omega. With the pack hierarchy settled in my mind I could be laser-focused on only one other thing. "You said January, though. Why?"

Her hesitation was making me squirm. I just knew something truly horrendous and uncomfortable was coming. "Well, you are mated now. You'll go into heat this spring. That's kind of a given."

And ... that would do it! "Oh my God!" I threw my head back and looked at the worn upholstery of the ceiling. "I'm a fucking dog!"

"Chloe, I know it might sound bad."

I cut her off. "Bad! No, it's worse than bad. Before we go back, we're stopping for birth control. I am in charge of my body, whether he likes it or not."

Her eyes got all wide and she worried her lip with her teeth.

"Oh, shit! What now?"

"The pills will work when you're in this form, but they won't when you're a wolf."

I gagged and wanted to jump out of my skin. "Gross. You're telling me Raff is going to get me pregnant while I'm an animal! And this is just a done deal!"

"Please don't yell," her voice was sympathetic. "I'm regretting telling you."

"You're right," I breathed in and out a few times. "It's not fair to kill the messenger. I need to save this energy to castrate Raff."

Akela laughed nervously while constantly checking to make sure I wasn't entirely serious. She parked the car and winced once she looked at me fully. "Coffee and comfort food?" she asked hopefully.

"Hell, yah, let's do it." I unbuckled and hopped out fully planning on drowning my confusing feelings in warm buttery goodness.

Chapter Ten

The coffee shop did not disappoint on the scones, but my heart just wasn't into it. I couldn't continue to bombard Akela with questions while around strangers, and I couldn't muster up enough enthusiasm to talk about anything else. I felt like a bullet train on a short track. I finally accepted the reality of my situation. I'm not human. Fully embracing my new life, though, was a lot to ask from someone recently kidnapped. I mean, I hadn't even been gone long enough for my apartment rent to be past due.

"You gonna finish that? Or do you want to hit the road?" She was bouncing her leg and shredding her napkin into tiny pieces.

I guess I wasn't the only one agitated today. "Sorry, I don't mean to keep you from anything."

"You're not." She patted my hand affectionately. "Aunt Val likes to ride my ass. I know I'm going to hear it about the coffee."

I wrapped up the rest of my scone and grabbed my cup. "I'm done. Let's get out of here."

Akela tossed a few bags of freshly ground coffee in the back seat and breathed a sigh of relief when the car started and she was back on the road.

"I guess Valentina is taking it easy on me, then, huh?" I peered over at her.

"What do you mean?"

"You said she rides you. She has been nothing but sweet so far with me." I was curious about the woman that apparently everyone assumed would be my mother-in-law.

"That's only because you belong to another pack.

If you had been raised with us, the minute you showed signs of being an alpha female, she would constantly be testing you too."

"Wait!" I swiveled to face her. "You're an alpha too? Does that mean you need to leave like Raff did?"

She shook her head in the negative. "It's different with females. We don't try to kill each other fighting over territory. I just need to show my neck and keep my head down till it's the right time for me to move on. But there will be a time when I have to. My wolf strays when we shift. I end up alone quite often. It's dangerous for me. Sooner or later, I need to accept my mate."

She said accept, not find! Would this be the time to bring up Tate? "Does this mean you're on a manhunt, then?"

She snorted and groaned simultaneously. "Ugh, not quite."

"You seem close to Tate."

Akela gave me a strange look I couldn't decipher. "He grew up in my house. In every way that counts, he is my brother. Did you know that?"

"No." The information deflated my hopes a bit.

"I love Tate. We are even closer than my biological brothers are to me. The twins always had each other. I had Tate."

"Do you have romantic feelings for him?" I felt strangely compelled to probe.

"Not in the slightest."

I didn't doubt the sincerity in her words. "Oh…" I felt foolish. "I was thinking about my job responsibility in matching up the guys and not feeling up to the task. I couldn't contemplate having someone go through what I did with those injections. You're already a wolf."

"Girl," she huffed. "You have so many things wrong. First, don't put the cart before the horse. Those guys have zero interest in getting paired up right now. They will either come to you when they're ready or you will just know. Second, I'm an alpha. That means I have to form my own pack or go lone wolf. No other options for me long-term. And finally, Tate is gay."

"What?" My jaw dropped thinking about my gentle giant.

"Don't look so surprised. I did mention the high male population? Actual wolves in nature pair up same sex too."

"He just doesn't show it."

"That's 'cause you haven't found him the 'one' yet. Or haven't seen him in a human bar when the opportunity presents. I have." She laughed loudly at my jaw hanging open.

"See!" I throw my hands up in the air. "I'm going to be terrible at this. Are any of the other guys gay? I don't want to put my foot in my mouth."

"In your pack, just Tate."

"All this pack stuff is truly complicated. I'm in an episode of the *Twilight Zone*."

"It's a shame you weren't brought up pack. I never understood why your mother felt she had to leave. Especially since she found her mate."

"I doubt my dad was her mate. She never mentioned him. She dated tons of men. He couldn't have been that special to her. Even my sister's father had more to do with our lives."

"Wolf shifters can only procreate with other wolf shifters. It doesn't work with humans."

"That doesn't make sense. My mom has two kids and we have different dads," I countered.

"I feel as if I should not be dropping any more bombshells your way." I watched her grip the steering wheel and avoid eye contact with me.

"Spill it. You're the first person who hasn't given me vague answers. Please don't start now."

"You and your sister have the same dad. Your family's story is well known in our pack. Especially after how he died."

The sight of unshed tears pooling in Akela's eyes made me take a steadying breath. "Please," I begged her. "Tell me everything. I can't bear to be in the dark anymore."

"I don't know, Chloe. Maybe this is a better story for Raff or even Valentina to share with you."

I crossed my arms over my chest and pinched my lips together. Raff already should have shared this stuff with me. "They won't. I need you to."

Akela chewed her lip, clearly torn. "Your parents were destined mates, like you and Raff," she began. She gave me the side eye when I snorted at her statement. "Your mom grew up in the same pack as Valentina and your dad left his pack to join with Austin when he became an alpha and needed a pack. Your pop met your mom when Austin was convincing Valentina to leave her parents and join him. Valentina was only eighteen at the time and wanted to wait, but hormones got in the way and soon Austin had his alpha female and the pack bonds formed. Your mother, swept up in it all, agreed to join our pack about two years later and she moved in with your dad. The story goes that she found it hard to be part of the pack and not feel the bond of the pack. Your mom could sense that your dad was special to her, but she was jealous watching her best friend fully mated and heading a pack. She disappeared one day and your father was frantic. He searched for her for months, never giving up, thinking she was in trouble, only to find her working at some diner pregnant with you."

We pulled up too soon to the large family house

and a commotion out front stopped Akela from continuing with her story. "Oh, shit," she squeaked as Raff sailed over the porch and ran toward us. Valentina and Austin were standing at the front door, while Tate and Rollin raced out of the house at the noise.

Before I could process what was going on, Raff swung my door open, pulled me out of the car, and was doing a ten-point inspection. I was intensely caught up in my own emotions and the lightning bolts of revelations, I hadn't noticed the extreme level of anxiety radiating through the bond.

"Where were you?" his words came out clipped and short. "What happened? I woke up and you were gone. Then,"—he gulped and grasped at his chest as if in pain—"I could feel how upset you were." His eyes grazed over me searching. He took in the bags of coffee Akela was reaching for from the back seat. "You left without a word. You can't do that."

I shoved him off me and glared. "I didn't realize my prison sentence was also without any in-and-out privileges."

"I don't treat you like a prisoner." He ground out through clenched teeth.

"Really? Then where is my cell phone? If I was allowed to have one, then you could have texted me, I would have texted back, and problem solved!" I spat back at him.

"You know it's not that simple. You're still adjusting." Raff put up his hands as if I should slow my roll.

"Adjusting to my Stockholm syndrome, you mean. You're just freaked out thinking I might have managed to be free of you." Raff gasped and had the nerve to look wounded.

Tate and Rollin reached us then. "Not fair,

Chloe," Rollin's tone was near a whine. "The bond was going haywire with strong emotions. We thought you might be hurt somewhere. Weylin is out in the woods searching for you. We were really worried."

"No." I shook my head. "You're only worried about your need to have me with you. If you worried about me, I wouldn't have been kidnapped against my will! I wouldn't be kept from information about myself!" I couldn't stop the scream tearing from my throat. Raff reached for me again but I evaded and took a step back. "I wouldn't be wearing this damn necklace displaying for the world we are engaged, when you never fucking even asked me!" I yanked with all my might at the pendant. The clasp gave, bruising my neck with the force. As I hurled it at Raff, a sharp pain lanced through my chest.

"Chloe, I'm sorry." Akela looked stricken as she placed a hand on my shoulder.

"Thank you for getting the coffee, Akela." Valentina strode forward taking the bags from the younger women's hands and looking properly pissed. "I think you've done enough for the day. Why don't you head home now?"

Akela opened her mouth twice, but neither time did any words emerge. She gave me a forlorn half-smile, huffed out a breath, and walked toward her house.

"She didn't do anything wrong," I protested. "She's the only one who's been honest with me."

"I have been nothing but honest, darlin'. I have never lied to you." Raff bent and picked up the necklace at his feet. A sad twinge thumped at my heart.

"Sins of omission then." I refused to let him off the hook. "Care to tell me the entire story about my parents? Or how about the little tidbit about getting pregnant as a wolf? Oh, better yet, that I will go into heat, like a dog."

"You just finally believed this was real!" He stood his ground. "How the hell am I supposed to spring all that on you in one sitting? You turned into a wolf and still didn't believe it. I was trying to take it slow for you."

"Says the kidnapper," I snapped.

Raff roared his frustration at the sky. "You are impossible! I need to cool down. I'm going to tell Weylin he can stop looking for your body in the woods." He nodded to Tate and Rollin. "Make sure she doesn't leave."

"Says the prison warden!" I screamed at his retreating figure. I was panting. Anger and rage like I had never experienced before flooded me. The bond between us feeding off the other. Yet underneath, it was thick with fear. My eyes involuntarily traveled to Tate and Rollin. Rollin looked more stoic, but Tate was absolutely devastated. It was his fear I was feeling.

"We're finally a pack, Chloe." His voice was hoarse, thick with emotion. "Don't you want us?"

Feeling his pain deflated my crazed anger like a pin puncturing a balloon. The story of his own family not wanting him because he wasn't strong enough or didn't fit the mold they expected, caused a boatload of guilt to settle on me.

"Lowe should be all done making breakfast." Valentina handed the bag of coffee to Rollin. "Go give him this to get a pot started." Rollin nodded and headed off at his mom's request and Austin followed behind him into the house. Only Tate and I remained outside with her. She placed a hand on both our arms.

"Tate, you know Chloe is going to take more than a few short days to adjust to a life she never knew existed. And Chloe, my dear, you do deserve to know the whole truth. Each day shouldn't be a shock to your system." The alpha's words calmed us both.

"Let's all go inside. Tate, I know you're hungry, I could hear that belly rumbling from outside. And Chloe, I'll tell you about your folks. Honestly, besides your mom, no one will know the story better."

Chapter Eleven

I could hear the clatter in the kitchen as all of Raff's brothers along with three of my guys settled in to eat. Valentina steered me into the living room and settled a heavy leather-bound photo album on her lap. She flipped through a quarter of the way, leaned back against the couch till our shoulders were touching, and showed me the photos inside. My breath caught. There was a photo of my mom, she could not have been more than twenty. Her violet eyes, so like my own, were sparkling, and her mouth was wide open in a full belly laugh. The man looking lovingly down at her must be my father. Akela was right. He was the spitting image of my sister Kate. I took after my mother with dark wavy hair, long legs, pouty lips, and the same unique lavender eyes. This man's skin coloring, eyes, and nose made him look like my sister's brother in the photo. We did have the same dad.

"How can this be?" I breathed as my fingers trailed over the image in the photo. "My mom never spoke of him. My sister thinks another man is her father, yet Kate looks just like him."

Valentina chuckled humorously. "There was a time when your mother and I could finish each other's sentences, but I will never understand why she rejected JT."

"JT?"

"Your father's name was Jerimiah, but everyone called him JT. He was a good man. A little too selfless and too much in love with Dianne."

It was hard listening to this woman, who was a stranger to me no more than a few days ago, talking about my parents. It felt like I was seeing my mother for the first time. "Akela said they were true mates."

Valentina nodded sadly. "JT knew right away. It was love at first sight for that man. She was smitten too, but without the ability to feel the bond, the pull is nowhere as strong. It's how she was able to leave him, but never able to settle down and be happy with another man. For Dianne, the bond was like a drug, she liked it but thought she'd be better off never experiencing it. For JT the bond was air. He couldn't live without it."

"What happened to them? They look happy in this photo."

Valentina flipped a few more pages to reveal my mother again, very pregnant, next to a young Valentina, also pregnant. It looked like a baby shower. Presents strewn all around the floor and both women held up crochet baby blankets. One was pink, the other blue.

"I was pregnant with Baree then, and that's you."

"I was born here?" This couldn't get any weirder.

"Not quite." She sighed softly. "When Dianne found out she was pregnant, she kind of freaked out. Got in her car, without packing a single thing, and drove off. It took JT five months to find her. He was a mess, thinking another pack had taken her. She was in Kentucky working at a greasy spoon joint, barely able to support herself, but determined to stay away from us. JT stayed with her there, driving back before every full moon and returning when he could. It was killing him to be separated from the pack. I think your mother did it to him intentionally, proving her point about how hard it was for her not to feel a part of our pack. Yet for JT, being away from your mom was the harder of the two.

"I convinced her to come here for the baby shower and holidays, but besides those, she stayed in Kentucky. That's where you were born. And your father stayed there too, until your mother got pregnant again with your sister. JT finally convinced her to come home. We didn't know if you or Kate would be able to make the shift, and JT reasoned it would be cruel to keep you away if you could."

After retrieving another photo album and handing it to me, Valentina encouraged me to open it. "That's yours. I kept it after your father passed."

Dumbfounded I turned the page. Pictures of me as a baby, and my sister, filled the album. My mother only had a few pictures of us that she kept framed on her nightstand, but they matched these. I had never known where they had been taken and my mother was always less than forthcoming. I recognized the alpha's big porch swing in one of the shots. My mom had both my sister and I on her lap. I was about four and my sister under a year. The childhood photos seemed to peter out when I looked about five. Then just a few of my sister by herself till about the same age. A series of random photos were shoved in after—me at my high school graduation taken from far away, my sister winning a spelling bee competition from the newspaper, an ad I was in for a local fast-food joint from my college days, and my sister in her wedding dress.

Tears pooled in my eyes and I took a series of short sharp breaths. "Why did he stay away?"

"A promise," Valentina's eyes mirrored mine in their wateriness. "Your mother agreed to return to the pack on one condition. If you girls could shift, she would stay. If you could not, then he would let her leave and allow her to raise you with no knowledge of our kind. She was convinced if you never knew about us, then you wouldn't feel the emptiness of the missing bonds. She would raise you as human."

"And that meant my dad couldn't see us? Why?"

My question was a broken sob.

"She pleaded with him to let her move on. If he was in her life, it would be too hard to keep her resolve and not return. Dianne didn't want you or Kate to live with the intense longing to belong and a life she believed as an outsider. JT wanted nothing more than his daughter's happiness and abided by her wishes."

One of the pictures of my sister nagged at my memories. She was holding hands with a man that looked almost like my father but not quite. "Oh my God! That's Frank. Kate thought he was her dad."

"He's your uncle. JT's brother belonged to the pack JT was born in, but at his brother's request, he brought your sister here for visits until it was clear she would not change either."

A fire in my stomach replaced a bit of the sadness. "My mother said he had joint custody. Then one day he stopped coming. Kate cried for months asking what she had done wrong. My mother never offered an explanation." I stared at the photo until my tears dried and the burn in my stomach became a desire to confront my mother. "How did my father die?"

"Oh honey," Valentina said and shook her head. "It's better left in the past. Know that he loved you both, was so proud of the strong women you became, and never stopped loving you."

"He was what? In his early fifties. Was it an accident? Please tell me," I begged.

"I don't want to turn you against your momma. She did what she thought was best for you girls. I think…"

"No!" I interrupted. "I want to know the truth."

At first, I thought she would refuse my demand. I could sense ordering another alpha in her domain was a misstep, but I was sick of secrets. Valentina sucked on her front teeth and frowned before shaking her head and speaking. "As much as the pack supported him, missing your mom was like a sore tooth he couldn't stop touching. He would secretly watch you all. Each new boyfriend or husband Dianne would go through would be followed by a bout of drinking. He would drink until he blacked out to escape the pain. Liquor turned to drugs. This latest husband of hers prompted JT to overdose. He died in his sleep."

The words were a punch to the gut. My mom just recently had gotten married, that meant I missed meeting my father by only a few months. He had died this very year. I hunched in and struggled for air. Valentina rubbed my back while I battled to control my emotions. "Thank you for telling me."

"You deserve to know your heritage. I always disagreed with my dear friend on how she handled you girls."

"Is that why you sent your son after me?" My open wounds were many. The lies of my mother cut the deepest, the loss of my father the freshest, but Valentina deciding what she thought best was a wound that still would not heal.

"I didn't know you would be true mates," her voice shook as fresh tears glistened. "I had felt it was possible and so I sent him your way... JT's death removed any guilt I felt about your mother's wishes. We always considered you and your sister pack."

I pulled away from her touch. "Promise me you will not think about taking my sister!"

"*Chloe*?"

The shock in her tone did not mollify me. I needed a promise.

"I would never separate a family. Your sister is an omega, it;s why she worked so hard at adopting those kids. They give her purpose and settle her. You, however, were floundering. Despite your mother's best efforts to have you be raised as a human, you were not one. You had trouble conforming to society rules, your inner alpha challenging all authority, and your dormant wolf driving you to lone-wolf behaviors. You may never thank me for pushing my son into your life, but I had to think of the good of our pack and yours. My boys were out there in the world without a pack, not truly living like they should. When you become a mother, you will understand. Mothers might not always know what's best, but they will do anything for their children if they believe it to be best. Being an alpha, like we are, is a blessing and a curse. I saw my boy alone and I just sensed sending him to you would fix it. I could not help myself." She patted my knee, eyes watery with an apology she would never utter out loud.

I stood abruptly. "I'm gonna take a shower and lie down."

"Okay, honey. I'll bring you up a tray and put it in your room in case you get hungry." Valentina wrung her hands. Her lips were pinched with worry lines.

I nodded wordlessly and numbly walked up the stairs. She wanted me to tell her I was fine, but I just wasn't. Everyone decided what should be done with me while leaving me in the dark. I'm not a child, and my mother, Valentina, and Raff needed to treat me as an equal.

Chapter Twelve

After a long shower where the hot water turned ice-cold and my skin pebbled in goose bumps, I was too numb to feel, I sat on the bed absentmindedly brushing my hair until it was no longer wet. I felt betrayed by my mother. All I could think about was the years of infertility my sister suffered through. She constantly cried wondering why it was happening to her, when some random crack whore could have seven children. The overwhelming sense of the unfairness made her incredibly depressed. Even though she was able to grow her family through adoption, none of the earlier pain she went through had to happen. My mom needed to be held accountable for that.

Raff entered our room. In the back of my mind I remembered he had stormed off earlier, but that seemed like a hundred years ago. "I need to see my mother," I announced.

The weight on the bed shifted as Raff sat down next to me. He pried the hairbrush from my hand, stopping my compulsive brushing. "She's no longer pack. We leave her alone now."

"She's my mother, Raff. Do you honestly expect me to go the rest of my life and never see her?" I stared at him, grim determination causing me to grind my teeth.

"I don't want you around her."

"That's not your decision to make." I folded my arms across my chest.

Raff scrubbed his hand through his hair and gave a long, aggrieved sigh. "For now it is. You're still adjusting. We haven't had our second shift together yet. Our bond is new and it still needs to develop into something truly solid. Hell, I thought you up and left today."

I wanted to shout and scream and demand, but I sensed through the bond he was hurting. "You can come with me."

His eyes searched my face, but he must have found something lacking. His eyes turned cold. "No."

"Expand on that no." I pointed at him. "Is that, 'no, I'm not coming with you'?"

Raff laid down and threw an arm over his face. "Can we not fight anymore today? It's too early to have another round. Not even noon yet, for Pete's sake."

"I'm not even sure why it would be a fight. I need to see my mother. The entire pack can come. I'm not threatening to run away. It's pretty straightforward." I was proud of how reasonable and calm I sounded.

He groaned as he stood up and began pacing. "She caused harm to my father's pack. She broke your poor father. Her words about us are poison. There is nothing she can say to justify her actions. There's nothing you need from her."

"Does she even know my father died, then?" I felt a pang in my chest at the thought.

"As if she would even care," he snapped.

"Listen, she wasn't always the best mom, moving us around and changing guys as often as bed linens, but she was loving. And what about my sister? She deserves to know the truth."

"Absolutely not!" His voice raised loud enough to make me wince. "Your sister is married and raising children. The truth would not set her free. It would cage her to a life she may not fully want. It would be cruel, and the fact you don't see that means it's too soon to see her. Look how long this took for you to accept. Your sister is going to think you're crazy and your mother is poison."

"Next month, after the shift. I can wait that long, but no longer." I set my terms and planned to stick with them.

"More like next year for your sister and only for a visit, not an information dump. I was close to your dad, and watching him kill himself over your mother doesn't warm me to the thought of ever seeing her." His frame loomed over me while I sat on the bed. He was the epitome of aggressive and domineering.

I hopped up, so I was standing on the bed and my head was higher than his. "Unacceptable. A month is more than generous, considering every instinct I have is screaming at me to get in the car and go now. I cannot move forward until I confront my mother. It. Is. That. Simple."

We glared at each other, our heavy breathing the only sound in the room. I could tell he had no plans to back down, but I didn't care. This was my family we were arguing about it. He had no right to dictate to me. If I was no longer a prisoner, then it meant I should be free to make my own choices.

I said he could come with me!

A knock on the door brought an end to our staring contest. Weylin sauntered in with Lowe trailing behind him. I felt a pang of guilt thinking Weylin had been searching the woods praying not to discover my body, and Lowe looked miserable. His lips were tightly pinched and his eyes red-rimmed and teary.

While I looked at the guys on the way in, Raff's laser focus never left my face. "I didn't say you could come in," he ground out.

"Come on, Raff," Weylin tugged at his shirt collar while he spoke. "We can feel ya' fighting from three houses away."

"Please be kind to Chloe," Lowe pleaded. "She's new to our ways. She's in pain."

"New or old, she's as stubborn as a mule." Quicker than lightning, Raff snatched me off my perch on the bed and into his arms in a tight embrace. He set me down, my body sliding and caressing his until my feet hit the floor. Some of the fury in his eyes simmered into desire.

"Don't get any ideas!" I poked him sharply in the chest. "This isn't finished."

Lowe lifted the untouched tray of food that Valentina had left me. "You didn't eat." He pouted. "I'd made all your favorites."

Anyone saying omegas are weak would be a liar. Lowe controlled me like no man before ever could. He made me feel like absolute shit when I didn't do things he wanted. "Sorry. I wasn't hungry."

"How about now?" His question was filled with hope.

I plastered on a smile. "Starving."

He put the tray on the bed, sat down himself, and looked at me expectantly.

I sighed as I settled in next to him. Looking up at Weylin, I found his eyes on my tray. "Did you eat?"

"Naw. I just got back." He left out the part where he was fruitlessly searching for me. I was grateful. "I was coming to see you before I got anything."

"Well." I patted the bed on the other side of the tray. "Lowe overloaded it for me, and I had scones at the coffee shop. Come join me."

Weylin smiled like a boy being offered sweets. Raff remained with his arms folded across his chest, lips pinched, and a slight twitch in the eye. "And what about me, darlin'? Am I left out of this picture of domestic bliss?"

I rolled up a pancake with a sausage inside and jabbed it in his direction to emphasize my point. "You're lucky I'm even speaking to you right now. Go be alpha somewhere else."

Both Weylin and Lowe paled a bit at my brashness. Lowe jumped up. "I'll get you something, Raff. What would you like?"

"No! Lowe, if you don't want to stay, that's fine, but Raff was leaving anyway." I tore off a bite in an angry tug.

"You ordering me around?" Raff looked far less put out than his words conveyed.

"Until you come to your senses and respect my most reasonable request? Damn right!"

Raff shouldered Weylin aside and leaned over the bed, his hands placed on both sides of me. Using his favorite intimidation tactic of getting extremely close to my face, he smiled showing all his teeth. He looked to be about to speak, but jerked his head to the side and captured my rolled pancake right from out of my hands. Standing up he shoved the entire thing in his mouth in one bite and licked his fingers obscenely loud. Looking mighty smug, he winked at me and strode out of the room.

He left, but it didn't feel like a victory. That's how it was with Raff. Too much the alpha to give me my way completely. I wondered if he would crack at all on seeing my mother. If not, I would have to find a way to leave him. I refused to live like a prisoner in this life.

"Here, Chloe." Lowe distracted me from glaring at the door. "I made maple bacon, nice and crunchy the way you like it."

I took the offering from his fingers and a buzz of contentment zipped through me. Weylin was munching happily at my side and Lowe smiled at me fondly once I took a bite. Leaving was no longer about an escape plan and finding my opening. Leaving meant shattering my soul and walking away with only the jagged remains.

Weylin's warm hand settled on my shoulder. He gave a gentle squeeze. "He's worried about losing you. We all are. Just give him some time. He'll come around."

"And if he dictates I never see my family again?" I pressed. "Would you help me?"

Weylin's dark eyes clouded over and Lowe could only stare at his hands. My chest constricted. "That's what I thought." All this talk about me also being alpha of the pack meant nothing if they only supported Raff. Or if they simply stayed silent when they did not feel he was being fair. Of course they would respect and listen to the man they saw as their leader over me.

"It's not like that, Chloe," Lowe barely whispered. "We can't come between the two of you and choose sides. Packs don't function that way. You have to work it out with Raff."

"Then why is what he wants more important than what I need?" I pressed.

"You don't need to see your mother," Weylin answered. "You have a desire to confront her. You feel hurt and want to talk things through. All this is understandable." I started to interject but Weylin held up his hand. "It is. It feels like need, but it's simply *want*. She won't be able to give you a satisfying answer. You are being hit with so many things. Give yourself time to process. Give us time to make this a family for you. Let us be your home. When all that settles, Raff will know. He'll take you to see your mom."

Unlike Raff, Weylin was all rational and calm. It was hard to not listen to his request. "I've given up everything I was before to be here with you all now." I downed some iced tea to mask the catch in my voice those words created. "I'm willing to give it more time, I offered that, but I'll never be okay with anyone else deciding when I'm ready to see my family. When I want to go, I'll go."

I felt the spike of fear my words created pulsate down the bond. I drew my line in the sand and the guys were wise enough not to press me.

Chapter Thirteen

Raff and I managed to avoid seeing each other for the rest of the day. I escaped for a long walk in the woods with Weylin. He pointed out various plant life around us, noting the scientific name and describing any medical or rare properties. He was the next best thing to having a search engine when no cell phone could be found or in my case, given. I found his chatter calming and I liked learning about things he was passionate about.

When we returned, Raff had gone out with his father to meet with another pack alpha. I could only hope I wasn't the main topic of the meeting. Our story wasn't a very successful one at this point. He was still away by eleven. I kept nodding off watching reruns of *The Office*. Tate was the only one keeping me company. He looked beat too.

"I'm keeping you up." I nudged his knee with my foot to get his attention.

"Nah, I watch TV till I fall asleep most nights." A slight blush accompanied his words. I marveled at how such a giant of a man could be shy and timid.

"But this living room is your bedroom, I'm overstaying my welcome." I yawned as I stood, stretching out the kink in my neck as I assessed him. "You look as tired as I feel. I'm off to bed."

"Night, Chloe." Tate reached for the handmade afghan at the end of the sofa and draped it over his large frame. "And there will never be a time you overstay your welcome."

If I was planning to fully commit to this life, finding someone for Tate was going to be first on my list.

There was a loneliness about him that none of the others had. "Night, big guy." I couldn't resist ruffling his soft mop of hair before leaving. He sighed contentedly and offered me a sleepy smile while I traipsed up the stairs.

After such a trying day, I thought I'd be up thinking about the flood of information I received or waiting for Raff for another game of who's in control. My body had different ideas. I didn't even remember turning out the lights before I was out like one.

Butterfly-soft kisses fluttered on my cheeks. Large hands cupped my breast as the weight shifted on the bed. I woke in increments to Raff's silent seduction. The bond was hungry and needy, a broken ragged thing that wanted to be mended. I instantly felt flushed. Desire pooled low in my belly. Being half-awake made it difficult to distinguish his wants from my own.

"Raff, I don't think…" I started.

"Don't think," his voice was a plea. "Shut it all out and just feel. Let us be." His mouth claimed mine. I could taste the whiskey on his tongue. It was as sweet as his soft caresses.

This undeniable thing between us was the only thing in this strange life that felt right, even though every part of our journey felt wrong. It wasn't hard for him to convince me to give in. I wanted to shut off my brain. I wanted to just feel. I knew in the back of my mind when the sun rose all our issues would come flooding back, yet for this moment I could let it go.

The moon shone brightly through the window casting an ethereal glow over his skin. Raff had removed all his clothes. The light worked its magic and amplified all the peaks and valleys his physique had to offer. My hands roamed up his thighs. The delight my small gesture evoked was evident as his skin pebbled and his eyes dilated. He would see this as a victory, but I didn't care. I wanted him inside me, I needed to feel like we could make this work and the future wasn't something to dread. Terrified of my instincts and crazy choices I made, I craved the comfort the bond would infuse me with.

I whipped off my tee and pushed down my panties, impatient with need. Raff wasted no time settling over me and pushing inside. I closed my eyes and focused on his coarser skin gliding over mine. His warm breath ticked the hair around my neck causing me to shiver in delight. He had me floating in mere minutes, crashing down only to rise again. My climax was intense, the aftershocks of it pushing him over the edge. The warm glow didn't fade. It stayed wrapped around us, offering sweet oblivion for the remainder of the night.

****

Sure enough, a jumble of emotions and uncertainty was my sole companion upon waking. Raff must have slipped out of bed early. There was no longer any residual warmth on his side and the bathroom door was open showcasing its vacancy. It almost left me wondering if I dreamed last night, except I was naked and certainly had not gone to bed that way.

His absence put me in a foul mood. I wasn't a fan of the "love 'em and leave 'em" technique for avoiding round two of our argument. The boys said I needed to work this out with Raff, but I couldn't if he kept skipping out and only returning once I was unconscious. Coming for me when my defenses were down and taking exactly what he wanted! Never mind I was willing. It was just plain rude!

I stewed about it a bit more while I steamed up the bathroom in a marathon shower session. Then it simmered to a quiet rage as I waited for my coffee. The pot was emptied out when I made my way down to the kitchen. Lowe sprang into action, offered to put on another pot, but I waved him away impatiently.

"I can make it myself," I groused. "There's no need to hover."

Lowe took that as an invitation to duck and cover and hightail it out of there. The only other kitchen occupants were a few of Raff's younger brothers, and they also discreetly let themselves meander out shortly after Lowe.

My nail tapped against the side of the empty mug while I watched the coffee drip, slowly filling up the pot. It was almost trancelike. *Tap. Drip. Tap. Drip. Tap. Drip.* I didn't see Rollin enter the kitchen. I jumped almost a foot in the air when he spoke.

"Is that done yet?" He yawned and scratched at his chest. He was shirtless, wearing only a pair of boxers. I quietly assessed him as he cocked his head to one side looking pensive. "What's eating you? I thought you kissed and made up last night."

I turned to face him, resting my lower back against the countertop. Did he think that because Raff had told him? Or was this what the bond told them all? I found it strange that a man as hot as Rollin standing in front of me practically naked did nothing for me. Between Rollin and Raff, Rollin was by far the hotter one. He wasn't as tall, but his skin glowed with a golden-brown hue, his face perfectly symmetrical, stunning blue eyes, and teeth pearly white and evenly formed. He was a sculpture come to life, walking art. Yet, all I could see was he wasn't Raff. He lacked the gruffness. The rugged charm and sharp chiseled features. The scars that marred Raff's skin only added to the intrigue and excitement I felt when he was near.

Was this all the bond making me feel for him? Was it the alpha appealing to me where Rollin's beta ways made him appear less than he really was? Wouldn't it be easier to have a man like Rollin, a man I could bend my will on, as a mate? Being with Raff was constant turmoil, a battle of wills, a struggle always for dominance. Should life be that exhausting?

"Chloe?" Rollin sounded uncertain. "You all right?"

I huffed. "What do you think?"

He gulped and treaded carefully. "I think you had a hell of a day."

"Just one?" I nudged.

His striking blue eyes warmed as they crinkled at the corners. "It's been a crazy ride for sure."

I didn't reply. Instead I stared out the bay window behind him. Raff must have gotten up before dawn since the sun wasn't too far from the horizon. I continued to idly tap at my mug. There was a man walking out from the woods that had the same build as Raff, but he was still too far away to be certain. I watched as he approached wondering if he was hiding out from me or not.

Rollin stepped in closer. His hand rested against my shoulder, startling me for a second time that morning. "It's not like you to be silent when you clearly have something to say. You know we would do anything for you, right?"

The gesture was incredibly brotherly. A sense of calm support echoed down the bond. I looked at his hand on my shoulder, but before I could muster up a response, I noticed the figure halted on his journey to the house. I could clearly make out it was Raff now, but he was too far away for our eyes to connect. I knew he could see into the kitchen—his brother naked from the waist up and me standing close to him. Is that what made him pause? Could I create a little discord among the boys with something as easy as jealousy? Would that change their allegiance to one hundred percent Raff to possibly being annoyed enough with him to listen to me?

I didn't give it much thought before I put the plan into action. Seize the moment and all that jazz. I set down my mug, inching closer to Rollin. Sucking in a breath and pushing out my boobs, I inched even nearer. I licked my lips and offered my bartender-patented sultry gaze. "Define *anything*?"

Rollin sucked in a breath of his own and took a step back. His brows furrowed. "Is something wrong?" he asked genuinely concerned.

I advanced, laying a hand on his bare chest. His muscles were well-defined and rigid and I wanted to pull my hand away the second I made contact, but I forged on. "Why would there be anything wrong?" I asked, the picture of innocence. My skin was crawling and when I leaned in more to move my lips closer to his I started to feel overwhelmingly nauseous. The look of pure horror on Rollin's face made me feel even worse.

"And on a scale of one to ten, how do you think this is going?" Raff chuckled from the doorway.

I dropped my hand and whirled to face him. I immediately felt better once I was no longer touching Rollin. Raff's poor brother looked white as a sheet. "I think I'll skip the coffee after all." Rollin looked ill.

Raff reached over and poured a cup. The machine had finally finished while I was making a fool of myself. He handed it to his brother. His signature shit-eating grin spread wide on his face. "Don't sweat it, bro. Our lovely alpha female was up to some of her old tricks. She's mad at me and thought I'd get jealous. She hasn't gone crazy overnight. I promise you."

Rollin released a ragged breath and shook his head at me. "We're pack."

As if that said volumes. Perhaps it did. What the

fuck do I know anymore? "Is that why my skin was crawling and I felt like throwing up?"

Raff nodded to his brother signaling he should leave. Rollin happily complied after grabbing a banana, looking back at me one more time, and snickering to himself. Once he was gone, Raff's hands settled on my hips. The heat of his hands caused my own to skyrocket. My toes curled in my slippers when he pulled me tight against him.

There was not an ounce of jealousy or anger in his eyes. He was utterly pleased with himself and amused. "You know they say wolves mate for life?"

"So?" My response was petulant at best.

"The bond between mates is even more powerful than the pack bond. When I said you were *it* for me, I meant it. That horrible feeling you felt touching my brother? It's the same for me. No other woman but you will feel right in my arms. From the first time we were together, my fate was sealed."

"My mother has been married several times," I scoffed.

"You father felt exactly the same way you did just now. The bonds are muted for the shiftless, but still strong enough to keep her from being able to settle with one man for very long. It's why she constantly moves on. Eventually being near these men makes her nauseous too. Now that you're a full shifter, you feel it intensely."

"I've touched guys since then," I challenged.

He slowly moved his head in the negative. "Not with sexual intent. Of course our mate bond doesn't stop you from offering comfort or simply touching another being, but it will stop either of us from acting on anything of a romantic variety. Your body only truly wants mine."

"I don't want you." I shoved him away. The loss

of his hand instantly made me sad.

"You're still mad at me," he corrected. "You can't help the wanting of me." He winked as he filled my coffee mug, poured in the exact right amount of creamer and sweetener, and handed it back to me. We have known each other only a few months, but he knew me like no other. It made me all gooey inside.

I should have blown on the drink before my first sip, but I was flustered by yet another thing different in this new life of mine. My own body betrayed me now. My head tells me to be angry, and with good reason, but my heart is full to bursting. With burnt tongue, I set the cup down quickly, even more irate. "You're just loving all this, aren't you?"

The egotistical arrogance melted away. "Not really, no." His somber words surprised me. "In a way, I'm just as much a victim. Before the serum you felt the bond, but nowhere near the strength you do now. But I did. The first time with you was a bolt of lightning for me. It freaked me out, knowing if I didn't change you by injecting you, my life would be as lonely and miserable as your father's was. I fell for you instantly, my brain telling me all the way to tread carefully and be cautious, and my body telling me it didn't give a fuck. The mate bond is powerful. Your father drowned himself in alcohol and drugs to suppress it, knowing your mother wanted him out of her life. I tried to stay away. I couldn't do it. My need for you allows my heart to beat."

His hands returned to me then. One reaching around my neck, his thumb stroking my chin. The other circling around my waist, while his eyes bore into my soul. "And when I had to watch you suffering, I died a little. Knowing I was the one that did that to you, knowing you probably would always hate me for it, and realizing I'd do it all again. Seeing your reaction to the bond, having you want me despite everything you tell yourself, was something I never truly thought I would have."

I closed my eyes. His gaze was too intense for me. Tears burned down my cheeks and he kissed them away, soothing me when I had planned only to rage at him. "I'm not sure what is real anymore. You're right. My brain tells me one thing and then you override all my senses with your presence. This is messed up."

"Is it?" Raff hugged me, not letting me answer. He talked into my hair. "Nothing feels more right in the entire world then when I get to hold you. No time in my life has been better than this moment with you in my arms."

I rested my head on his shoulder and sighed in contentment. I let my anger fade away and the bond hummed happily between us. I felt not only Raff but my other guys as well, joyful, peaceful, content. It was a heady mixture. My constant battle against it wasn't making any sense.

Why do I strive to be angry and miserable when I can be this happy?

Chapter Fourteen

Raff's entire family stood outside to say their goodbyes. A great many things had happened since we arrived, it felt like we'd been here longer than two weeks. His younger brothers gave me quick hugs while they threw insults and joked with Raff and Rollin. Austin stood to the side with his brother Lucas, and they both kept a watchful eye on Akela as she approached me.

"Sorry if I got you in trouble," I whispered as she shrugged off the apology. "I'm grateful, though. My entire life has felt like a secret. I'm glad to know the truth."

She winked. "Us alpha girls gotta help each other out."

It was a strange feeling for me to have a girl as a friend. I liked it. "Absolutely. If you need a place to hide out some day, come find me," I joked looking at Valentina.

"I might take you up on that," she said and laughed.

Raff's mom was continuously running in the house and grabbing even more food and packages for the boys to load up in our caravan of cars.

"Woman," Austin shouted to get his wife's attention. "It's only an eight-hour car ride to Swan Quarter. How much food are they possibly going to need?"

"Oh, hush!" She waved at him dismissively while approaching me next. "These, my dear, are for you." She handed over a stack of magazines. My first thought was it was kind of her to think I might need reading material since Raff showed no inclination of ever letting me hold my cell phone again. The second thought was to drop the damn things. They were all wedding magazines. "We can go over them at your next visit." She smiled delighted at the thought.

"Valentina," I groaned. "It's a bit much."

"Nonsense! We can make it a family affair only, no other packs need to come," she placated.

"That's not what I meant," I tried to clarify that a wedding *at all* was not really on the table, but Austin beat me to it.

"Give her a bit of time, my love." The alpha winked at his wife while pulling me in for a hug. "She won't give it up, though," he whispered softly. "Might be easier for everyone involved if you earmark a page or two."

I blew out a breath, completely dumbfounded about how I would deal with these alphas. Raff threw his arm over my shoulder, laughing at the look on my face.

"Mom, Chloe's not ready yet."

I almost corrected the assumption of *yet*, but Valentina jumped in. "A fall wedding would be so pretty, though!" She looked pensive as inspiration struck. "I guess we could wait and do one around the holidays. I'll check the lunar cycle. It would be a great way to bring in the New Year."

"Okay, what car are we taking?" I was ready to move as far away as possible from this conversation.

A few more farewells were uttered before Raff steered me into his truck. I saw Lowe and Tate getting behind the wheel of my car and the rest of the crew in another work truck. I dumped the magazines on the floorboard. "I miss driving. Mind if I take the wheel?" I held my breath wondering if this would be another fight.

"Not at all, darlin'." Raff handed me the keys and switched to the passenger side. He was flipping through a magazine before I even buckled up. "I got a lot of reading to do."

"Ha, ha. You're hilarious." I adjusted the mirrors. "Where the heck is Swan Quarter?"

"It's near the coast, by a wildlife refuge. A no-claim territory, where we can be assured of moderate safety. Head east."

His answer reminded me the full moon was only ten days away. My worry about Valentina force-feeding me wedding cake samples dwarfed in comparison to my fear of being killed as a wolf. Raff put a hand on my knee, rubbing in soothing circles.

"Everything's going to be fine. I've got you." When his comfort was met with silence, he pressed on. "We haven't had a wolf killed by hunters in twenty years."

"Hmph! There are tons of ways it could go bad. It's terrifying." I shifted the truck into first gear and revved the engine a little more than necessary before barreling down the driveway. Raff's easy meandering through the wedding mags halted as he grabbed the "oh shit" handle above the window.

"Damn, darlin'. Where's the fire?" He laughed. "We have a better chance getting in a car accident, and I mean a much better chance, than getting hurt as our wolves."

I eased off the gas a bit since he was white-knuckling it. His truck had a good deal more pickup than I was accustomed to. Tate was a mere speck in my rearview mirror. "Near the coast? What state?" Highway signs up ahead caused me to realize I hadn't asked.

"North Carolina. Red wolves are still seen there in the wild, but they are endangered. We will have maximum protection from the government that way. Not many of the red packs are left and we tend to stay between Tennessee and North and South Carolina. Tate's kind are a bit more spread out, but as populations grow our territory options become smaller."

"It's going to be whitetail hunting season soon. You don't think that will be a problem?" I chewed nervously on my lip. What if something did happen to us? My mom and sister would never know. Even while angry at my mother, I hated not having my sister aware that I was alive and well. At least for now, that is.

"We're no strangers to hunting season. I've been shifting since I was a small boy. We take precautions, go to more remote places. You'll have to trust me."

I was still working on the trust thing. That warn gooey center that was my bond pulsed with comfort. I knew it was a form of coercion of sorts, but it was damn effective. My pulse slowed, a sigh escaped me as my anxiety deflated, and my shoulders, stiff with tension, sagged. I started to take in the lush greenery surrounding the road. We basically had several hours on I64 before I even needed to contemplate more than just driving.

Three hours later and my bladder was telling me a stop was in order. I saw we were close to Asheville, where my life used to be, only a little over a month ago. Without giving it too much thought I signaled my exit. Much to my utter annoyance, Raff had continued to read every wedding magazine his mom handed me. He was on the last one when I left the highway. A raised eyebrow followed by a glance at his gas tank, prompted me to speak. "I need to pee."

"I'm craving a burger." He dropped the mag on the floor with the rest and shifted in his seat to pull out his cell. Out of the corner of my eye I could see he was looking where to stop.

"I know a good place," I offered.

"Will there be people you know there?" The

question was direct and caught me unexpectedly off guard. Even though I was literally in the driver's seat, he was keeping close tabs on me. He asked for my trust in him, but I still was not afforded the same courtesy.

"No," I snapped. "I only ever ate there once. No one to come to my rescue."

Raff's eyes crinkled in the corners as his face pinched. "I just don't want this to be hard on you. Answering questions about where you've been and who we are. You may not be prepared to answer to friends."

"Don't you mean former friends?" I couldn't stop being a bit miffed. "You're the one that wanted a burger. I just need a gas station to use the bathroom."

"You know a good place, we should go there. The boys like to hoard Mom's cooking for our place and eat as much junk as they can on the road. I'm sorry I brought it up at all." Raff uncharacteristically backpedaled, perhaps sick of fighting.

I made sure our caravan was complete before pulling into the sports bar on the corner known for its killer burgers. As usual the guys were starving even though all they did was eat. The poor waitress had to make five trips to carry everything. The crew seemed pumped about getting their own territory and finding a permanent home. The nomad life had always appealed to me, but perhaps that was my lone wolf coming out. I wasn't particularly hungry, but I grabbed a fry knowing the boys would not start the chow fest until I did. Lowe was the only one besides me not stuffing his face. His left eye was a bit red and swollen and when he rubbed at it he winced.

"Lowe." I peered at him closely. "You have something in your eye? It looks infected."

He grimaced. "When I was dicing up peppers a seed flew and hit me straight in the eye. When I went to get it out, I still had the juice from the dang things on my fingers. It made it all worse. Its killing me now and I can barely think about anything else."

The guys winced in sympathy but collectively thought it was funny. "Oh..." I scooted closer and rubbed his back. "You poor thing. There's a pharmacy right down the road. We can see if they have something to help flush it out. In fact, I'm not that hungry, I can go and be back by the time you all are done."

It went perfectly quiet and the eating stalled. It dawned on me, I just asked to leave on my own. Do they trust me? Do they believe I will be back? Raff looked at me pensively, but Lowe interrupted before I could find my answer.

"That is sweet of you, Chloe." It's like his eye knows we are talking about it and tears up fiercely. "If you think the pharmacy will have anything that can help, I'd like to go too. The faster this stops burning like hell, the better."

"Of course," I use my most comforting tone. "That makes sense. Come on. I'll drive."

"Here, Chloe." Tate tossed me my own car keys. "Raff's truck is filled in the back." He points with his chin out the window of the diner where we parked the car in plain sight. "Best take the car instead."

It's a weird feeling having them tell me to use my own car, surreal even, as if all my possessions belonged to everyone. I threw my purse over my shoulder and stood. Raff's hand shot out and encircled my wrist, but his eyes were on Lowe. "You got your cell on you?"

"Yup," Lowe said and nodded.

Raff's thumb stroked back and forth over my pulse. He took a steadying breath. "Be safe."

I couldn't help but roll my eyes. "We are going to the pharmacy five minutes from here."

"Well, then. Perhaps for once, you can follow instructions." The cocky grin I hadn't seen since our last big fight emerged.

"Don't ever count on it, big boy," I huffed while I patted his cheek and walked out.

Chapter Fifteen

The pharmacist was a little Southern grandma. She commiserated with Lowe, telling a tale of a similar hot-pepper-related incident. She had quite a few remedies that could help. Lowe and I sailed through the aisles picking up her suggestions. She chatted away while ringing us up. "First try the saline solution, it's the least messy, but if that doesn't do the trick I suggest whole milk."

"Milk? Really?"

She nodded sagely. "It breaks down the oil. You need to buy a shot glass too. Fill it up to the rim, put it over your eye, seal it tight, and flip it back."

"Huh…" I cringed a bit about putting my exposed eyeball in milk, but I suppose if it was burning enough, I'd try it.

"In fact, why don't you try the saline here? And you can move onto the milk if it's not better."

"Thanks," Lowe said and handed over the cash for our purchases. "Is there a bathroom?"

"Back of the store." She reached under the counter and handed him a key attached to a miniature neon green buoy. Lowe looked askance at me.

"I'll wait here. Go take care of that," I replied sympathetically. I watched Lowe trudge into the bathroom and when the door closed it hit me. I was alone for the first time since all this started.

"Is there anything I can help you with, dear?" the little pharmacist asked kindly.

I was about to reply in the negative but thinking about Raff made me ask an entirely different question. "I'm in the system, I believe. I was wondering if I could pick up my birth control today."

"Sure, dear. What is your name?"

"Last name, Toulou."

"Let me see. I have a Dianne Toulou."

"I'm Chloe. Dianne is my mom." My mom who lived only a few miles from here.

"I see you now! It looks like you don't have any more refills. Would you like me to call in to your doctor?"

"Oh, no worries." I acted like it didn't matter. Considering Akela told me it would not work on me anyway. "I won't be in town long."

"Here visiting your mom, then?"

The question should not have felt like a slap in the face. "Yep. I'm just on my way to see her." I smiled weakly and looked back at where Lowe disappeared.

I *should* have gone to see her! I needed to talk about all of this with her, and Raff was being unreasonable. Imagine wanting me to wait more than a year before I considered confronting my mom! I watched the door to the bathroom and started mentally counting. If Lowe emerged in the next thirty seconds, I'd stay. If Lowe took longer, I'd leave. I could be to my mom's and back before the guys even finished eating.

Thirty seconds came and went. I stayed frozen. It felt like a betrayal to leave Lowe. Yet, he did have a cell phone. It's not as if I would leave him stranded completely.

"Oh, no!" I breathed in dramatically. "I just realized I left my cell phone at the diner up the street." I patted around showing empty pockets to the pharmacist. "Would you mind telling my friend I'll be right back to get him?"

"Not a problem. I'll help him with his eye when he gets out and tell him to wait for you."

Without giving it much more thought, I pulled out my keys and shouted my thanks behind me. Guilt is a strange thing. It coated me like syrup as I made my way outside. I felt disgusted at myself. My heart was pounding as I neared my car. Violently shaking hands dropped my keys twice before I could get the alarm off. I practically peeled out of the parking lot, my adrenaline running high. My mother's house was less than two miles away. *I can be there before Lowe even leaves the bathroom.*

I broke a few moving violations getting to my mother's in under five minutes. A nearly twenty-year-old Mustang sat in the driveway of a weatherworn yellow house. My mother's car was once an electric blue. Now it had oxidized to a dull navy, coupled with never getting washed, it was more than a bit rusty around the rims. While I never lived in this house with my mother, as she moved more often than storm fronts, the car was the only real constant in her life.

She never answered the door during the day, afraid of having to speak with door-to-door salesmen, so I didn't bother knocking. A hanging plant off my mother's porch hid the spare key tucked away in a fake rock. I let myself in and stood at the doorway listening to where she could be.

"Momma," I called out as I stepped into the living room.

"Kate, you're early! You tell those kids of yours not to touch the collectibles! I haven't had the chance to put them away. I mean, I love my grandbabies, but those dolls are very expensive."

I shuddered while glancing at the "collectibles." My mother had a thing for rare ventriloquist dummies. It was like every horror show I watched as a kid multiplied by thirty. Thank God she didn't see the need to collect these while I was growing up. They were scary as fuck. I couldn't imagine Kate's kids wanting to go anywhere near the things.

"It's not Kate, Momma."

"Chloe! Oh my God, girl! Where have you been?" My mother raced out from her bedroom with one side of her hair perfectly straight, while the other still a wet mass of black curls.

I was prepared to confront her with an angry tirade about my father dying and it was all her fault that I never got to meet the man. I thought I could yell at her and berate her for keeping secrets, but when my mother looked me over from head to toe with a worried glint in her eyes, I became a little kid needing her momma.

"Why did you never tell me?" I choked out as tears started flowing. I fell to my knees sobbing.

My mother knelt in the thick shag carpet next to me. "Baby, what is it? What has you so worked up?" Her voice was soft, soothing me enough to take a shuddering breath. I placed my hand over my heart as if trying to rub the ache away. Her eyes settled on the necklace from Raff. She audibly sucked in a breath. "Where did you get that?"

"My mate gave it to me."

The term created a wall of silence between us, tall and thick. She stared into my eyes, my accusations laid bare. I held my breath wondering what she would say. Will she confirm this crazy nightmare is my new reality? Will she deny it all?

"You're with a wa'ya?"

Well, shit!

"He's the son of Valentina. I believe you were once friends?"

Tears pooled in her eyes. "The best of..." she trailed off gazing out the window as if she could see her past. "How is our alpha?"

"She's not my alpha," I stated more calmly than I felt. "I'm a member of her son's pack. I'm an alpha."

Her eyes went wide with wonder. "You can shift, then?"

A shudder raged through me as I nodded, confirming my full freak status, not only to my mother but more importantly to myself.

"Oh, honey! That's amazing. How wonderful for you!"

"What? You think finding out I'm a walking horror movie is wonderful?" To say I was incredulous at her reaction would have been an understatement.

"Of course it is! You're my daughter, and I love you. But I am so jealous of you right now I could chew nails!" My mom's confession had her blushing to her roots.

"Let me get this straight. You're jealous of the fact I turn into a dog every month?" I couldn't seem to close my mouth. It was permanently fixed open in shock.

"It's a wolf, Chloe. And yes! You're complete in a way I never was. Both your halves exist as one. I've never felt completeness my entire life. Look at me. The endless wanderer unconsciously searching for my lost self, even while knowing I will never find the feeling of being home." She grasped my arm firmly. "How did it happen?"

I stared down at my mother's desperate grip on my arm and truly saw her. She had spent her life jumping from one thing to the next. Places to live, husbands, and jobs were all like outfits she tried on and discarded, never once happy with the fit. Was I not like that too? She spoke of the feeling of being at home. This was exactly what Raff and the guys were. No matter where we were, they were home. Guilt slammed into me once again for leaving Lowe at the drugstore. I just needed to get closure with my mother and go back as soon as I could.

"A formula has been developed to make the dormant genes work again. I'm no scientist like Austin, so don't ask me to explain it."

It crushed me to see the spark of joy light up my mother's eyes knowing I would extinguish it. "It's dangerous," I added. "A few girls died trying it. Austin thinks it only works on mated females. Something about the biological imperative forcing things along." At that statement her eyes truly glowed. She swallowed loudly as if afraid to ask her next question. I needed to pull the BAND-AID off quickly.

"He's dead, Momma."

"JT?" She covered her mouth with her hands. Her shoulders slumped. She rocked back and forth a bit trying to get in control as tears ran down her cheeks. "No, that can't be true. Someone would have told me."

I placed a soothing hand on her shoulder offering her comfort even though it's what I came here in need of. I didn't understand my mother. Her grief felt like a palpable thing. How could she have loved a man enough to have children with him and then walk away, only to still want and love him every day? Why would she waste her life in torment because her dream wasn't perfect? It still could have been better than the reality her life was. "It's strange. I came here half-hoping you would tell me this was all in my head, that there's no such thing as shifters, and I just needed proper medical care. Or that Austin was the leader of a cult and I've been heavily drugged this entire time." I chuckled brokenly.

"Why?" She gazed at me as if she couldn't comprehend my actions. "You have a mate and pack bonds. It must feel amazing when you're together. Do they not treat you well?"

"They do. The fellas dote on me." I cringed a bit thinking how upset they all must be right now. Lowe certainly called Raff. He was going to be pissed and take forever to trust me again.

"Is your alpha too aggressive? Does he hurt you?" She inspected me again looking for signs of abuse.

"No, Momma. He loves me. He is an asshat most days, bossy and demanding—"

"Well, he's an alpha, Chloe," she interrupted.

"And he kidnapped me. I didn't go willingly into this life. I resent him for my lack of choice." I stated it mournfully, knowing even if I could forgive him one day, it would still be this thing between us. Yet, how could I judge my mother for obstinacy if I allowed it to fester in myself? I was happier with him than without him in my life.

"For the survival of our race, sacrifices should be made." My mother got a bit prissy and folded her arms looking dour.

"Well, Mother dear. You never told me I wasn't human! So, big surprise when I didn't feel this earth-shattering desire to save something I didn't know existed!" Some of the anger I shelved seethed back out. "You certainly did not stick around and do your part!"

She averted her eyes and winced. "That's on me. I thought you would be better off not knowing what you were missing. When I became pregnant with you, I knew I had to leave before anyone figured it out. They would expect me to stay. Be near the pack but not a true part of it. I didn't want that for you. JT convinced me to come back, though, on the off chance you could shift. Then Kate came into the picture and I was in deep. The minute it was clear you were like me—shiftless—I knew I had to leave. I thought if you never knew, you might find happiness, and not live with this gaping hole of loss all your life."

"Oh, Momma!" I cried. Wasted time was the only thing her actions had delivered. "I was very angry at you when I found out." My admission caused her to drop her eyes. "I never had a chance at knowing my father, and your life jumping from place to place made no sense to me."

"I'm so sorry, Chloe. I thought I was making a sacrifice so you girls could have a better life. But I lost JT for you as well as me. You don't know how sorry I am." She covered her hands over her face as her body shook from silent sobs.

"Actually, I think I do know. I've been fighting this thing between Raff and me. That feeling of being home is amazing, yet I'm ready to toss it out the window every time I get pissed. I haven't given my pack a fair shake. And they don't know where I am right now. I wanted to see you. They didn't want me to until I was more settled in and trust was built between us. I destroyed it by running off." I stood up from the floor and pulled her with me. "I don't have a cell phone to let them know I'm coming back. They said it was too soon for me … on that, Raff was wrong. Seeing you made me realize I do love him. I couldn't bear the pain you're feeling right now. I should get back before they think I fled for good."

"I understand." She pulled me into a tight embrace. When she pulled away she went into Mom mode. Fixing my hair and using her sleeve to dry my eyes. "Don't be a stranger. I can't lose you too."

"I won't, Momma."

Chapter Sixteen

It was a wonderful feeling getting into my car and returning to my new family. I knew Raff was going to be pissed, but through our bonds he would feel I was ready to fully commit to this life. I would tell him first thing. He might watch me like a hawk for the next year, but I won't mind. I was his now. They were mine. I was ready.

A few lights away from the drugstore, I caught a red light. As I came to a stop, a car screeched behind me. I braced for impact, placing both hands firmly on the wheel. My back fender was nudged but not too violently. Still, there was damage, so I couldn't drive away like I wanted to. "A cell phone would be super darn helpful right now!" I grumbled out loud.

As I was about to open the door, the passenger from the vehicle behind me hopped into my car. "What the hell?" I turned and my heart stopped. The barrel of a 9mm handgun was pointed at my chest.

"Drive!" a familiar voice growled.

The light switched to green, I hesitated, and the gun moved closer to my temple. "Don't make me repeat myself."

Gripping the steering wheel hard enough to turn my knuckles white, I placed my foot on the gas. My brain was in a bit of a fog as the world appeared to rush by me. The gun lowered to rest back on his lap, still pointing my way.

"What do you want?" I squeaked. I had no idea why he chose to single me out. We didn't have a pleasant first encounter, but I was surprised to see Tate's brother.

"Same thing most pack alpha's want. A mate." The giant's gravelly voice chilled me.

My gaze rested on the beast of a man but darted away when his glare carved a tunnel of ice in my stomach. The drugstore parking lot was just to my right. I searched it frantically.

"They just left," Miles sneered.

"I'm not sure what you want," I repeated lamely. A sense of dread slowed down my thought process.

"I just told you," the hulking alpha spat the words at me.

"I mean, what do you want with me? I have a mate," I spoke softly afraid to enrage him.

"I'm not interested in Raff's sloppy seconds," Miles huffed. "You're a means to an end, sweetheart."

"Where am I driving to?" I imagined if I kept him talking the odds of him using the gun on me would diminish.

"Just keep straight. I'll tell you when to turn."

The command made me bristle. I knew it was foolish but my mouth had a will of its own. "There are easier ways to get a ride, you know. I could call you an Uber."

"Funny," he deadpanned.

"Seriously, Miles, how is kidnapping me going to get you a mate?"

My question was met with silence.

"Austin might be willing to share the formula with you. You don't need to go to extreme measures."

He snorted derisively. "I don't need his vile of poison. My mate isn't a genetically broken shifter."

"Well, if you don't want the formula, I'm not sure what kind of leverage keeping me hostage will provide you. I doubt it will make all those perfect shifters cream in their pants to be with you either."

"You're a snarky one." Miles's appraising stare swept me up and down. "Raffy boy got his work cut out with you, eh?" His glare turned sharp. "Almost makes me feel sorry for the douchebag." He raised the gun slightly using it to point. "Turn left up ahead."

"Do you mind not pointing that thing directly at me?" The fear twisting my gut could not override the alpha in me. It was drowning out my common sense.

"Shut up. Follow instructions. Play your cards right and we can both get what we want. Simple as that." His tone was cold. I couldn't get a sense of what threat level this was. Would there be any benefit in killing me? Was this purely a hostage situation?

I turned left at the light and tried to breathe slowly. "Now what?"

"Now we are going to put enough distance between you and your pack."

I really did not like the sound of that. "Why?"

"You are so new, you're like a pup. When the bond is stretched over distances, it gets weaker. Raff knows you're close. He can feel your fear. He's looking for you. I'm going to make sure he isn't going to find you." He shrugged as if his words wouldn't affect me.

"What is it you want Raff to do for you?"

"I don't want anything from him. I just need him to stay out of the way. I need to make a trade."

All the fine hairs on my neck raised. "Who are you going to trade me to?" I whispered the question. My head filled with gory possibilities.

"It's who I'm going to trade you *for* that matters. Get on the highway."

My mind was whirling a thousand miles an hour. If he wanted to trade me, then maybe he wouldn't shoot me. If he wouldn't shoot me, then I shouldn't be driving myself to some unknown destination with a dangerous man. Would he trade me to the government to experiment on? Another shifter pack? Raff said the grey wolves and the red wolves were often at odds.

I slammed on the breaks. Stopping the car before entering the on ramp. "I'm not going to make this easy on you."

"Bad decision," he grumbled low. Shifting the gun in his hand he brought up the handle to the side of my temple faster than I could react. My vision went dark and spotty. I felt the driver's side door open, and a brief sense of relief that help arrived as giant hands pulled me from my seat. It was the driver from the car behind me, same car that had hit me. I had been focused on Miles. I missed that we were being followed.

Shoved into the back seat, I struggled with heavy lids. The hit to my temple made me feel sluggish. No amount of adrenaline could combat the concussion I was sure to have. My head lolled back when my neck could no longer properly support it. Despite the danger I was in, my body shut down, and I faded from consciousness.

Chapter Seventeen

"Oh my God, what have you done to her!" a feminine shriek filtered into my dark haze.

A deep rumble followed. "I thought I explained it pretty well over the phone."

"I want to see her," the firm voice sparked a memory, but my fog-filled brain could not process.

"By all means."

I could hear the car door open and the cold air from outside rush in. Soft hands examined my face and titled my head side to side. The movement caused me to wince. "You are such a bastard," the woman murmured. I started to blink my eyes, straining to figure out my situation.

"Chloe, can you hear me?"

"Akela?" I croaked. My throat felt filled with sawdust.

A sigh of relief accompanied my question. "Yeah, it's me."

Holding up my hand to shield my eyes, I considered my situation. I was still in the back seat of my car. By the look of the sun low in the sky, I guessed it was morning. Meaning I had passed out since yesterday early evening. I cringed as I sat up, my head spinning. We looked to be on the side of a dirt road. There wasn't a single structure in either direction.

"What's going on?" I swallowed thickly around the clog lodged in my throat. Akela was in the back seat with me, but I could see Miles standing at the open door, with a gun tucked into the front of his jeans. Another giant-ass dude stood beside him—he had driven the car that hit me.

Akela put her hand on my arm and rubbed it reassuringly. "I'm here to make sure you get home."

I perked up a bit at that, but something didn't feel right. "I thought there was going to be a trade."

Miles snorted a laugh. "Not too bright, eh?"

Akela kept a tight smile in place while my eyes widened in realization. She was a female alpha born to naturally shift. "You're coming with me, right?"

She evaded my question. "How are you feeling?"

I held my hands up in surrender. "No way! Are you crazy! I'm not trading my life for yours."

Her mouth tightened and a stubborn glint filled her eyes. "Your pack needs you."

"Miles is a psycho! You can't stay with him." I gripped her arm and shook my head as I pleaded with her.

"Okay, enough girl talk," the psycho himself spoke. He wrapped an arm around Akela's waist and yanked her out of the car. With his other hand he pointed the gun at me. "Get out!"

"Miles, don't be an ass! You hit her hard, she can't move yet. She might have a concussion." Akela struggled in his grip, elbowing him to release her. She was no match for his giant tree-trunk arms, though.

"Tough shit. We are leaving. Now." He kept the gun pointed at me as I scooched out and gingerly tried to stand. "Give me your cell phone."

"I don't have one," I replied, but it was Akela he was scowling at. He released her and waited.

Pulling it from her back pocket, she looked at him hopefully. "Are you going to let me give it to her? I can't leave her here until I know she'll get help."

It looked to me like Miles was seconds away from just smashing the thing. Yet, as his eyes flickered back to Akela's, indecision showed in them.

"I'm not going to leave her with it," he ground out. He held out his hand, but Akela stubbornly shook her head. "I'm not playing, woman."

"That's not the best way to start *this*, you know?" she shot back.

"*This* started years ago. You left me no other choice. It's not the start, this is the *finish*." Miles leered as he yanked the phone out of her grip.

"Damn you! She's family, and you hurt her! I'm not leaving her in the middle of nowhere." Akela was yelling directly in his face and clawing at him to get her phone back. She was in a rage, but Miles barely registered her swats. His wingspan far surpassed her reach.

I watched it all in a distant haze, my head still foggy and the pain in my body a dull pulse. Miles, with a speed quite shocking for his large frame, snagged both of Akela's wrists with one hand, firmly subduing her. With the other free hand, he sent out a text. He showed the screen to Akela. "Satisfied?"

"Hardly," she ground out.

He drew her in even closer, his nose lightly touching the column of her neck. "I guess I can work more on that later," he whispered, his voice husky.

Akela snorted in response and averted her eyes. Miles turned and chucked her cell phone a hundred feet away into the long grass. Akela cursed him under her breath, but didn't seem surprised at his actions. Miles turned to glare at me.

Lifting a finger, he pointed down the road. "Get in your car and drive in that direction. About forty miles down the road is a coffee shop called Blake's. I sent your pack the address."

The other miscreant that aided in my kidnapping tossed my keys at me. I could barely register the throw and flinched when they landed by my feet.

"She's not well enough to drive, you asshole!" Akela attempted to walk over to me, but Miles held fast to her arm.

"She's fine! She can sit in her car till her head clears. We need to go." Miles started to drag her to the other car, but Akela dug her heels in.

"Give her some money, then," she hissed.

"What?" Miles replied more annoyed than baffled.

Akela held open her palm expectantly, brow raised in challenge, and lips a thin line of displeasure. I had no clue what was going on. Miles shot daggers from his eyes at me, yet he pulled out his wallet and placed a few bills in Akela's waiting hand. She huffed out a breath, shrugged out of his grip, and walked to me.

I blinked, completely stumped about why money was needed right now. Akela offered me a watery smile and bent to retrieve the keys at my feet. She handed my car keys to me with about thirty dollars. "It's gonna take the guys over an hour to get here. You've been gone since yesterday. Raff is going out of his mind, so he might make it quicker when he reads that text. Get some food and wait inside the coffee shop. Everything is going to be fine."

"Come with me." I swallowed and glanced up to see Miles's perpetual scowl. "You shouldn't get in the car with them. He's dangerous."

Miles sauntered over, fingers resting menacingly on the holster of his gun. "Just get in the damn car, Chloe. This is none of your concern."

"I can't let you do this," I begged Akela.

Akela surprised me with a tight hug. "Take care, Chloe."

The nameless thug got back into the car that

collided with me, while Akela and Miles walked over to her car. I sprinted after them. Miles held his hand out keeping me at bay, while he assisted Akela into the passenger seat. "Back off. She's keeping her end of the deal, so I will keep mine and let you go. Don't make me regret it."

Akela sat rigid in the seat not making eye contact, resigned to her fate. I stared at Miles with fury blazing. "I swear to God if you hurt her…" I panted and clenched my hands into fists. My impotent threat hung between us.

He patted me condescendingly. "Don't worry that pretty little head. I'll be taking nice care of her." With those parting words, the jerk flipped me the bird and hopped in the driver's seat. I uselessly watched as he started the car and drove away in the opposite direction of where he told me the coffee shop was. Akela's eyes met mine from the side-view mirror. I held her gaze, tears streaming down my face until she faded off in the distance.

Chapter Eighteen

Somehow, despite dealing with a concussion, a broken heart from my friend's sacrifice, and a shit ton of overwhelming guilt that my rash actions caused all this, I made it to the coffee shop. The waitress delivered a massive amount of food after I numbly agreed to the breakfast special, but I still just stared at the offering with fork in hand. She came by for the fourth time, worry clear in her eyes.

"Everything all right, sugar? You need anything?" She was a kind-faced, middle-aged woman. Average height but a bit portly with grey strands showing through her black short-cropped curly hair. I knew I looked a mess. The woman probably wondered if I was on the run.

I fidgeted under her concerned stare. "Thank you, everything looks great." I made a show of eating so she would leave me alone. She nodded and backed away.

I wished for the thousandth time I had a damn cell phone. There was a pay phone at the restaurant, but I didn't know any of the guys' numbers. Akela said it would be a while before Raff found me. I'm not entirely sure how long it took me to drive here. My head was swimming and I think I blacked out again before I started the engine. Then I debated about following in the direction Akela had gone versus heading here. My heart wanted to see Raff so badly that I abandoned the idea of chasing after his cousin. Another failure of mine I could dwell on later.

Halfway through my plate of food, I started to feel immensely better. My head was clearing and the despair in my heart weighed less. Then it hit me. My heart rate sped up as I felt the bond again. They were close. I threw the money I had down on the table and jumped up when I saw Raff's truck tear into the parking lot. "Keep the change!" I shouted to the waitress, not wanting her to think I was dining and dashing.

I shoved the heavy glass door open and ran directly into Raff's arms. I could not control the sobs that shook my entire frame. "They have Akela. We have to get her back."

"Shh," he hushed me. His hands rubbed soothing circles over my back as he pressed me close. I knew instinctively he could feel my frantic need as I continued to repeat Akela's name. Tate unbent his tall frame from the truck. The rest of the guys were not present, I noted with a sharp pang.

Tate edged closer to us. I could tell he was anxious to comfort me. There was a wariness, though. As I tried to pull away from Raff, my mate held me tight against his chest. "Not yet," I heard him mutter. "I can't share you yet." He trailed kisses from the top of my head to my cheeks. I felt underserving of his love and the tears spilled faster and heavier. The rest of the guys sped into the parking lot interrupting the scene. Rollin opened the car door and jumped out while Weylin was still putting it in "park." I could see Lowe in the back seat, his face pressed against the window, pain lancing his eyes.

I had left all of them without a word, but Lowe I had abandoned. The guilt I felt was heavy, I could barely lift my head. One by one my pack laid a comforting hand on me as they surrounded me. With their touch, the pain eased, and I felt forgiven.

"I'm sorry. This is all my fault," I blurted out. "I just wanted to see my mom."

"And I should have known denying you would drive a deeper wedge between us. I was being selfish."

Raff gripped my face in his hands. "I should have come with you when you asked."

And just like that, all the guilt and dread melted away. The bond hummed with contentment and I could feel and truly understand unconditional love.

Then the past hour flooded in. "Miles took Akela. We have to find her."

Raff pulled back clearly torn. He gritted his teeth before he spoke. "We can't, darlin'. We're running out of time to get to our new territory before the full moon. Miles knew very well what he was doing. They could be anywhere right now, and we can't risk not being someplace designated as safe when the change happens."

"But she's trapped with him because of me!" The sick feeling of guilt started to bubble up again. I'd believed with my pack around me everything would right itself.

"Miles is her true mate," Tate grumbled acting displeased with the information.

"What?" My question was voiced by Raff and I at the same time.

Tate kicked at a rock by his foot. "Akela's known since she was fifteen. She confided in me, but as long as she fought against it, I supported her. I kept her secret."

Raff rubbed his hand over his face. "Well, that's that, then," he sounded resigned.

"No!" I replied mulishly. "She needs us to rescue her."

"Chole, either way we're trapped. The safety of our pack is paramount. We need to get to a safe place before the shift."

"But it's a week away," I protested.

"We are heading to new territory. We need to explore it and prepare stash sites through the forest." He settled his hands over my shoulders. "Remember what you felt like waking up after the shift?"

Mutely I nodded.

"Waking up naked in a place we've never been is dangerous. The more we familiarize ourselves with the wilderness as humans, our wolves will stay in those familiar places. It's what keeps us safe as a pack. We need this time. Same reason Miles hightailed it out of here without a day to lose. He needs Akela to adjust too."

"What if that isn't what she wants, though? She didn't seem thrilled about getting in that car with him." My voice cracked as I remembered her driving away. I hated feeling helpless.

Raff sucked on his lips as he considered. "We might be able to find her after and bring her home, but if Miles is her true mate…" He grimaced at the thought. "Once she shifts with them, a bond will form with his pack. Those bonds are not easily broken. Akela knew that when she left with him. Unlike you, she knows exactly what is going to happen. Pack law does not allow us to interfere if they are true mates. Did she ask you for help?"

"No, but—"

"There is no 'but' to this." Raff stroked his hand down the side of my face lovingly. "Unless she perceives her life to be in danger from her pack, then we can do nothing. She is an alpha, Chloe. Maybe what those jerks need is an alpha like her to get them to be less like assholes and more like a pack. I don't envy her the job, but my cousin is tough. She can handle herself."

"It doesn't feel right." My response was flat and half-hearted.

"I know," Raff whispered searching my face. "But do you trust me?"

A million questions weighed into the one he spoke. I could feel them all: *Are you with us? Do you believe I love you? Will you follow me? Are you a part of this pack?*

I looked at all my guys and sent as much love as I could through our bond. Then I looked at my mate, the hope for our future glittered in his eyes. This was more than about surviving. This was about becoming a family.

"Yes." I smiled knowing I meant it with all my heart. "Let's go home."

Epilogue

A forehead was pressed tight against mine when I opened my eyes. I was laying on my right side, my head rested on a firm curled bicep. Behind my neck warm breath ghosted over my skin, as another body was pressed tight against me. My left leg was bent and my right stretched out. It was weighed down by yet another body using my calf as a pillow. I was essentially fully pinned. At least there wasn't a severed and bloody deer head staring back at me. So, all in all, a step up from last time.

I attempted to stretch out muscles sore in the strangest of places, but Raff groaned and snuggled closer, causing an impressive erection to spear into my thigh. Something I smiled at but would not be partaking in at this precise moment.

The sun was cresting on a new day, providing some much-needed illumination as to where the heck we might be.

"Rise and shine, boys," my voice was gravel. I cleared my throat. "Don't want to give any hikers the wrong idea."

Raff smiled while keeping his eyes closed. "What idea is that?" he mumbled sleepily.

"That they're interrupting a crazy mud-people orgy."

I recognized the dry laugh behind me belonging to Weylin. I shook my right leg and dislodged Lowe from my calf. With his weight removed, I managed to sit up, despite Raff's protests. We were in a small cave. At the mouth of the cave a large mound snored away. Tate could sleep through anything.

"I don't see Rollin." I worried my bottom lip with my teeth. My anxiety spiked as I tested our bond seeing if I could feel him. I must have yanked at it hard, because a second later he stumbled in with a camouflaged knapsack slung over his shoulder.

Unlike the rest of us, Rollin was wearing clothes. He was still shivering as he crouched down to enter our little shelter, though.

Dropping the bag, he rubbed his hands to warm them. "Jeez, it sure as shit is cold out there. I seriously might have frozen my balls off walking the half-mile to find this pack." Unlacing the bag, he pulled out the dried apples and jerky from the top and tossed them at Lowe to open and pass out. The first article of clothing, a tightly balled-up heavy navy thermal Henley, he offered me with a wink. It took a moment to register I wasn't even bothering to cover up my exposed breasts. My brain was still foggy transitioning from wolf back to human, and nudity hadn't felt strange.

"Thanks." I blushed slightly while pulling on the garment.

Raff was right. Spending the last week familiarizing ourselves with our new territory gave me an advantage this time. I recognized this cave. I had come here at least three times in the last week, thinking it would offer protection from the elements. My wolf must have taken my advice to heart.

I accepted a handful of dried apples from Lowe and tried to shoo the cobwebs out of my mind. "Are we three miles from the cabin?"

Rollin finished handing out the clothes. He looked back over his shoulder to the forest. "Yeah, just a little bit over that. Shouldn't be too bad of a walk."

I shimmied into my leggings, but paused to watch Raff give a full-bodied stretch before he covered up.

Catching me ogling him, he gave me one of those sexy half-smirks that drove me crazy. "All yours, darlin'. Right after a hot shower," he suggested with a husky, just-waking-up tone.

I should have rolled my eyes, his ego needed to be taken down a notch, or twenty. Instead, I wiggled by eyebrows, extremely pleased with the idea he painted.

He laughed and gave me a playful swat on my butt. "Feeling is mutual." He kissed the top of my head and surveyed the weather.

The bond hummed. We were together, we were safe, and we were heading home. My heart ached at the thought. My mind wandered as it often did this last week to Akela.

I looked at Tate, sensing his mind was preoccupied with the same thoughts. I walked over to him and placed his hand in mine. "Maybe we can look for her now?"

He crushed me to him in a gentle bear hug. "Thank you for thinking of her too," he mumbled into my hair. "I worry about her. She's closer than a sister to me."

He released me and my eyes traveled over to Raff. "Can we at least try and see if she's okay?"

He looked at me with so much love in his eyes. How could I ever have thought him indifferent? "Of course, Chloe."

"But not today," I amended. "Today we celebrate our new home and…"

"A hot shower," injected Weylin.

"A pound of bacon and pancakes," added Lowe.

"I just want to watch Sunday football and not move from the couch." Rollin titled his neck from side to side. "I feel like we ran ten marathons."

"Agreed," Tate said and laughed. It lifted my

spirits to see it. "All of the above, please."

The guys started heading out. Raff circled his hand around my arm halting me. "I would like to add to the order," he whispered in my ear.

"Oh?" I replied innocently.

"There are a few muscles I believe still need to be put through their paces."

My laugh sprung forth as my skin pebbled in awareness. "Promises, promises…" I teased.

Raff clasped his hand in mine, lifted it to his mouth, and kissed it tenderly. "Every and all promises for you, darlin'. You are worth it."

"Come on, sweet talker." I licked my lips slowly. "I plan to hold you to that."

The End

ACKNOWLEDGMENTS

Thanks to all my readers! I have truly appreciated the messages and encouragement. Your reviews mean everything to me, so please leave one when you can. Special thanks to Evernight Publishing for all they have done to get my stories into your hands.

www.mariamercurio.com

MARIA MERCURIO

EVERNIGHT PUBLISHING ®

www.evernightpublishing.com